MARK ROBSON

SIMON AND SCHUSTER

For Timothy—
may your life be rich and
full of good times.

SIMON AND SCHUSTER
First published in Great Britain in 2006 by Simon & Schuster UK Ltd
A CBS COMPANY

5 7 9 10 8 6 4

Simon & Schuster UK Ltd
Africa House
64–78 Kingsway
London WC2B 6AH

A CIP catalogue record for this book is available from the British Library

ISBN-13: 978-1-4169-0186-0

www.markrobsonauthor.com

www.simonsays.co.uk

Typeset by Rowland Phototypesetting Ltd,
Bury St Edmunds, Suffolk
Printed and bound in Great Britain by
Cox & Wyman Ltd, Reading Berks

DRAMATIS PERSONAE

In Shandrim, Capital City of Shandar

REYNIK – Legionnaire of the General's Elite Legion. One of only two such elite Legionnaires yet to reach their eighteenth birthdays.

TRENNON – Legionnaire of the elite First Legion.

SIDIS – File Leader of the elite First Legion. Companion to Femke during her journey to Thrandor.

FEMKE – Talented young spy for the Emperor of Shandar. Mistress of disguise.

TYMM – Legionnaire of the elite First Legion. Friend of Reynik.

NELEK – Veteran Legionnaire of the General's Elite Legion.

LORD TREMARLE – Powerful 'old school' Lord of Shandar. Father of Lord Danar.

LORD LACEDIAN – 'Old school' Lord of Shandar. Best friend of Lord Tremarle.

LORD DANAR – A handsome young playboy of the Imperial Court. Only son of Lord Tremarle, a powerful 'old school' Lord. Killed by Shalidar during Femke's mission in Mantor.

LORD FERDAND – Master Spy. Mentor of Femke. Missing, presumed dead for two years. Now the Guildmaster of the Guild of Assassins.

OTHER ASSASSINS – Brothers: Scorpion, Firedrake, Falcon (deceased), Viper, Cougar, Fox, Bear, Dragon, Wolf Spider.

SURABAR – Ex-military General of the Shandese Legions, now Emperor of Shandar.

SHALIDAR – Member of the Guild of Assassins (Brother Dragon) and long-time adversary of Femke.

LADY ALYSSA – A phantom. That is, an alias of Femke. A spoilt young woman known to be the daughter of a rich merchant Lord from a coastal city.

VERSANDE MATTHIASON – Proprietor of The Silver Chalice, a high class inn located in the centre of Shandrim.

RIKALA – Dressmaker and friend of Versande Matthiason.

LORD KEMPTEN – 'Old school' Lord of Shandar. Regent of the Shandese Empire in Emperor Surabar's absence.

LADY KEMPTEN – Gracious lady wife of Lord Kempten. Known affectionately as Izzie by her husband.

COMMANDER SATERIS – Commander of the Shandese First Legion.

COMMANDER VASCILLY – Legion Commander who gives daily reports to the Emperor.

ANEKI – A servant to Serrius, retired gladiator of Shandrim.

SERRIUS – A deadly gladiator. Reputed to be the best swordsman ever to fight in the Shandese arena. Retired. Tutor to Reynik.

DERRYN – An ageing street entertainer and expert knife thrower. Tutor to Reynik.

DEVARUSSO – The debonair leader of Shandrim's foremost band of actors. Tutor to Reynik.

DIKARIS – File Second to Sidis in the elite First Legion. Stickler for discipline and personal hygiene.

TOOMAS – An unscrupulous tattle tout.

SHANTELLA – True name of Brother Fox – the only female member of the Guild of Assassins.

JARRON – A guard at the house of Lord Lacedian.

DAKREAS – A guard at the house of Lord Lacedian.

SASSO – A servant of Lord Tremarle.

MERRIK – A lord of Shandar.

SHEDRICK – An informant – agent of Femke.

LUTALO – Legion Commander. Assigned to the elite First Legion after the assassination of Commander Sateris. Father of Reynik.

TAM – A legionnaire.

JURRE – A servant in the Guild complex.

GAETAN – A wagoneer.

CHAPTER ONE

'Well, lads! What do we have here? If it isn't the Emperor's golden boy returned from his holidays. Did you have a nice time in Thrandor, Reynik? Did you bring us all presents?'

All eyes in the barrack tent turned to focus on the young man in the doorway. He met their combined gaze with a confidence at odds with his years. Reynik had yet to celebrate his eighteenth birthday, but already he was no stranger to military action. During his first ceremonial guard duty there had been a skirmish with traitorous rebels. Reynik's skill at arms during the fighting had brought him to the attention of the Emperor, who had then chosen him for a special escort mission. The acid welcome at Reynik's return was no more than he had expected.

'Thrandor was hell! Fine wines, beautiful girls and a luxurious room with my own bathtub – a complete nightmare. You'd have hated it, boys,' he responded, his grin making him look more a boy than a man. 'I spent all my money on memories, so you'll just have to make do with my stories as gifts.'

'Bah, you wouldn't know what to do with a beautiful girl if she came with written instructions!' one of the older men spat.

'At least they didn't worry about over-exciting me for fear of my heart packing up, Trennon,' Reynik retorted swiftly.

There was a round of general laughter at that. Reynik was relieved. Outwardly he strove to give the impression of confidence. Inside, he trembled. He knew from his recent training that anything perceived by the group as special treatment made for bad feeling. His father had taught him group dynamics well. He knew that brazening it out was the best way to tackle the situation.

If he could tell them the *real* story of what had happened in Thrandor, then his re-acceptance by his fellow soldiers might be easier to achieve. Sadly he was sworn to secrecy. The Emperor had made it clear to both himself and Sidis that they were not to discuss the events of their trip with anyone. Sidis had been a miserable companion for the entire duration. Given that he was a File Leader and Reynik was a junior Legionnaire, Reynik had hoped that Sidis would take time to teach him something new of soldiering during their journey. He had not. He had been sullen and unfriendly throughout. After he witnessed Reynik tackle an assassin in front of the entire Thrandorian Royal Court, the File Leader's disinterest in progressing Reynik's soldiering skills turned to active obstruction. During the return journey Sidis had been all but unbearable.

2

'If only Sidis was more friendly,' he thought. Having someone, anyone who he could talk to about the time in Thrandor would have helped. The only person with whom he could talk about the trip was Femke, the Imperial Spy who had posed as the Shandese Ambassador, and that was awkward on several levels. Thoughts of Femke were not helpful. They were distracting and he knew he had to keep his focus. He had to show his fellow soldiers that he had not lost his identity as a member of the group.

Reynik heaved his heavy pack in through the opening of the tent and put it in the nearest corner, to the left of the entrance flaps. The spot closest to the door flap was the worst in the tent. It was the draughtiest, the most difficult to keep clean, and the place liable for the most disturbances during the sleeping hours.

'So, what's Thrandor really like, Reynik?' asked one of the other more junior soldiers.

'Much like Shandar, Tymm,' he replied with a shrug. 'The trip was pretty boring for the most part. File Leader Sidis and I got to play nursemaid for an Ambassador during the journey. When we got there, we were largely left to our own devices until it was time to come home again. I got to see a fair bit of Mantor, which was good fun. The Royal Guards in the Thrandorian Palace were up for a bit of weapon play, so I learned one or two new tricks. Aside from that, it was as dull as a duty watch in the early hours.'

'In other words, a holiday then,' grunted Nelek from the back of the tent. 'You'd better not have gained any bad habits or sloppy ways, youngster. If the File Leader picks us up for anything on your account, there'll be hell to pay.'

'Welcome back, Reynik,' Tymm muttered quietly with raised eyebrows, making sure that the comment was quiet enough for Nelek not to catch it. The rest remained silent and appeared to lose interest in his return.

'I'll do my best not to let anyone down,' Reynik said, emptying his travel pack and constructing his narrow canvas bed. It would take some time to be fully accepted again. In the meantime, he knew he had to concentrate on the basics of soldiering and blend back into the background.

All Legionnaires were trained to look after themselves in every sphere of life. There were standard ways of making up a bed, of storing one's clothes, of cutting one's hair and of cleaning one's personal kit. There was even a 'Legion Standard' way of making one's cup of klah in the morning. To become a Legionnaire was to become more than just a soldier; it involved taking on a whole way of life. For Reynik, the Legion standards were something he felt born to. He had learned many of them at his father's knee since he had first begun to walk and talk.

Reynik's was a distinguished military family that boasted generations of fine soldiers. Most recently, both his father and uncle had been Legion Commanders, the highest military rank barring General that a soldier could aspire to. His father was still a serving Commander, but an assassin had killed his uncle some years ago.

Reynik had witnessed his uncle's murder and had seen the man who killed him. He had never expected to see the killer again, but recent events had caused their paths to cross. He now knew the man's name was Shalidar. Having recognised the assassin, he had hoped to avenge his uncle, but the chance had not materialised. His consolation was that he and Ambassador Femke had foiled Shalidar's attempt to dissolve the peace talks.

The assassin was still on the run. No one was sure how, but he had eluded all pursuit and escaped the Royal Palace in Mantor. Reynik was quietly pleased at this, for whilst foiling Shalidar's plans had held a certain satisfaction, it had not sated Reynik's desire for revenge. He wanted to face the assassin blade to blade. He wanted Shalidar to understand why his hatred for the man burned so deep. Then, and only then, he would kill him – if he could.

It was unlikely that Shalidar would be foolish enough to return to the Shandese capital. The Emperor had put a bounty on the assassin's head large enough to keep any sane man away. Shalidar was not mad. On the contrary, he was one of the most calculating men that Reynik had ever met. As Reynik was not at liberty to pursue him, thoughts of vengeance appeared futile.

'Atten . . . shun!'

The File Leader's voice boomed into the tent, causing an instant response. Everyone sprang to attention at the end of his bed space, upright and taut.

'Form up outside. One minute. Move! Move!'

The men spun again and began gathering relevant kit. Fortunately for Reynik, he was already dressed in all his gear. All he needed to do was to strap on his sword and he was ready. He used the few extra spare seconds to re-secure the straps on his pack. Then he stowed it neatly next to his bed space.

Once outside, the Legionnaires formed three ranks

swiftly and silently. The File Seconds checked the spacing before taking up position ready for the File Leader's briefing. Reynik assumed his old position in the back rank, and the others rearranged themselves accordingly.

Tent city for the Legions was located outside the South West Quarter of Shandrim. It was beginning to feel like a permanent extension of the city. Rows upon rows of canvas constructs were set out with exacting precision. The plan had been to camp briefly, draft in conscripts and then to mount an invasion of Thrandor. Instead, the men were being used to supplement the city militia and maintain public order in the aftermath of a dramatic change of Emperor. The capital was still reeling from the strange sequence of events that had led to a General taking the Imperial Mantle.

The new Emperor was General Surabar, founder of the elite Legion to which Reynik belonged. The soldiers revered him as a leader, so they had good reason to aid him in securing his rule. There had been no coup. However, now that a distinguished soldier with a reputation for being honourable and fair had taken over leadership of the Empire, they were keen to see him keep it.

Those members of the Legion participating in today's exercise marched out in ten groups of sixty to the huge training grounds at the edge of the tented area. The rest of the men were all on duty around the city. A File Leader led each group of sixty, and there was a drummer at the front of every second group beating out the cadence of the marching pace.

It felt strange for Reynik to be marching to the training

grounds again. After the extended period away from the Legion it felt good to be back. When they reached the training grounds, the File Leaders each briefed their group on the schedule of training for the morning. Reynik's group was ordered to start with individual weapons practice, then move to the drill area for manoeuvre training.

Reynik gritted his teeth when he was paired with Nelek. The veteran was an excellent swordsman, but he had never been friendly towards Reynik. The man appeared to enjoy inflicting pain on the younger members of the Legion.

Reynik knew the next half hour would be hard work. He was under no illusions as to who was the superior swordsman. Nelek moved with incredible speed and grace. He also had the instincts of a killer. The veteran had survived several battles during his career, despite having been in the thick of the fighting for hours. When Reynik had first joined the Legion, one of the more friendly veterans had recounted a tale of Nelek in the grip of battle fury. The man had claimed to have witnessed Nelek carve his way through a mass of fighters as if they were so many dead trees to be chopped down. Whether the story was true, or exaggerated, made little difference. The fact remained that he was a truly talented fighter. What Reynik needed to know right now was his weaknesses, not his strengths.

'You and me then, Nelek,' Reynik said brightly, hoping to spark some sort of response.

Nelek grunted, grabbing two training swords from the pile and tossing one to Reynik. They moved into a suitable space and faced one another.

7

'How would you like to warm up?' Reynik asked, rolling his shoulders to limber them in preparation for the punishment he anticipated ahead.

Nelek gave no answer. Instead he attacked. He gave no warning. He just launched straight into a barrage of hard, fast strikes with his wooden blade. Instinct and lightning fast reactions were all that saved Reynik from a mass of bruises in the first few seconds. The veteran was hitting with full force.

Leaping away from Nelek in an effort to regain some poise and balance, Reynik found he was instantly pursued. Nelek was not giving him space to think. The barrage of strokes continued and started to get past Reynik's guard. He took a sharp rap to the ribs and a second on the arm, but there was no let up. Nelek showed no external signs of spite or anger. If he had, then Reynik would have yelled the yield call that would have forced the man to stop his attack. But Reynik was not ready to yield.

It occurred to Reynik that Nelek was trying to prove something. But what? It did not matter. If this had been a real fight with proper blades, Reynik would already have been severely wounded, perhaps mortally. But it was a training bout. There were rules. Nelek had already broken one by neglecting to salute. Would he break more? Reynik decided to find out.

Leaping backwards again in apparent retreat, Reynik anticipated that Nelek would continue his relentless pursuit. This time, though, rather than looking for breathing space, Reynik used the momentary disengagement to change his stance and deliberately leave his head vulnerable to attack. Nelek took the bait and swung at the side of Reynik's head. Reynik blocked the stroke and then executed his premeditated plan. He had deliberately landed such that his weight was forward. As the wooden swords met, he spun under and inside Nelek's guard to drive the elbow of his left arm up into the man's solar plexus.

It was a trick that one of the Thrandorian Guards had played on him during a practice bout at the Royal Palace in Mantor. It proved as successful for Reynik as it had for the Thrandorian. Nelek doubled over, only to have his face meet the back of Reynik's fist, which rapped the bridge of his nose firmly enough to bring more pain. Nelek staggered back. Before he had a chance to recover, Reynik had disarmed him and placed his practice blade against the veteran's throat.

'That's quite enough of that,' a stern voice interjected.

Reynik backed away from Nelek and saluted before turning to face the File Leader. Sidis was looking on with a face like thunder. 'Nothing new there,' Reynik thought grimly.

'What exactly do you think you're playing at, Reynik?' Sidis asked, his voice filled with outrage and fury. 'This is a training ground. We do not deliberately attempt to inflict injuries on our training partners here. You are a Legionnaire, not a back street brawler. You deliberately struck Nelek in the face. Blows to the head are strictly forbidden for good reason, Reynik. If you think you are above the rules because of your recent mission, then think again. You are hereby placed on restrictions for seven days. Additionally, you are designated to jacks duty for the same period. Maybe a week of digging toilet trenches will grind some sense of reality into you. If I see you do anything like that again, I'll not hesitate to have you transferred out of the Legion. We harbour no snakes here.'

Reynik said nothing. He looked the File Leader in the eye and saluted him, but he did so in the most perfunctory manner. Sidis turned and stalked off.

Inside, Reynik was seething, but there was nothing he could do. He knew Sidis well enough to know that the man already disliked him. Protesting would only make matters worse. The fact that Nelek had struck at his head with a training sword mere seconds before was irrelevant. All he could do was to accept the punishment and try to avoid further altercations.

'Amazing!' he thought, sick to the stomach. 'I've been back little more than an hour and already I'm in a whole mess of trouble!'

'Ready for another bout, *boy*?' Nelek sneered.

For a moment, anger erupted inside Reynik as if someone had lit a heavily oiled torch in his belly. He clamped down on the feeling with an iron discipline, replacing the heat of anger with a cold, calculating fury. He turned to face Nelek with an icy stare that looked strange on the face of one so young. For a moment the veteran's snide grin froze on his face, but he was quick to cover up the discomfort. The trickle of blood from his nose was Reynik's one consolation. 'It was a shame I didn't hit Nelek a fraction higher,' he thought. 'A finger's width higher and he would probably have sported double black eyes.'

10

With a mocking salute, Nelek initiated a new fight and Reynik knew that there was to be no mercy from his opponent now.

The trumpet call to signal the change of discipline could not come fast enough. By the end of the session, Reynik had taken so many blows to his arms and body that he fully expected to be black and blue by the evening. The following drill session was agony. Trying to maintain a stiff, smart stance after having been battered with a wooden training sword for half an hour was no small challenge. He could feel the File Leader's eyes following him during the session. The sour old soldier was watching for him to put a foot wrong, ready to pounce on him like a cat on a rodent that had been a trifle too brave.

Reynik did not oblige him. Somehow he survived to the end of the session without fault, though it took every ounce of concentration he possessed. Even during the march back to tent city, he knew he could not relax. The sensation of being watched was relentless. It had never been this bad before. Neither during training, nor when he had first joined the unit, had he been forced to endure such scrutiny.

If he had been able to focus on anything other than keeping in step and swinging his arms to the regulation height, whilst maintaining the perfect distance from the man in front of him, Reynik might have noticed the first signs of spring around him as they marched back to the tents. The air was crisp, but had lost much of the bite of winter. The hedgerows were beginning to show the first buds of green whilst the sun rode a shade higher in the sky.

But the only elements of the change in season that made any impact were the negative ones. The sticky mud, churned by thousands of boots on their daily march to and from the training grounds, was no longer stiffened by the frost. Instead, it sucked and squelched underfoot like a live thing, clutching and dragging at him, draining his energy still further with every step.

Far from the fresh-looking, positive young man who had returned from his travels to join his colleagues a mere two hours beforehand, it was a battered, weary and mud-stained one who stumbled back into his tent after the morning's training. He was sure it had not been this hard before he left, but maybe something of what Nelek had been intimating was right. He was out of shape. He knew it. Despite trying to maintain his fitness levels whilst he had been away, he had not done so with the same iron discipline inflicted by the Legion's training staff.

'Well, if I ever need a reason to keep in shape in future, today will give me one,' he mumbled as he collapsed into his bed space in the tent.

There was not much time. He knew he would have to clean his boots and make his uniform more presentable before lunch. He allowed his body a moment or two of respite before getting cleaned up. It was a mistake. His muscles, stiff from the discipline of the intense drill and the long march to and from the training area, protested by flooding his limbs and torso with cramping pains. The bruising from his battering at the hands of Nelek served to intensify the discomfort.

'Shand's teeth!' he swore, groaning as he rose.

Tymm laughed from where he was sitting nearby. 'You sound like a man three times your age! What's wrong with you? A little light exercise and you fall apart. I thought you were made of sterner stuff.'

'Yes, well you thought wrong,' Reynik replied grinning. 'I feel greener and more sore than I did after my first week as a recruit. Nelek made sure of that. I guess it's going to take a few days to get back into the training rhythm. It'll come back to me soon enough, and when it does . . .'

Reynik left the phrase hanging and Tymm laughed again. 'I hear you landed a week of restrictions within minutes. Good going, Reynik! I think that must be a new record.'

'You know how it goes,' Reynik said with a shrug. 'These things happen. File Leader Sidis has never liked me. Our trip to Thrandor together did little to improve our relationship. I must have annoyed him somehow, though I'm not sure what I did to earn his dislike. I think today was his way of reminding me that we're back in Shandrim where the rank gradient between us is more applicable. Sort of a welcome home present really.'

'Nice present! What are you going to give him in return? You remember what we gave Sevarian when he was out of order?' Tymm asked, his face sly.

'Oh, no! I'm not going down that road. It would be too obvious. Who else would have a reason to set him up with something unpleasant? It would make matters worse, Tymm. I need to keep my head down and my nose clean.'

'What if it were to happen to Sidis whilst you were being monitored on your restriction duties? He couldn't blame you then. I'm game for a good stunt, but it would have to be spectacular.'

'No! Definitely not! It wouldn't matter if the Emperor himself were my alibi right now. Sidis would find a way to nail it on me regardless. Please don't do anything stupid, Tymm. I appreciate the sentiment, but it wouldn't be a good idea.'

Tymm sighed. 'You're right, of course, but it would have been fun.'

'For you, maybe. You wouldn't have to endure the repercussions. Thanks for the idea, but I think that this time it would be better if I just ride out the storm and look to re-establish my place as quietly as possible.'

By evening, Reynik was ready to change his mind. He had endured the afternoon training sessions through gritted teeth. Now he was spattered in excrement and stinking to high heaven from having filled in the old jacks trenches. But that had only been the beginning. He, and the other unfortunates designated to this duty, were still struggling to dig the new trenches. Regulations stated that the trenches had to be five spades long, a spade wide and a spade deep and Shand help any duty group who tried to skimp on the regulations. History had proved time and again that poor sanitation had killed more soldiers than any battle, which was why jacks duties, and all other matters of personal hygiene, were taken extremely seriously.

After the physical activities of the training sessions, the task of digging in the heavy, muddy ground was torturously hard work. Reynik's arms, back and shoulders all protested with every stab and heave of the spade. Every time his spade struck a large stone, the jarring impact reverberated through his body, amplifying his aches and pains. Time dragged, every minute stretching into an eternity. He felt as if it would never end. It was almost full dark before he finished.

'Good enough,' the supervising File Second admitted grudgingly, as Reynik demonstrated the dimensions of the trench with his spade. 'Go and get cleaned up. I'll see you again at first call after training tomorrow. Dismissed.'

Reynik was so tired he could barely scramble out of the trench. He staggered over to place his spade with the others, being careful not to upset the neat stack. Then, with as much dignity as he could muster, he marched wearily back to his tent.

It was not far. By the time he arrived his sole desire was to fall into his bed space and sleep. But, much as his body craved the rest, Reynik knew he had to push on just a little longer.

The others in the tent ignored him when he entered. Not even Tymm looked at him when he ducked through the canvas doorway. 'So this is how it's going to be,' he thought glumly. 'Well, so be it. It won't be for long. I know the drill.'

Stripping off his filthy clothes, he folded them into a pile and put them by the doorway. Then he pulled on a spare pair of briefs and, gathering his dirty clothes together with a small square of drying cloth under his arm, he forced himself to duck out of the tent again into the chill evening air. He knew it was not wise to go out so scantily dressed, but he did not want to make any more clothes dirty.

15

He desperately needed to wash before touching any of his spare uniform. The File Leader was out to make life difficult, looking for any little excuse to pick on him. Reynik was determined not to make it easy for him.

Washing in the cold water was uncomfortable. Scrubbing his filthy clothes whilst still not fully dry was even more so. However, it did wake him up and stimulate his body enough that he found the energy to hang up his wet uniform in the appropriate drying area before retiring back inside the tent.

Still he could not rest. Experience told him that unless he got something hot to eat and some fluid into his body, he would pay the price in the morning. He had to get to the field kitchen. So, ignoring the deliberate snubbing of his fellow Legionnaires, he dressed and went out in search of food.

The walk was not a long one, but he felt every step like a bee sting. Not for the first time since he had joined the military as a recruit, he questioned his reason for being a member of the Legions. Did he really want this life, or was he just stubbornly following his father's footsteps because it was expected? Would he have been better off trying his hand at becoming a merchant, or at learning a respectable trade? After a moment or two of negative thoughts, he laughed aloud and dispersed his melancholy mood.

'Of course I want this,' he muttered determinedly under his breath. 'I was born for this. I couldn't be more suited to the military life. I will not allow the pettiness of a few individuals to stop me living my dream. Bring on the pain. Bring on the tiredness. I will not let Sidis break me. It won't take the others long to see that I'm above his little vendetta.'

CHAPTER TWO

'Dead? Danar is dead? How?'

Lord Tremarle sat down with a thump onto his chair, his complexion draining of colour until he was ashen grey. The lines on his face deepened as the weight of the grim news settled on his features. Lord Lacedian wondered for a moment if the tidings would be too much for his old friend.

'I'm not exactly sure, Tremarle. My source wasn't flush with details. Rumour has it Danar was poisoned, but I stress this *is* only a rumour.'

'First Espen, now Danar. My sons are spent. My line has failed.'

Tremarle fell silent. His shoulders slumped and his eyes became distant. Lacedian looked on in helpless pity. What consolation could be offered at a time of such loss? Danar had been Tremarle's first-born son. It had been but a matter of weeks since his younger son had been killed in a hunting accident. Tradition was that upon the death of a

Lord the eldest living son would adopt the name of his father's House. Lord Tremarle had daughters, but a daughter was not allowed to inherit the leadership of a House. He was too old to father more children. Without sons his death would see the end of the House of Tremarle. The House, together with the family estates, would be taken over by the family of his eldest daughter's husband, thus ending a four hundred year history. It was a bitter blow.

The silence dragged into minutes. Lacedian's eyes started to rove restlessly around his friend's expansive study and he wondered if he should take his leave. Should he go and allow his friend to deal with his pain in solitude, or stay to offer him comfort in his time of mourning?

'Was there a woman involved?' Tremarle asked woodenly, causing Lacedian to jump at the unexpected question. Tremarle had never displayed an active disapproval of Danar's dalliances with the young Ladies of the Court, but he had long felt that if anything, a woman would prove to be his son's undoing.

Lacedian shook his head. 'I don't think so, old friend,' he said soothingly. 'As I said, information is sparse, but I wanted to save you hearing the news from the Emperor's lips. I didn't want you to say anything that we might all regret.'

'Of course, Lacedian. I understand. Thank you.'

Lord Tremarle did understand. Everyone who had been involved in the movement against the new Emperor, Surabar, was on edge at the moment. Several of the Lords had been hung for treason in recent weeks by order of the Emperor's Regent, a man they had thought to be one of their own. The Emperor had returned from his trip to Thrandor. There was every reason for caution.

'Shall I leave you in peace, Tremarle?'

'No, Lacedian. Stay. There are things that we need to discuss, questions I would like to ask.' Tremarle looked at his friend and noted the discomfort in his face. He smiled encouragingly. 'Don't worry, old friend, I don't expect you to have answers to the questions, but it will do me good to ask them anyway. Thank you for taking the responsibility for bringing me these tidings. It was bravely done.'

The old Lord gestured for Lacedian to take a seat in one of the large armchairs. Tremarle leaned forward and pushed up out of his own chair. He walked across to the drinks cabinet.

'Drink, Lacedian?' he asked, opening the front of the cabinet and taking out two glasses.

'It's a bit early for me, Tremarle, but under the circum-stances a drop of something would be welcome. Thanks.'

Tremarle took out a crystal decanter of dark red wine. With care, he filled the two glasses with generous measures. When he had finished pouring, he wiped the neck of the decanter clean with a pristine white cloth before replacing the stopper and putting it back in the cabinet. The old Lord handed one of the glasses to his friend and returned to his armchair. For a moment they sat in silence again, gently sipping at the wine.

'Have you any idea what Danar was actually doing in Thrandor?' Tremarle asked quietly. 'He came to me with some foolish story about him being sent as an Ambassador. There wasn't an ambassadorial bone in my son's body. He was a playboy with little sense of responsibility. I know he was concealing something, but I don't know what.'

Lacedian shook his head. 'I don't know,' he said slowly. 'But he gave you that warning just before he left, didn't he? Surabar had found out about your involvement in plotting against him and displayed that awareness through Danar.'

'That's right.'

'Well, my guess is that Surabar was probably black-mailing him into doing something dangerous. If I were to theorise, I would say he was sent as a spy into the Thrandorian capital. There have been several message riders from Thrandor over the past few months. Surabar gave no reason to the Court for his sudden visit to Mantor. There are those who are saying he's in league with the southerners. A General he may have been, but it looks like he's lost his taste for military action. He's made it plain that he intends no strikes against Thrandor despite their slaughtering of our people.'

Tremarle considered Lacedian's words for a moment. He suspected that his friend was not far from the truth with the blackmail theory. Emperor Surabar had no noble blood in his veins. It was only natural that he would utilise gutter tactics to secure his followers. It was hard to imagine Surabar conspiring to ally with the Thrandorians, especially given that thousands of Legionnaires had recently died at their hands in a bloody battle, but there was a perverse sort of logic about it. Maybe Lacedian was right about it all. Surabar did not have the unanimous support of the nobility here in Shandar. Indeed, he had few friends among them. If he was to make his position as

Emperor secure, he needed powerful allies. As he didn't have them here, he could be looking to the neighbouring countries to help him tighten his grip on the Mantle. Anger growled within Tremarle as he considered this. If Surabar was seeking powerful aid from outside Shandar, then it made the need to get rid of him even more urgent.

'It's a good theory, Lacedian. It has a ring of truth about it. But how can we prove such things? It will not be easy.'

'Do we need to? Dispose of Surabar and we gain both vengeance for Danar and an Emperor that the nobility can respect.'

'Have the others united behind a single candidate then?' Tremarle asked, his anger turning momentarily to surprise.

'No, not yet, but the number of players is whittling down gradually. Pereth dropped out of the running yesterday. He finally realised that he didn't have the backing enjoyed by the others.'

'So, there are what – four left? Five?'

'Four. Nobody takes Miranthel seriously.'

'Well, they'd better hurry up and decide,' Tremarle rumbled, his tone ominous as his anger returned. 'They haven't much time. Find me an assassin, Lacedian. I want to place a contract on Surabar. The Guild of Assassins will not touch a contract on the Emperor. Their creed will not allow it. But someone will take up the mark. There's always someone willing to kill if the reward is great enough.'

The circular hall was dim, lit only by the torches mounted in brackets around the walls. Shadows danced and flickered in the niches and alcoves, tormenting the vision of any who were unfamiliar with the vagaries of the chamber. It was a strange place. Secret. So much so that one could be forgiven for sensing paranoia in its design.

The central floor space was empty aside from an enclosed, raised podium, large enough for a single man to stand in. Next to it was a dark hole in the chamber floor, concealing a flight of tightly spiralling steps that descended into blackness. The podium was like a pulpit in design, though no priest had ever visited this dread place. The staircase that plunged beneath the floor led to the most secret places of the inner sanctum – the chambers of the Guildmaster. Few had seen what those chambers held.

The ceiling of the hall was high and domed, but not ostentatiously so. Although the craftsmen who had delved this place into the rock had carved decorated, arching buttresses that met at the centre point of the chamber roof, the room had been designed to be practical rather than ceremonial. Twenty alcoves had been carved into the chamber wall. Each was independent of the others, with no immediate access from one alcove to the next. A wall, built to an average man's waist height across the front of each alcove, made them look almost stable-like from the centre of the chamber. All were identical in design and size save for the carved insignia on the wooden access gate through the front wall of each recess. None was internally lit. The architect's intent was clear. Those in the alcoves were to remain anonymous and be considered equals, with no prospect of being promoted above another except to the position of Guildmaster.

A sudden movement in the centre of the chamber grabbed the attention of those seated silently waiting in the alcoves. The shadow that marked the well of descending stairs bulged upwards as a black shape flowed from the forbidden depths. It was the Guildmaster, hooded and cloaked in the traditional black garb of the Assassins' Guild. All of the assassins were similarly dressed, their identities concealed from one another by their deeply cowled hoods and the darkness of the alcoves.

The shadowy figure climbed smoothly up onto the podium, rising up the steps as if floating on a cushion of air. If the chamber had been quiet before the Guildmaster's appearance, it was deathly silent now. A torch guttered, the sound of it amplified by the stillness. The figure in black looked around the room, slowly turning full circle as he paused to focus his gaze into each of the alcoves in turn. Most were occupied. It was the most complete gathering of the Guild for many months. That fact alone gave testimony to the serious nature of the meeting.

'I accept . . .' the Guildmaster prompted.

As one, the assassins began chanting the litany of the creed by which they lived.

> I accept that as a member of this Guild:
> I must accept the ultimate authority of the Guildmaster.
> He is my guide, my father and my conscience.
> He will maintain me on the path of light.
> I will accept his orders without question,
> And carry out his requests, regardless of cost – even be it
>   my life.

I will accept only those contracts that have a just purpose.
I will accept no contract that I foresee may cause the
   destruction of the Empire.
Those who offer contracts that do not clearly demonstrate
   a just purpose,
Or that work against the greater good of the Guild
I will report to the Guildmaster.

I will kill only to fulfil a just contract,
Or to cover my tracks, such that none shall learn more of
   the Guild.
I will kill at the Guildmaster's direction.
He is the discerner of truth, my leader who seeks only to serve
   righteousness.
I will kill anyone who kills indiscriminately,
Regardless of status, age or sex.
These evildoers deserve the ultimate punishment.
I will never kill for pleasure, revenge, in anger, or out of
   jealousy.
I accept that doing so would place me at the mercy of the
   Guildmaster.
I offer up a tenth of all contract monies to the maintenance
   of the Guild.
As is fair and just.

I state this creed in the full knowledge that should I break it,
My life will be forfeit.

The echoing mantra finished and silence descended once
more.

When he began speaking, the Guildmaster's voice was

warm and friendly, in stark contrast with his bleak appearance and dread position. Some amongst the Guild had thought him a strange choice when he had risen to lead them, as his voice gave the impression of a gentle grandfather taking care of his family. None, however, disputed his reputation as a professional killer. Deception was one of the key qualities of a successful assassin. The Guildmaster possessed this skill in abundance.

'Brothers, it is good that so many of you are in attendance. I cannot stress the gravity of this meeting enough. The outcome of today's discussion will shape the future of our Guild more than any since I became Guildmaster. In over six hundred years, our brotherhood has never faced such a crisis as the one confronting us now. We have news to discuss, options to consider, and difficult decisions to make.'

The Guildmaster paused for a second to allow his opening words to sink in. He was not prone to exaggeration.

'Please bear with me if you are familiar with any of the following, but I think it important that everyone knows the facts before we debate any course of action. I'm sure that all here are aware that the Emperor returned last week from Thrandor. The true purpose of his visit there is not known, but the common perception is that he went to negotiate peace. He sent an Ambassador to Mantor some months ago. Brother Falcon infiltrated the party under contract by a fellow Brother. This was an unusual arrangement, and not one of which I approve. An assassin contracting a fellow assassin to serve a personal goal flirts dangerously with breaching the creed.

Any considering employing such an arrangement in future should consult with me first. I will not have Brothers believing they are above our laws. We have maintained our reputation over the centuries by following the creed. If we abandon it, then we will become no better than common murderers. I am not willing to be painted with such colours.'

He paused and there was a gentle mutter of agreement from around the chamber.

'Let's save discussion of that internal matter for another day.' The chamber fell silent again, save for the sound of his voice. 'Matters have arisen that require us all to focus our attention outwards. The new Emperor has been initiating policies during the last two days that impact hugely on the Guild. Brother Scorpion, would you please make your report to the Brothers?'

'Of course, Guildmaster, though I'm sure most here are already aware of my tidings.'

Where the Guildmaster's voice was warm and friendly, full of expression and rich with variations in tone and pace, Scorpion's was cold and lifeless. Words fell from his lips like dead wood from a tree – a thudding, inert mass, shed without feeling.

'At the eighth hour yesterday morning, the Emperor sent forth his criers with news to the citizens of Shandrim. Part of the proclamation concerned us directly. The Emperor has declared the Guild *anaethus drax* – illegal and outcast for as long as his reign shall last. Any assassin caught in Shandrim after the midday call of the next rest day shall be summarily executed.'

'But that's only three days away!' a voice exclaimed from the other side of the chamber.

'Indeed, Brother Firedrake, which is why this meeting was called at once.' The Guildmaster spoke gently. 'There was more, but Brother Scorpion has stated the worst of it. Let us debate our response to this declaration before we consider anything else, for it is the crux of why we're here.'

'Kill the Emperor,' a voice stated immediately. 'His reign will then end and his proclamation will be void.'

Mutters of approval and otherwise echoed around the chamber.

'A tempting proposal, Brother Viper, but not one that we can implement without destroying our integrity,' the Guildmaster replied. 'I'll not deny that removing the Emperor has crossed my mind, but it would breach the creed on several counts. Firstly there is no contract. Secondly by killing the Emperor we would risk the collapse of the Empire. The creed specifically prohibits us from knowingly initiating a chain of events that has a high chance of destroying Shandar. We have our place in society, but it is not for us to dismantle the Empire by our actions. Thirdly, and finally, this proclamation looks likely to have been sparked by one of our own. The creed does not allow us to strike back in such a case.'

'One of our own?'

'Who?'

'Why would a member of the Guild do such a thing?'

Questions came from all directions like bolts from a dozen crossbows. The Guildmaster stood firm and un-moving in the crossfire, allowing the wave of questions to wash over him. When the eruption of voices died away he spoke again.

'It doesn't matter *who* caused it. The Emperor would have made this proclamation before long regardless. He is prejudiced against the Guild. Let that be reason enough. The question we should be asking is what are we going to do about it? I have already given the reasons why we cannot kill the Emperor, though that option will be kept under constant review. I will not discount the idea as a last resort.'

'If we cannot kill *him*, then let's strike where it would hurt him most,' purred a female voice.

'And where would that be, Brother Fox?' the Guild-master asked, smiling beneath the deep shadow of his hood as he attempted to anticipate her proposal. He knew her to be a natural strategist with a sharp mind. Whatever she proposed was likely to be worth listening to.

'The Legions, Guildmaster. Let us hit the Legions. Surabar has devoted his life to the armies of the Empire. That is where his heart is. Soldiers go to battle. They die. It is what they're paid for. The average man on the street will care little if we pick off a few key Commanders. It will not cause much public outcry, but Emperor Surabar will feel the pain of their passing as if they were close family. He does not like unnecessary death. He will get the message quickly enough.'

The Guildmaster nearly laughed aloud. Trust the Fox to see past the obvious and find a cunning solution. She was a fox indeed, and a worthy bearer of her symbolic predator's insignia. The Legions were the perfect place to strike. It would not be difficult to find people willing to pay a small fee to see particular Legion Commanders die suddenly. That would satisfy the creed. Yes, it was a good plan. It was easy to implement, unlikely to outrage either the common people or the Nobility, yet sure to give the Emperor the desired message.

'Your suggestion has a lot of merit, Brother Fox. If we are to take the offensive, this seems a positive way ahead. I say "if", for we should at least consider the Emperor's standpoint. If I were to play his advocate here, then I would have to ask what our role is in today's world. Has the Guild outlived its purpose? Are we a relic of the past that has survived beyond its time? The Emperor would have us believe this is so. The Assassins' Guild has been a part of life in Shandrim for a millennium. It's easy to see how the Bakers' Guild and the Merchants' Guild have a consistent role to play, but does today's society really need assassins? The Emperor would argue it does not. He sees us as murderers, or hired thugs who act as a destabilising influence in society. Do any here feel empathy for this point of view?'

There was a long moment of silence before the woman spoke again.

'Guildmaster, there are none here who do not believe in our purpose. We have a creed that has stood the test of a thousand years. We have as much of a right to exist here in Shandrim as the merchants, the bakers, or any other trade you care to name. We do not kill indiscriminately. If a Nobleman had taken the Mantle, this decree would never have been made.'

'Yes, the military have always displayed ignorance of our

role here in the city, and around the Empire,' agreed another.

'Aye, they bleat that we are murderers, yet they slaughter men far more innocent than many we are contracted to kill.'

The Guildmaster nodded. 'It is well that you're all in agreement. Who here feels we should seek to make our point by taking contracts on military targets?'

A wave of 'ayes' sounded through the chamber, echoing slightly with the chorus.

'Those against?'

Silence.

'So be it. I will seek those wishing to place such contracts and will make assignments over the next few days. Now, on to other matters . . .'

Femke knocked on the door of the Emperor's study. At the prompt order to enter from within, she wasted no time in obeying. Nothing had changed in the room since her last visit. It was a bleak workspace, with nothing to give it warmth. The large desk, behind which the Emperor sat, was the main feature of the room. A few crossed weapons on the walls were the only items of décor, and these seemed to add to the cold, imposing atmosphere rather than detract from it.

The Emperor smiled warmly as she entered and indicated with a wave of his hand that she should sit down. Femke bowed and looked around to where Surabar's wave had directed her. There were a few wooden chairs positioned against the wall nearest the door, so she moved one of the chairs out towards the desk and carefully sat down.

'How are the injuries healing, Femke? I can see from here that you're still suffering some discomfort,' Surabar asked gently.

'They're getting better slowly thank you, your Imperial Majesty. It's frustrating to feel like an invalid, but I'm moving much more freely now. My ribs appear to be knitting back together well. They're sore, but that is to be expected.'

'Indeed it is. I cracked a couple of ribs once; a glancing blow to my breastplate with an axe – not a pleasant business. At least you're looking more yourself again now the bruising around your face has receded. Might I suggest that if you ever decide to take on someone like Shalidar in hand-to-hand combat again, you use your hands to deflect his blows, rather than your head? It tends to be less painful, you know.'

'Really, your Majesty? I'll try to bear that in mind,' she replied, maintaining a completely straight face.

The Emperor laughed and shook his head. 'You're one extraordinary young woman, Femke. I cannot help but be impressed with how you handled the business in Mantor. I find it hard to imagine anyone else proving their innocence under such circumstances. Somehow, you did. You saved Shandar from the political embarrassment of having to own up to spying on our neighbours. You saved me from having to order your execution, which was not a task I relished. You broke more Thrandorian laws than I care to imagine. Shand alive, you even robbed the Thrandorian Royal Treasury! Yet the King of Thrandor likes you. Young lady, you deserve whatever reward I can give, but you know that I can't do anything publicly for fear of compromising your role as a spy.'

Femke smiled. 'Give me something to do, your Majesty. That would be the best reward I can imagine right now. I'm bored witless with sitting around and recuperating. I need to be doing something. Anything! Please, give me another assignment.'

'You're not fit—'

'Your Majesty,' she interrupted, giving a smile to apologise for her impertinence. 'I'm not asking for you to give me a *dangerous* mission. I simply want to be useful again. I think I'll go insane if I have to endure any more of the medics' patronising exhortations to rest. I need to get my fitness back. I need to move around and do something. Surely there's some little bit of information I can go looking for that will not put me in harm's way?'

Surabar looked at her with his calculating gaze. Her young face still showed slight signs of the battering it had taken at the hands of Shalidar, but her eyes were bright with intelligence. Femke knew exactly what she was asking. She knew that there was no such thing as a 'risk free assignment'. He could set her an administration task, but that would be like asking a freshly graduated soldier to stand and guard the supplies whilst all his colleagues went off into battle. He would do it, but would resent the duty. That resentment would then fester against the person who gave the order. The Emperor needed Femke's help too much to alienate her. No, she would need something to do that would utilise her skills, yet not be likely to result in physical confrontation. As he thought about it, he realised he had the perfect task.

Shalidar was a picture of calm. He sat in the simple, windowless chamber, painstakingly stroking the whetstone along the blade of his dagger. The steel blade glinted in the dim light as he turned it from side to side, taking care to apply an even effort to both edges. The slow, rhythmic, grinding ring of stone on metal was almost hypnotic as the assassin waited for the Guildmaster. It was not a meeting he was looking forward to, but he knew it was necessary if he were to avoid being hunted by killers far more deadly than any the Emperor had in his employ.

The Guildmaster, hidden in the shadows outside the open doorway, observed him silently for a moment. 'Shand, but you're a cool one, Shalidar!' he thought. 'If you weren't so damned talented, I'd have you killed where you sit. It would be a terrible waste, but it would save me a host of trouble.'

He looked at the lean figure sitting in the wooden chair, one leg casually crossed at ninety degrees over the knee of the other, and he felt cold anger build within his gut. After jeopardising the future of the Guild with his recent antics, Shalidar must know that his life hung by a thread. The Guildmaster held the power to snuff him out like a candle with a given word, yet Shalidar sat, cool as ice, and apparently unconcerned with the precariousness of his situation. How could anyone be so arrogant and self-assured? For a moment, the Guildmaster considered slipping away and ordering Shalidar's termination. 'No,' he thought. 'I'll give him one chance to explain his actions first.'

It was likely that Shalidar knew the Guildmaster was there. He had not become a deadly killer without having a keen awareness of his surroundings. The Guildmaster had made no noise, yet he knew that to Shalidar it was almost like a sixth sense, an awareness of being watched that would alert him to his master's presence.

There was little point in further delay. He stepped forward into the chamber and Shalidar got smoothly to his feet. The assassin was careful not to make any sudden movements that could be misinterpreted. The dagger and whetstone he placed on the small wooden table beside him as he rose. Once standing, he bowed his head deferentially and waited for the Guildmaster to speak.

'So, Brother Dragon, you decided to return to us. I admit I'm surprised to see you. I had thought you would be far away by now, and unlikely to make an appearance in Shandrim for some years. After the trouble you have caused the Guild, you're fortunate I've not already ordered your death. I will allow you this one chance to explain yourself. What did you do in Thrandor that caused Emperor Surabar to declare us *anaethus drax*?'

'I, Master? I can't imagine that any of *my* actions would have caused such a thing. It's true that some of my recent plans in Thrandor went awry, but it's difficult to imagine how the consequences of my personal circumstances could result in such a reaction from the Emperor.'

The Guildmaster watched Shalidar's body language carefully as he spoke. Under the depths of his black, cowled hood, he pursed his lips. If Shalidar was lying, then he was doing it extremely well.

'The Emperor has over-reacted, Master,' Shalidar continued. 'I could not have foreseen this. As you know, I have a legitimate business in Mantor, a trading business formed with the money I earned through my work for the Guild. I've hidden nothing of these activities, as there has been no reason to. A couple of the Thrandorian Noblemen were interfering with my business in Thrandor to the point they were becoming a severe disruption. As I was constrained by the creed from acting independently, I contracted Brother Falcon to travel to Thrandor to deal with the problem. You should have received my message to this effect.'

'I did,' the Guildmaster replied coldly. 'I was not happy with the contract arrangement, but we will talk about that when you have finished your explanation.'

'There is little to tell, Master. Brother Falcon travelled as a servant to Thrandor and carried out his contract, for which I paid him at the agreed rate. Sadly, events then quickly spiralled out of our control. The Shandese Ambassador was blamed for the deaths. This was unfortunate, for it caused a diplomatic incident that in turn sparked dialogue between the King of Thrandor and Emperor Surabar. Aside from the diplomatic embarrassment caused by the implication of the Shandese Ambassador in the deaths of two Thrandorian Noblemen, it transpired that the Ambassador was a spy, sent personally by the Emperor. He, therefore, had a keen personal interest in seeing that his spy was not compromised, as this would have been even more damaging to international relations. The spy was clever. She managed to find a way of implicating both Brother Falcon and me in the deaths of the two Noblemen. Though her evidence was fabricated, it convinced the King. It was she who named both Brother Falcon and me as assassins. Whether she knew it to be the truth or not is immaterial. We were compromised and forced to make a break for freedom. I managed to escape. Brother Falcon was not so fortunate.'

The story sounded feasible. The Guildmaster reviewed it, looking for anything that sounded false. Shalidar had not tried to hide anything with clever words or fancy language. He had simply stated a sequence of events, many of which were verifiable. If he was lying, then he was doing so in perfect control and following the best practice of keeping his lies simple. Killing people was the Guild's business. Shalidar had arranged to have two people killed. There were always consequences to deaths. The question here was: were the consequences of these two hits foreseeable? From the stated sequence of events, the Guildmaster did not see how they could be. He would have to verify what he could of the story, but he doubted he would find any holes in it. True or false, Shalidar would have covered his tracks sufficiently to blur the truth.

'Brother Dragon, you know that you skate on thin ice. I will look to verify your story. If I find you have lied to me, you will die swiftly. I'll not tolerate those who seek to use the Guild to their own ends. You've done very well from your membership of this elite brotherhood. If I find that greed has corrupted you from adhering to the 'creed, I'll show you no mercy. How did Brother Falcon die? His icon returned here some time ago.'

Shalidar shook his head sadly. 'They hung him the day after they caught him, Master. I could do nothing.'

The Guildmaster fell silent for a moment. 'That is . . . unfortunate,' he said eventually. In his head, he continued, 'but very fortunate for your cause, Shalidar. Had he been alive, it would have been easy to verify the tale you have just spun. Instead I must waste precious time and resources checking out your story.' Aloud, he added 'I'm assuming you're aware of the price the Emperor has put on your head?'

Shalidar nodded.

'Then can I also assume that you intend to reside here in the Guild complex for a while?'

'Yes, Master.'

'Very well. You'll be given assignments like all the others, which I expect you to fulfil. They will be made more difficult because of the bounty on your head, but that is your problem. If I were in your position, I would avoid taking on any business outside of your Guild duties. It would be best to wait until the dust has settled and the bounty hunters have given up chasing shadows.'

'Yes, Master.'

The Guildmaster turned to leave.

'But, Master?'

'Yes, Brother Dragon?' he answered, pausing and looking back over his shoulder.

'What about the spy who exposed Brother Falcon and me? It is ultimately her fault this situation has arisen. It is she who is responsible for the Guild being pronounced *anaethus drax*. Will she be punished for her actions?'

For a moment the Guildmaster said nothing. When he did speak, he began by quoting in the chanting strains of the creed. '*I will never kill for pleasure, revenge, in anger, or out of jealousy.* We are not going to take revenge, Brother Dragon. That would lower us to the gutter. Don't even think about the spy. She is as ancient history to you now. Spend some time reciting and contemplating the creed again tonight, Brother. Make it sing in your blood. Ignore it and you will die. It is that simple.'

Shalidar bowed his head in acceptance and the Guildmaster walked swiftly from the room, his black robes merging quickly into the shadows of the corridor outside. When Shalidar's head came up, there was a set of defiance on his face that would have chilled even the Guildmaster's blood.

The meeting had been a dangerous gamble for Shalidar. He had thrown the dice of life with an outward confidence not mirrored by his heart. He had thrown and won again. Rather than come back straight away, some in his position might have travelled to foreign lands and utilised their talents there. There was always a demand for talented assassins. But Shalidar knew that if he had done this, he would always have been the outsider. Suspicion would always have fallen at his feet if there were trouble. It was human nature to suspect the stranger. Coming back to Shandrim was fraught with difficulties, but Shalidar knew how to blend in here. True, it was dangerous – particularly with the huge bounty the Emperor had placed on his head –

but every road held danger in his chosen profession. It was only the degree that varied.

Drawing back his sleeve, he contemplated the gleaming silver wristlet that bound him to the Guild. The engraved dragon there appeared to mock his inspection. There were times when he wished he could take it off and throw it away, but he knew that to do so was to invite instant death. In accepting his icon, he had bound himself to the Guild for life, or until he was retired by the Guildmaster. His life force was magically tied to the wristlet. He did not know how. It had never been fully explained. He could remove it, but he could move no more than a few paces from it without his life being forfeit.

There had been some who had tried to run in the past, but they had all returned, or died. The icons had to be placed against the binding stone once every year. If this contact was not made to refresh the bond, the icon automatically returned to the binding stone the moment the year was up. Unless the current holder of the icon was standing next to the stone at the time, he died instantly. As a safeguard against infiltrators, new members of the Guild were not told of this limitation until an initial probationary period had been completed. Shalidar remembered the shock he had felt when he had been told. It had left him wondering what other secrets the Guildmaster held. Although the Guild could not forcibly cause him to return to the headquarters at any particular time, he could no more leave the Guild than he could learn to fly.

By long-standing tradition, Guild members met to refresh their icons at midsummer's eve and midwinter's eve every year. Those who could not be there refreshed their icons as soon as they returned to the complex after these dates.

Only the Guildmaster held the means to remove an icon safely, but how that was done, Shalidar had never been able to discover. He covered it again angrily. At times the wristlet felt like a shackle. This was one of those times.

He had won his first gamble today. He had been accepted back by the Guildmaster. He knew he would have to tread carefully, but he had no intention of forgetting what Femke had done in Mantor. He would take his revenge. It might take a while to manipulate events to achieve it, but Shalidar could be patient when he had to be. He had always paid lip service to the Assassins' creed. It had never bound him as it had the others. If the Guild ever found out about any of his breaches of their law, he would be executed. It was partly the thrill of this danger that had led him to twist the words of the creed time and again. At one time or another, he had flaunted almost every critical phrase, but he had always covered his tracks meticulously. His fellow assassin, Falcon, would have died in Mantor regardless of the outcome of events there. He had learned too much of Shalidar's activities. By hanging him, the Thrandorians had saved Shalidar the job and provided the perfect cover.

'Your turn will come, Femke,' he whispered softly. 'Your turn will come.'

CHAPTER THREE

'All done,' Reynik said wearily.

'Show me,' the File Second ordered.

It was over. The last trench was dug. Tomorrow he would return to the relative normality of a training routine without all the extra evening duties. The relief at that thought brought a warming feeling to his stomach. Reynik jumped down into the trench, his knees threatening to buckle at the shock of the impact. A moment later and he had demonstrated the dimensions of his hole to the satisfaction of the supervising File Second.

'Very well. Stack your shovel with the rest, then go and get cleaned up. I don't want to see you in the restrictions party again, Legionnaire.'

'Thank you, File Second. I'll do my best to stay out of trouble.'

Reynik climbed out of the freshly dug toilet trench and walked over to the pile of tools by the equipment tent. He placed his long-handled shovel with the rest and sighed with relief as he gently rubbed his blistered hands together. 'If I never dig a hole again, it will be too soon,' he decided.

It was as he turned to leave that he spotted the lone figure walking between the tents not far away. Despite an overwhelming wave of tiredness, something about the silhouette instantly registered in his mind as being wrong. A shiver shot down his spine and he knew he could not ignore his premonition that whoever the figure was, he was up to no good.

'Walk away. Don't get involved. It's nothing to do with you.' The thoughts tumbled through his mind. 'If you're wrong, there could be consequences. You might end up back on restrictions again.'

But it was not that easy. The feeling would not go away and Reynik found his eyes returning to the figure now rapidly fading into the shadows of the dusky camp. The man was dressed in uniform, but Reynik could not see his Legion insignia at this distance. It would have been hard in full daylight at this range, but in the poor light of dusk it was impossible to make out. That walk; the way the man stepped. It was familiar.

'That's it!' Reynik breathed. 'He's not marching like a Legionnaire. No one from the General's Legion marches like that. He's making an effort, but it doesn't look natural. He's no Legionnaire. He walks more like ... Shalidar! No! It couldn't be!'

The shocking thought that he might be looking at his sworn enemy galvanised Reynik into action. Any concerns about potential repercussions were cast aside. If that was Shalidar walking bold as brass through the camp, then

Reynik wanted to ensure the assassin did not escape. His hand went automatically to his hip, seeking the comfort of his sword hilt. He cursed softly. His sword was in his tent, which was in the opposite direction from where the figure was disappearing. There was no time to go and fetch it. He didn't even have his knife with him, as it kept getting in the way when he was digging. Should he follow without a weapon? Should he follow at all?

His curiosity said yes. Also, his instinct told him he might not get another chance. It was now or never. With a quick glance back at the File Second to see if he was watching, Reynik picked up his long-handled shovel again and set out after the retreating shadowy figure. The shovel was unwieldy, but it could be used as a weapon at a push. Adrenalin began to flow as he dashed silently between the nearest rows of tents in an effort to close down his distance from the figure.

'Be careful,' Reynik told himself silently. 'Shalidar is bound to be on his guard for signs of pursuit.'

The dim, dusky light made it easy for him to flit from shadow to shadow as he raced to catch up, but Reynik knew that if Shalidar detected him, he could easily find he had switched from hunter to hunted without warning. Darkness would fall quickly now. This would make tracking the killer both more difficult and more treacherous. In order to keep the assassin in sight, Reynik would be forced to follow him more closely, thereby increasing the danger of discovery. There was no wisdom in this, he concluded, but his resolve to follow did not waver.

'What brought you back to Shandrim, Shalidar?' he

wondered. 'With half the bounty hunters in Shandar salivating over the reward the Emperor has placed on your head, why would you choose to return? It's got to be something important.' Even more intriguing was the question of what he was doing in the heart of the campsite of the Emperor's own elite Legion. Did Shalidar have a friend within the Legion? It would not surprise Reynik if this were the case. Assassins and spies all seemed to have friends in unlikely places.

He was catching up fast. The killer was apparently in no hurry to go anywhere, but he was moving steadily between the tents towards the edge of the city. If Shalidar had a friend in the Legion, then he had already paid him a visit.

It was an abrupt rumpus erupting behind Reynik that fitted the main piece into the jigsaw. The assassin wasn't here on a social visit. He was here on business. By the sound of the confused shouting behind them, Reynik guessed Shalidar had already concluded that business and was now coolly walking away, as if nothing had happened. Who had been the victim? It was impossible to tell from the noise.

'Well, it isn't over until you disappear, Shalidar,' Reynik said under his breath. 'And you're not going to disappear so easily today.'

The assassin accelerated his pace slightly. He was still showing no signs of undue haste, and certainly not enough to draw attention to his movements. Reynik felt that his stealthy movements were more likely to draw attention than the bold, striding pace of the assassin. It was annoying, but necessary. He could not afford for the assassin to notice that he was being followed. If he was spotted, Reynik was as good as dead. It would not take much for the assassin to drop out of sight around a corner and set an ambush for his pursuer. With the element of surprise, even a half competent assassin could kill anyone he chose with ease. For an expert assassin like Shalidar, it would be as simple as drawing breath.

'Looks like you're heading for the guard post on the main South West Avenue. Now why would you want to be seen there, Shalidar? Do you think you're going to stroll out of the camp with no one the wiser?' Reynik was amazed at the man's audacity. Surely one of the guards would notice he was not a Legionnaire.

Having worked out where the assassin was going, Reynik turned and ran silently between the lines of tents at ninety degrees from the direction of his destination. Once he was far enough offset from Shalidar's route to avoid detection, he turned and paralleled the assassin's track. It didn't take long to overtake him. By the time Shalidar reached the guard post at the edge of tent city, Reynik was in position, concealed nearby to watch what happened.

The assassin stopped and began talking in a low, urgent voice to the guards. His body language conveyed his message beautifully. Reynik was not close enough to hear what he was saying, but he did not need to be. He got the message loud and clear. Something bad had happened in the centre of the camp and the guards were to increase their alertness.

'Very clever,' Reynik conceded silently. 'As the bearer of the news, you put yourself above suspicion. Decision time. If I let him go into the city I will most likely lose him, or be discovered. If I call out, others might die.'

It was a difficult choice, but Reynik could not in conscience let the assassin go. He drew a deep breath and then launched into a sprint from his hiding place.

'Stop that man!' he yelled. 'He's an assassin. Stop him!'

The guards looked around in surprise, but if the assassin was surprised, he showed none of it. The momentary confusion of the guards was enough to give him the advantage he needed. Before Reynik had covered half the distance to the guard post, two guards were down and the other two had backed away in shock, giving the assassin the space to make his break.

He ran. Reynik ran after him, yelling for the remaining guards to follow as he went past. They didn't move. Seconds later a glance over his shoulder revealed them to be dithering; paralysed with indecision. He would receive no help from them, he realised. It was one on one. In his dreams, Reynik had imagined this meeting, though this was not quite as he had envisioned it. In his mind, he had thought to meet Shalidar face to face with a sword in his hand to duel with him to the death. Not surprisingly, he had never pictured himself dog-tired, chasing the assassin with a shovel as his only weapon!

Shalidar was fleet of foot, and it was taking every ounce of Reynik's flagging strength for him to keep his quarry in sight. The shovel was hardly an easy implement to run with. Its length alone made it awkward to carry, but the imbalance of weight due to the metal head made it worse. Reynik tried swapping positions as he ran, but he could not find a way of holding it that allowed him to run freely.

Within a couple of minutes, he realised that the assassin was getting away from him.

The streets were largely empty. The road they were running along was one of the major routes into the heart of the city, but it was late and the merchants had stopped trading more than an hour before. Most people were at home preparing their evening meal. There were a few folk abroad, mainly men in small groups on their way to the local taverns for a drink. Those that were abroad observed the chase with interest, some pointing and laughing at the sight of a filthy soldier carrying a spade chasing another who sported a sword and dagger at his side. Not one of them moved to interfere in any way. If he could, Reynik would have solicited help from them, but he did not have the breath left to shout. It was all he could do to keep running.

The aroma in the streets was pungent. An evil brew of rotting waste in the gutters mixed with the open sewerage channels. It was little wonder that the peasants in the poor quarters had a short life expectancy, Reynik thought as he pounded through the filth. Even panting hard as he was through his mouth, it was impossible to ignore the stench totally. It clung to the back of his throat like treacle. However, despite the choking odour he retained his focus, never allowing his attention to shift from the chase.

Shalidar turned left off the main avenue into a side street. He had a good sixty pace lead now. Blundering forward, Reynik ran straight at the corner. It was only in the last few paces that he realised his mistake and swung wide to avoid being too close to the blind spot as he rounded the building. It was well that he did, for his quarry was waiting for him.

Instinct and a slice of good fortune saved Reynik from being butchered in the opening exchange. The assassin leaped, swinging his sword down at him in a deadly overhead stroke. Even as the blade whistled at him, the young Legionnaire twisted and raised the shovel to block it. The blade bit deep into the handle of the shovel about an inch below the metal head and jammed in the wood. The shock of the impact drove the handle down and in towards Reynik's body, but the resistance that he offered, together with the pivoting effect of the blade sticking in the wood some distance from his hands, carried the tip of the sword clear of his body.

Reynik was quick to respond to the situation. Even as the shovel tip touched the ground he shifted his weight and reversed the pivotal movement of the handle, wrenching the assassin's sword arm back up and over in an arc. The handle of the sword was twisted from his fingers, but Reynik did not stop the momentum of the shovel and he smashed it down onto the cobblestone street. The deep cut in the handle had weakened it such that the handle splintered on impact, sending the sword and the head of the shovel spinning across the road.

For a moment, Reynik and his assailant faced one another. As he looked into the assassin's eyes, Reynik realised to his astonishment that it was not Shalidar staring back at him, but a complete stranger. For a split second the two paused, each as surprised as the other. How circumstances had changed in those few action-packed heartbeats!

Reynik's attacker had gone from having the advantages of both surprise and superior weapons to being unarmed and facing a soldier armed with what now looked like something between a staff and a spear.

Shalidar he was not, but if Reynik had been a gambler, he would have put money on the man being a paid killer.

'You ... are ... under ... arrest ...' Reynik started, panting out the words and lifting the lethal-looking wooden handle threateningly.

The man growled. There was no other description that adequately conveyed the sound that issued from his mouth. It was a low-pitched rumble of anger and frustration that erupted from the man's throat like the ominous grumble of a big cat. Then he took advantage of Reynik's surprise and fatigue by spinning and running away in one swift movement.

Reynik hesitated to follow. He was tired. The fire of vengeance that had burned in his belly had been doused by the discovery that he was not chasing his sworn enemy. He was in no fit state to follow further. The man still had a soldier's knife, which if wielded competently could be every bit as deadly as a sword. All Reynik was left with was the remains of the shovel – now more of a pole.

Reynik glanced across at the sword lying in the road, but realised that grabbing it would lose him more time. Duty and fatigue battled for supremacy in his mind. It was a swift conflict. Duty won. He did not know what the man had been doing in tent city, but judging by his actions when pursued, he was unlikely to have been doing anything good.

Gritting his teeth and forcing his body onwards, Reynik took up the pursuit again. The side street was narrow and darkening fast. Dusk was already giving way to night. Reynik's laboured breathing, together with the echoing footfalls of their running feet, sounded loud in his ears. An alley cat yowled and ran to one side as the assassin approached it. It gave a spitting hiss at Reynik as he passed by a couple of seconds later, clearly annoyed at being disturbed from its evening hunt.

The man turned right into a narrow alley between two rows of tall, overhanging terraced houses. Reynik once again took the wide approach to avoid another surprise attack, but the man had not paused this time. He was progressively stretching his lead. There was nothing Reynik could do, but doggedly press on after him.

It was so dark in the alleyway that Reynik could no longer see the man he was chasing. It was a clattering noise followed by a frustrated curse that told him the man had tripped and fallen. The noise brought a feeling of triumph to Reynik, though it was tempered with caution. He slowed his pace a touch as he approached the area where the assassin had tripped. The step that had caused the man to fall almost caught Reynik as well, but he spotted it at the last second.

There was no sign of the assassin, so Reynik knew that the man must have got up and continued running. The alleyway curved slightly ahead and then opened into another side street. Reynik moved forward cautiously, slowing to a walk as he approached the end of the alley. He could no longer hear the assassin's footfalls, which meant he had either stretched his lead further, or that he was hiding somewhere.

As he emerged from the end of the alley, his caution proved well placed. The man attacked from the right, lunging towards him with the long soldier's knife. Reynik's survival instincts again served him well. He whipped his wooden pole around, connecting hard with the man's knife wrist and deflecting it. As an extension of the movement, he continued to spin, bringing his left foot up into a high kick, expecting to drive his boot into the side of his assailant's head.

To Reynik's surprise, his kick did not land. Instead his attacker blocked the kick with his forearm, throwing him off balance. There was a scrabbling scuffle as both men fought for position. A rapid sequence of attempted blows followed. Each was blocked and counter-attacked by the other.

It quickly became apparent that Reynik's wooden pole was the superior weapon, particularly as it was wielded with exceptional skill. In desperation, the assassin threw his knife. The throw was rushed and not as accurate as it could have been, but despite twisting to avoid it, the blade sliced Reynik's left upper arm as it passed. Again off balance and feeling the hot slice of metal tearing through his flesh, Reynik was caught off guard as the assassin grabbed hold of his makeshift staff. There was a brief struggle for possession, as the two men wrestled back and forth for control.

In a pure surge of adrenalin, Reynik yanked his attacker towards him with the staff and smashed his forehead down

52

into the bridge of the man's nose in a vicious head butt. The assassin's head snapped back and a plume of blood flew from his nose. He was given no time to recover as Reynik heaved his body backwards, rolling onto the ground and dragging the man forwards – straight onto Reynik's waiting feet. With a heave of his legs, Reynik flipped the assassin over his head, sending him crashing down hard onto the stone street.

This was too much for the hired killer. The wind rushed out of his lungs and he writhed on the ground in pain, letting go of the staff in the process. Reynik wasted no time. In a flash, he was back on his feet and before his assailant had time to recover, Reynik dealt him a cracking blow to the temple with the thick end of the pole. The assassin went limp, completely out cold.

Reynik heaved a sigh of relief and staggered over to the wall of the nearest house. He let the wooden shovel handle fall to the ground and then he sat down with his back against the wall to catch his breath. He touched his left upper arm where the assassin's knife had cut him, wincing as pain lanced up through his shoulder. There was a rapidly growing area of dampness on his shirt where the blood was flowing unchecked.

'It wouldn't do to pass out from blood loss,' he thought dully. 'I'd better bandage it before it gets too bad.'

His chest was still heaving from his exertions. First the run and then the fight had sapped what little resources of energy he had retained after his first week back in training. It was likely that Sidis would give him a hard time for having ripped his shirt, regardless of the circumstances.

Then it occurred to him that the assassin was wearing an identical shirt of a similar size with no such rips.

'Excellent!' he muttered. 'I might not come out of this so badly after all.'

He rested for a minute, applying direct pressure to his sliced arm the whole time, in order to restrict the flow of blood. When he had recovered his breath sufficiently, he grabbed his wooden handle and used it as a prop to help get back onto his feet. His legs felt weak and his knees threatened to give way as he wobbled over to where the unconscious assassin was sprawled on the ground.

Reynik prodded him gently with the pole, looking for any signs that the man was acting. There were none. He was out cold. Having established this, Reynik went and recovered the man's knife from where it had skittered to rest a little way down the street. He removed his shirt, wincing at the fresh pain as he peeled the blood-soaked sleeve from his arm. Looking at the wound made him feel light-headed. It needed stitching, but he could not do it on his own.

Using the knife, he cut several strips from the back of his ruined shirt. The first he folded into a pad. Then he bound the pad of material over the wound with the second. It was not an easy task. He fumbled for some time trying to get the bandage to take hold. Working one-handed made it all but impossible to get a suitably tight finish, but having managed to tie it off, he concluded that it would do until he could get back to the Legion medics.

The temperature was dropping as the darkness of night deepened, and Reynik shivered as the cold fingers of the evening breeze stroked his back. Again, he was cautious as he approached the man. The last blow he had struck with the wooden pole had been hard and accurate. Looking at the man's face closely, Reynik began to wonder if he had hit him too hard. Judging by the damage to his left temple, it was possible that he might never regain consciousness. Stripping him would not help his cause, but Reynik was not about to freeze for this man's comfort.

The task of removing the unconscious man's shirt was not an easy one. It took several minutes of manoeuvring and tugging awkwardly at the fabric, but Reynik finally held the shirt in his hands. He donned it swiftly, ignoring the pain as he forced his wounded arm into the sleeve. The fit was not quite perfect. It was a little on the loose side, but that was all to the good under the circumstances.

Having regained a degree of comfort, Reynik bent over the man to take a closer look at something curious he had discovered underneath the man's shirt. It was a sort of pendant. A leather strap around the man's neck sported a most unusual talisman. As Reynik looked more closely, he realised that it was a silver replica of a wolf spider. He had never seen a live one, but his father had an artist's impression of one in his study at home, so he identified it immediately. As a boy he had asked his father about it, and he vividly remembered what his father had said.

'The wolf spider is an amazing predator, son. It is not like other spiders. It doesn't weave webs with which to trap its prey. It hunts like a wolf, running down its victim and killing it with a venomous bite. Nasty creatures, wolf spiders.'

'Nasty creatures, wolf spiders.' The words echoed in his mind like a prophecy. He shivered again, but not from the cold this time.

Thinking to take a closer look, Reynik lifted the leather necklace over the man's head and walked a short distance down the street towards the nearest oil lamp. As he walked away from the man, the necklace began to tingle in his hand. The sensation was strangely alien, and Reynik's instinct was to drop it immediately.

As it struck the ground the spider glowed briefly with a sparkling energy that was not natural. Then it dissolved to nothingness, leaving the leather thong as the only evidence of its existence. At the same time, the man laying on the street suddenly convulsed and groaned as if in extreme pain before going limp and deathly pale. Reynik did not have to check his breathing to know that he was dead.

'What in Shand's name . . . ?'

Assassins, he could cope with, but this weird magical stuff was a totally different prospect. The supernatural was something he had always left well alone. Had he killed the man by hitting him with the handle of the shovel, or was there something more sinister at work here? The silver wolf spider talisman had clearly been more than just a decoration, but what had its purpose been? It was a mystery that he suspected would not be easily solved.

It took Reynik a long time to drag the man back to the guard post at the end of the South West Avenue. He had not realised they had run so far. When he got there the entire Legion campsite was in uproar. Fortunately, the two guards who had failed to help pursue the assassin were still a part of the group on duty. They were quick to relieve him of the body without too many questions.

'What's going on?' he asked. 'I'm guessing all the activity is due to our friend here, but who was his target?'

A Legionnaire with File Leader rank markings on his sleeve answered the question. 'Our Legion Commander has been murdered. If this is his killer, then you've done well. None of the others have been apprehended.'

'I'm afraid he won't be answering any questions, File Leader. He didn't want to come quietly and I inadvertently rapped him on the head too hard. He's dead. You mentioned others, File Leader. There were more victims, or more assassins?'

'Three other Legion Commanders died this evening, aside from our own. I can't imagine this man was responsible for all four deaths. It would be impossible for one man to travel that far in such a short time. It's been a disastrous night for the Legions.'

The File Leader's information brought a bitter flood of bile to Reynik's throat. 'My father is a Legion Commander. Do you know the names of the dead?'

The File Leader returned Reynik's gaze apprehensively. 'I don't know all of their names,' he said warily, 'but I do know which Legions they commanded. Which Legion does your father command?'

'The Third Legion.'

'Then as far as I know, your father still lives.'

Reynik heaved a grateful sigh and sank to the ground as his body flushed warm with relief. For a moment, he had felt sure that he was about to hear the worst possible news.

His mind was racing with memories of his uncle's murder. Assassins were the worst kind of killers, he concluded: cold blooded, and motivated solely by monetary reward. It was good that the Emperor had declared them *anaethus drax*. Now the assassins had given their response. It appeared that the Emperor had instigated a war of sorts. The assassins had fired the first volley, making sure it was the military that took the casualties. It would be interesting to see how the Emperor would respond.

The File Leader thought it impossible for a single man to kill the four Legion Commanders, but an image of the disappearing talisman gave Reynik reason to doubt. This too sounded impossible, but it had happened. He was certain of it. Was there a connection? If there was, then new lines of reasoning could lead them towards any one of a myriad of unlikely possibilities.

'Are you all right? I can see you're bleeding. Do you need the medics?' The File Leader squatted down next to him.

Reynik looked at his arm and saw that blood had seeped through the bandage and stained his sleeve again.

'I could do with a few stitches. He sliced my arm pretty badly when we fought. I bandaged it with my torn shirt and took his since he didn't need it any more. I'll live, but I'd appreciate getting it seen to before it turns bad.'

'Looks like you could do with a hand getting there. Hey! You and you,' he called, pointing at two nearby soldiers. 'Help this young Legionnaire . . .'

'Reynik.'

'Help Legionnaire Reynik to the nearest medic's tent. I'm sure that someone will want to debrief you on how you caught this man. There is bound to be an inquiry. Who is your File Leader?'

'Sidis.'

'Sidis, eh?' A slight sourness in the File Leader's tone gave Reynik the clue that he was not fond of Sidis either. 'Well, I'll speak to File Leader Sidis later. Go and get seen to by the medics, then you'd better get some sleep. I think you're going to need it.'

CHAPTER FOUR

Lady Alyssa had been back in Shandrim for a few days, and everyone who was anyone knew about it. She had been up to all her usual tricks. Her trademark high-handedness and imperious manner had brought quiet havoc back to the Silver Chalice.

Versande Matthiason, proprietor of the inn, was not sad when the young Lady announced that she was returning home. He was flattered that she had returned to his inn, for she was notoriously difficult to please. That she would choose to return spoke volumes amongst those who followed which establishments were in fashion. He was also happy to extract large quantities of the young Lady's gold from her seemingly endless wealth, but her visit had once again proved a trial to his normally imperturbable demeanour.

From the moment Alyssa had arrived, she had sent him an endless stream of demands. He had organised soirées in the inn's private function room for the Lady's chosen guests. He had organised visits by perfumers, merchants of cosmetic paints, clothiers, merchants who sold ladies shoes, and had called on the services of Rikala, the dressmaker, to make another outfit for her. He had been harassed about every little detail of how the private function room should look for each of her elitist gatherings. Florists, specialist food suppliers and artists – all had been required to make the room 'just so'. It had been exhausting.

As she left, Lady Alyssa, sweet as a rose, politely thanked Versande for his services. 'Sorry if I've been a little picky,' she said with a coy smile. 'I do get a bit carried away sometimes.'

'You are always welcome at the Silver Chalice, Lady Alyssa,' Versande replied, wondering how forced his smile looked as he clenched his fists behind his back. 'Have a safe trip home.'

Femke, consummate actress though she was, had a difficult time maintaining a straight face at Versande's parting words. The man was a treasure – utterly professional and wholeheartedly determined to uphold the reputation of his inn. How he had kept from cracking under the pressure she had applied over the last four days, she did not know. She had made sure he earned every last gold sen of his outrageous fee for her short stay.

Playing the part of Lady Alyssa was always fun. This time had been no exception. As she rode along the Eastern Avenue, her servant led the baggage horse ahead of her. Mentally she compiled her report for the Emperor. It had been a productive week. She had wined and dined many of the sons and daughters of the more influential Nobility of Shandrim. With a subtlety that few possessed, she had pumped them for information about current affairs, attitudes to the new Emperor and the Assassins' Guild. Asking anyone about the final subject was a risky business. If the Guild got to hear of her enquiries, they might decide it would be in their interests to eliminate her. Femke had picked her guests with a great deal of care. She did not wish to inadvertently draw attention from the wrong quarters. Had an interrogator watched her, he would have marvelled at the indirectness of her questions. She made the acquisition of useful information look to be an art form of the highest order.

Although Femke's activities had left her none the wiser about the location of the Assassins' Guild headquarters, she had not really expected to get that lucky. Likewise, there were none who speculated on the identity of the Guildmaster. Doing so would have been tantamount to inviting death to dance. However, the information she had gleaned would be interesting to the Emperor. Attitudes were changing slowly amongst the Nobles. There had been a gradual, but positive shift of opinion over the few months since Surabar had taken the Mantle. He was winning them around with his firm, but positive approach to ruling Shandar.

Lord Kempten had won some over during the Emperor's trip to Thrandor. The fact that an old-school Lord like Kempten could be so won over by the ex-General's abilities had given many of his peers cause to reconsider. There was still a large cadre of Noblemen who were intent on replacing Surabar with one of their own. However, when

Lord Kempten had sent some of their more outspoken members to the gallows, the group had been forced to become a lot more circumspect about their activities.

Femke was still mulling over the information she had gathered when she and her servant left the eastern boundary of the city. Constant mental reinforcement of the names and other nuggets she had gathered was vital if she was to retain every detail. Writing them down was not an option. To do so was dangerous in the extreme. With hindsight, she realised that she should have been paying more attention to the road.

The sudden fizzing buzz of an arrow was followed by a sickening thud as it punched her servant from his saddle. He did not cry out as he fell. The arrow had caught him squarely in the chest. Femke's mind raced. If an assassin had fired the arrow then she would have been the target. It was more likely to be the fame of Lady Alyssa's wealth that was the motive behind this attack. Assuming this was true, she knew there was a chance of getting out of the situation alive.

It was easy to let shock and horror flood her features. She let out her best 'damsel in distress' scream, the high-pitched trill cutting through the surrounding trees with an intensity that would carry a good distance.

'Stop that noise now, or the next arrow will stop it for you,' ordered a deep voice to her left.

Femke clamped a hand across her mouth and loosened the knife up her sleeve in the process. She always had several weapons about her person. Whether she would attempt to use them would depend on how many adversaries there were. If the odds were bad she would continue to play the pathetic, terrified Noblewoman until a suitable opportunity arose for making her escape.

'There ain't no one else followin', boss,' came a second voice from some distance behind Femke.

'Good,' the original, deeper voice responded. There was a rustling noise in the bushes by the side of the road. Two men emerged, both wearing self-satisfied grins. One was barrel-chested with thick, black hair, a square jaw and strangely angular features. He was holding a sword as if he knew how to use it. At his side was a slimmer man sporting a bow. He was sly-faced with lank, greasy-looking hair. Femke had no doubt that it was he who had just killed her servant. His proud glance across at where the unfortunate man had fallen was enough to confirm that view. The third man remained hidden somewhere along the road towards the city.

'At least three of them,' she thought. 'But they're split, which helps.' She remained seated on her horse, as if frozen in place by fear. The two men approached her confidently.

'Get down off the horse, Lady,' the leader ordered, raising his sword until it was pointing at her. 'We'd like to get better acquainted with you and your money, and we can hardly do that while you are sitting up there shaking, now can we?'

Femke squeaked fearfully from behind her hand, her eyes wide. The two men glanced at one another and laughed. As was fitting for a Lady, Femke was riding sidesaddle. Her legs were towards the armed brigands, which was undoubtedly their intention. They did not want her to use the horse as a shield and try to run away. As she considered her options, Femke decided that with only two of them in sight she had more than a good chance of taking them by surprise. The third man's last call was from some way away. She decided to discount him as an immediate threat.

'You'll r . . . r . . . run me through if I jump down.'

'I'll run you through if you *don't* jump down! Get off that horse. Now!'

The man moved his sword to one side to encourage her. It was just the chance Femke was looking for. She did not hesitate, but pushed away from the saddle to bridge the gap between her and the big man. Her jump carried her inside the natural arc of his sword and she twisted just slightly as she descended. Femke landed hard, driving her left heel down onto the man's left foot. As she compressed her knees on impact her right hand grabbed the handle of the knife in her right boot top, whilst another appeared miraculously in her left hand from her sleeve. The roar of pain had barely begun to erupt from the big man's mouth when it cut off. Femke, rising out of her crouch, threw the knife from her right hand straight into the body of the thinner robber. In one smooth simultaneous action, she opened the bigger man's belly with a twisting slash of the blade in her left hand.

The big man dropped his sword in shock. Femke did not wait for a further reaction. The man's redoubled bellow of pain spooked her horse. It reared and galloped forward, frightening the packhorse into a gallop as well. Luck and quick reactions favoured her. She was just quick enough to turn and grab a handful of her horse's mane before it charged forward out of reach. Her arm wrenched in its socket as the terrified horse dragged her away. She skipped twice, the horse pulling her far faster than she could run. Using her momentum, she kicked hard off the ground on the second bounce, flipping herself back up and onto the horse's back.

Pain lanced through her chest as her partially healed ribs were first stretched by the overextension of her arm and then battered as they connected with the pommel of the saddle. The pain brought tears to her eyes, but she gritted her teeth and concentrated on staying on the horse's back. Trees and bushes flashed past in a green blur as her mount stretched out into its full gallop. The flapping of her dress against the horse's flank did not help, as it served to perpetuate the poor animal's fright. It took a few moments before she managed to gain a secure seat. By the time she had, the main threat of danger from the robbers was behind her.

The two men in the middle of the road were both badly wounded. Femke did not know if they would live from the injuries she had dealt them, but the knowledge that their partner in crime would get to them quickly salved her initial pangs of guilt. If they lived, she doubted they would be so quick to attempt robbing Noblewomen in future.

A short way up the road, she managed to pull alongside and catch her servant's horse. Then, with both horses and all of her belongings still intact, she continued to her pre-arranged rendezvous point. When she arrived, her contact was waiting. Femke changed quickly into nondescript clothing, warning her agent of the ambush that had awaited her outside the city. The man's expression was grim on hearing the fate of his fellow operative, but he did not ask for more information. He knew that this was not the time for chatting. The man put Lady Alyssa's travelling clothes into her bags with all of the rest of her belongings, took her two horses and left. Femke mounted her fresh horse, turned it away from the road and set off across the open countryside to circle around to the south of the city. There was little chance of her being attacked twice in one day, but she took the precaution of switching some of her less accessible weapons to where she could get to them quickly should the need arise.

A glance at the sun told her she was running ahead of schedule. 'Just as well,' she decided. 'It wouldn't be good to keep the Emperor waiting.'

When she arrived at the door to the Emperor's study later that afternoon, she was surprised and delighted to find Reynik also waiting in the corridor. After their adventures together in Thrandor, it was like an unannounced visit by a brother. He greeted her with a very gentle hug, clearly mindful of her healing ribs. Having crunched them against the pommel of her saddle earlier that day, Femke was very glad of his thoughtfulness.

'What brings you here today?' Femke asked in a whispered tone, noting that Reynik looked embarrassed after their brief embrace.

'Emperor Surabar summoned me. He probably wants to talk to me about the assassin I caught last night,' he replied with an offhand shrug.

'You caught one of them? Do you know who it was? Has

he given up any information about the Guild?' Before Reynik had a chance to answer her excited barrage of questions the study door opened, cutting short their talk. The Emperor was standing in the doorway looking grave. He waved them both inside.

'He won't be talking about anything,' Reynik whispered in her ear as they moved to comply. 'I killed him.'

Femke's head turned sharply to look at the young soldier's face as they walked forward, but he hid any emotion well. In the Emperor's presence, Reynik was every inch the young soldier. He marched forward smartly and came to an abrupt halt in front of the Emperor's desk, making Femke feel positively slovenly in comparison. A guard positioned outside the door closed it behind them.

'At ease, Legionnaire,' Surabar ordered. He sat down behind his desk, rested his elbows on the table and steepled his hands. His eyebrows drew together in a strange expression, halfway between a frown and deep contemplation. 'It seems that I cannot keep you two out of things even when I want to. I want reports from both of you, but as we are likely to be here for some time, you had better pull up chairs. Do the honours, please, Reynik.'

Reynik immediately went and fetched a chair for Femke. He held it for her in his best courtly fashion as she sat down, though he felt awkward doing so. Then he fetched another and sat down next to her.

'Thank you. Now, Femke, let's start with you, shall we? I asked you to do some quiet information gathering, yet I have been hearing nothing but tales of your lavish little gatherings at the Silver Chalice. I thought I was quite clear about what I wanted you to do.'

'You were, your Imperial Majesty. My orders were to gather information about the loyalties of the Nobility without drawing attention to the fact that I was doing so. I was further to ensure that I minimised any personal danger. That is exactly what I did. Nobody would suspect Lady Alyssa of being a spy. The gentry are far too caught up with her outrageous behaviour and her lavish lifestyle to think beyond the façade. I can assure your Majesty that there was no one at any of my little parties who suspected for one second that I was information gathering.'

'Lavish, yes. Outrageous, yes. Outrageously expensive tastes, I would certainly agree! I don't even want to think about what your little expedition cost, young lady. Please, next time you have the urge to spend half of the treasury, could you at least warn me first? I nearly had a heart attack when I realised what you were doing.'

'But, your Majesty,' she protested innocently, 'the results were clearly worth the expense. I can provide you with an extensive list of those amongst the Nobility who are now supporting your rule. Not only that, but a list of those whose activities border on treason. Surely this information is worth a few gold coins?'

'Indeed it is, but I doubt that the bill was limited to a few gold coins! I've seen the prices at the Silver Chalice. I'm sure that thief Matthiason charges for the ground you stand on from the moment you walk through the door.'

Femke laughed.

'When I write out the list of names for you, your

Majesty, I'm sure that you will feel every copper sennut was well spent.'

'Very well, I shall reserve judgement for now. I take it that everything was comfortable in your lodgings? I suppose I cannot complain that you were taking physical risks with your choice of accommodation.'

Femke winced as she thought about the attack outside the city that morning. There was no point in concealing things from the Emperor. If it ever came out later that she had been attacked and she had not told him, he would never trust her again. Strangely, trust was the primary basis on which effective spying was built. Betraying the trust of one's employer was the greatest mistake a spy could make.

'Actually, your Majesty, it wasn't such a great choice after all.'

'Really? In what way?'

'My apparent wealth attracted a criminal element that I hadn't anticipated. It was foolish. I should have foreseen it. My agent and I were attacked shortly after we left the city boundary. My agent was killed by an archer. The thieves sought to rob me. What their intentions were beyond that is unsure.'

The Emperor looked at her expectantly. Reynik was listening with fascination as well.

'So? What happened? How did you escape?'

'I was lucky. They did not expect me to be armed, nor to have the nerve to take the fight to them. I gutted one and left a knife buried in the belly of another. There was a third man whom I never saw. He was some distance behind me, and hidden in the trees as I made my escape. I made my rendezvous on time and changed identity, but I should have thought to take more of an escort. It's easy with hindsight to see how my character would attract such an attack. My agent was a good man. I will miss his loyalty.'

The Emperor gave her a hard look. 'You take too many risks,' he stated in an uncompromising voice. 'I don't want you back out in the field until your ribs have fully healed. I'm not going to accept any arguments, so don't even try. Clear?'

'Yes, your Majesty.'

'Now, aside from the list of loyalties, did you manage to make any progress on the whereabouts of the Assassin's Guild?'

'No, your Majesty,' Femke replied with a sigh. She hated to admit failure, but there was no point in glossing up the little bit of information she had gleaned from her subtle questions. 'None of those I spoke to appeared to know anything useful. A lot can be deduced from body language, your Majesty. I doubt those whom I questioned were such expert liars that they could hide the tell-tale signs one gives when not telling the truth. There were none amongst them who knew anything of great interest about the Guild. Some of the older Lords might. Have you asked Lord Kempten? He may know something.'

'Kempten knows nothing of use. I've already exhausted his knowledge. Reynik might be able to fill in some of the gaps, which is one of the reasons for his presence. Last night's strikes by the Guild of Assassins were clearly a message of defiance meant for me, but I'm not going to be intimidated. I will not be dictated to by a secret society of killers. They're an outdated throwback to a previous age. I do not accept that they're a desirable, or necessary part of Shandese society. My decision to outlaw them has now been validated by their actions. I intend to see them driven from Shandar. Can you tell us about your encounter last night, Reynik? It may give us an insight into the way they work.'

Reynik explained the circumstances in which he had spotted the assassin, how he had thought it was Shalidar and how he had tracked him with only a shovel for a weapon. He told of how the guards had failed to stop the man at the guard post, the chase, and his first short encounter.

Femke noted that for all his impassive face, the Emperor was clearly impressed that Reynik had survived that first meeting. Having parted the assassin from his sword during the fight the balance had swung in Reynik's favour, so it was strange that the assassin had chosen to attack a second time, when he could clearly have outdistanced Reynik and made a clean escape. When he had finished telling of how he had knocked the man unconscious, he paused, unsure of whether to tell the Emperor about the strange silver talisman.

'There is more to this story than you're telling, isn't there?' Surabar asked, his cold eyes boring into Reynik.

'Am I that obvious, your Majesty?' Reynik replied, flushing with embarrassment. 'You're right. There was something else – something most curious. The man was wearing a strange talisman around his neck. It was a silver replica of a wolf spider hanging on a leather thong.'

'So what happened to the talisman? Do you have it? It wasn't mentioned in my briefing by Commander Vascilly last night.'

'That's the strange thing, your Majesty. It disappeared. It melted away before my eyes, exuding a sparkling energy that did not look natural. I'm assuming that the talisman possessed magical properties, but its purpose remains a mystery. What's particularly interesting is that it should disappear at the same instant the man died.'

'Melted away, you say? When the man died – hmm, that is interesting. Have you ever seen anything like this before, Femke? Does Shalidar have one of these spider talismans?'

Femke shook her head. 'Not as far as I know, your Majesty. I've never heard of the Guild having any sort of symbol before, nor of them using magic. A magician in their ranks would be a fearsome adversary.' She paused in thought for a brief moment, then continued. 'If they've adopted the wolf spider as their mark, it's not something they've advertised. The wolf spider would be an appropriate symbol for their profession, but I find it hard to believe, given that we've not come across it before.'

Emperor Surabar scratched his nose thoughtfully for a moment. He looked first at Femke, then Reynik, then back to Femke again. There was much to consider, but he already had a plan in mind. The two young people had brought nothing new that would affect what he had in mind, so he decided to go ahead and put his strategy into motion.

'I agree, Femke. The disappearing spider talisman is interesting, but I'm not convinced that it has any real bearing on what I'm trying to achieve. I need to know more about the Guild of Assassins. I intend to destroy them, but only a fool destroys something without knowing all of the implications of his actions. By declaring them *anaethus drax* I've made clear my intention to drive the Guild from Shandrim. I didn't expect them to go quietly, but neither did I anticipate their strike against the Legions. It was a clever countermove on their part. Whoever leads the Guild is no fool. I need to know more about this Guildmaster whom I've set myself against. "Know your enemy" was a tenet I was taught very early in my military career, but how do you get to know an enemy you cannot find? It's a difficult question. I have a solution, but it involves risks. Risks to my person I would never shy away from, but my plan will involve risking the lives of others.'

When Surabar paused again, Femke smiled. 'By "others", would I be right in assuming you mean us?' she asked, indicating to include Reynik and herself. The Emperor nodded. 'Then what would you have us do, your Majesty? I am yours to command.'

'I too,' Reynik added, bowing his head.

'Another tenet I learned a long time ago was "Never volunteer for anything without knowing exactly what you're letting yourself in for",' Surabar said with an amused grin. 'I suggest that you listen to my idea before you agree. My plan will put at least one person in extreme danger. I will not order anyone to do it. I'll only accept a volunteer.'

'We're listening, your Majesty,' Femke encouraged.

'I want someone to infiltrate the Guild. I need a volunteer who is willing to become an undercover assassin.

Once we have someone on the inside, the two crucial pieces of information needed to bring the Guild down should be ours for the taking. It is of paramount importance to find out where the Guild headquarters is located. Second only to this is the identity of the Guildmaster. Once we know these things, breaking up the Guild will become relatively straightforward.'

Femke did not hesitate. 'I'll do it, your Majesty. I have the requisite background training. It will take me a little while to create a suitable new persona, but it should be possible with the appropriate support.'

'No, Femke – not this time. You're not suitable for several reasons. First, you have not fully recovered from your injuries. Do not think I'm going to cast aside my vow about your returning to the field before you are fully fit. Second, Shalidar must be a member of the Guild and he knows you too well. If he returns to Shandrim, you would be discovered and killed very quickly. We don't know what sort of induction procedures the Guild has, or how they screen their recruits. Your various personas have all been seen around Shandrim for some years. I wouldn't be surprised to find that you are already marked by the Guild.'

'Which leaves me, your Majesty,' Reynik said coolly. 'If I were to accept this mission, would I have to kill in order to be accepted into the Guild?'

'Yes,' Surabar said grimly. 'The hypocrisy of it galls me, but I am not blind to the necessity of giving you a solid cover. If it brings any comfort, I will feel any lives we are forced to take as darker stains upon my soul than any I gained for my decisions as a soldier. I can assure you that any targets I assign you will already have been marked for the death sentence. There are a lot of prominent Noblemen out there set on treasonous activities. I abhor the whole nature of killing for money, but it will be necessary for you to become a real assassin if you are to successfully infiltrate the Guild. Moreover, you'll need to do something spectacular if you are to grab the Guild's attention.'

'Your Majesty,' Femke interrupted, 'if I might be so bold, Legionnaire Reynik, for all his good intentions, is trained neither as an assassin, nor as a spy. He will be spotted easily.'

'That's why I'm making it your job to train him. You have three weeks. No more.'

'Three weeks, your Majesty! But that's impossible! Three months would be hard, but . . .'

'You have three weeks, Femke,' Surabar interrupted. 'Events are moving quickly. With hindsight, I was rash to declare the Guild *anaethus drax*. I should have waited until I had more information. Three weeks is as much time as I can allow. The longer we delay, the more people are likely to lose their lives for no purpose. Legionnaire Reynik will have to learn quickly. He has proved himself resourceful before. I've no doubt that he will be able to absorb enough information in that time to become convincing. Accept and your first hit will take place in three weeks. I will place any resources you require at your command. What do you say, Reynik?'

'I remain yours to command, your Majesty. I will do as you ask.'

'We will both do our best, your Majesty,' Femke added.

'See that your best is good enough. Good people are dying because of my miscalculation. A location and a name – that is all I ask.'

Reynik bowed, recognising the dismissal in the Emperor's final statement. As he turned to leave, his mind raced. In three weeks, he would be expected to kill someone in cold blood. It was not a thought that filled him with joy.

'How is your search going? Have you found me an assassin willing to kill the Emperor?'

Lacedian shook his head. 'No one has responded. Are you sure this is a good idea, Tremarle? Others have tried and been hanged for treason recently. It would only take one word in the wrong ear and it'll be us swinging from the gallows next.'

'I'm not about to back down. Find me someone who won't fail. I want revenge for the loss of my son and the loss of my House. Surabar must die.'

A shiver ran down Lord Lacedian's spine. There was a look of madness in his old friend's eyes. It was possible that the death of Danar had unhinged Tremarle's mind. Should he continue to act on the request? He wanted to see the Emperor replaced by one with true Noble blood as much as anyone did, but was an assassination truly the way ahead?

'I'll try, my friend,' he said finally, feeling forced to speak in order to break the pregnant silence. 'There are few who are likely to accept the hit, but I will enquire.'

'You can offer them four thousand gold pieces to see if that will help them to decide.'

'Four thousand! Have you got that much gold? There may even be some in the Guild who would overlook their creed for that sort of money.'

'Lacedian, I would beggar myself to see Surabar dead now. He has destroyed my family's future. I will not rest until he dies.'

By chance, a passing cloud eased in front of the sun. The light in Lord Tremarle's drawing room dropped dramatically. Lacedian shivered again. He was not normally superstitious, but the timing of the sudden darkness gave the feeling of an omen. No matter how Lacedian tried to shrug it off, he could not shake the feeling that he should back out now before it was too late.

He opened his mouth to speak, but nothing came out. He bowed his head and his heart sank. It was no good. He could not deny his friend. Doomed or not, Lacedian would find someone willing to take on the hit. Four thousand in gold would buy a lot of interest. The problem would be keeping the contract a secret from the Emperor's spies. If he failed, it would mean death – a powerful incentive to keep from making mistakes.

CHAPTER FIVE

'This way, Reynik,' Femke ordered, striding off through the corridors of the Imperial Palace as if she owned the place.

'Where are we going?' he asked, jogging for a moment to catch up.

'Firstly to find some civilian clothes for you to wear; then to find a man who can teach you to use a sword.'

'But I can already fight with a sword,' Reynik protested. 'I admit I'm not the best swordsman around, but I can hold my own.'

Femke stopped abruptly. Reynik tottered slightly as he fought to stop and maintain his balance. She gave him a hard stare and when she spoke it was in a low voice that would not be overheard.

'You walk like a soldier. You talk like a soldier. As far as I know, you probably fart and swear like a soldier! We have three weeks to beat that out of you, Reynik, or the Guild will see right through you. I don't want to think about what they would do to you then. I'm starting with the obvious. You will need to handle a sword differently. You will also need to acquire other less usual weapons skills. We'll not be able to hide your military training entirely in such a short time, but we should be able to build you an identity as a military drop-out. I see you as a disaffected soldier who has turned to killing for a fee. The trick to making this persona convincing will be to eliminate some of your military habits and style, but leave evidence of your past.'

'That makes sense.'

'Of course it does, so please don't question my judgement. Do as you're told like a good little soldier and things will be fine. I'll conduct some of your training myself, but for those things that I can't teach you, I'll find those who can. I happen to know of an expert swordsman who could do with a paying job right now. If anyone can teach you how to use a sword effectively, it'll be this man.'

Femke had a word with one of the Imperial Palace staff, and Reynik was given access to the guest wardrobes. Stores of clothing suitable for most sizes were kept in order to save visitors embarrassment in the event of their arriving during poor weather, or after a difficult journey, with nothing suitable to wear around the Palace. Reynik did not take long to find something in his size. An off-white tunic, black leggings, calf-length riding boots and a mid-blue jacket with silver decorative stitching suited him well.

They bundled his uniform into a bag and dropped it off at Femke's quarters. Femke took the opportunity to change into nondescript clothing before they set off again, heading out of the Palace towards the south west quarter of the city. It took a while to reach their destination. The streets were busy with the bustle of daily life. The smells of cooking meat wafted on the air, as food vendors began utilising the tantalising scents to lure in custom. Traders called out to them, extolling the virtues of their wares, and young boys tried to cajole them into inns and shops, undoubtedly looking to gain a commission for bringing the proprietors custom. Femke ignored them all with a single-minded intensity, leaving Reynik to deflect interest onto other potential customers.

Reynik had not spent much time in the commercial areas of the city when he was growing up, so he felt awkward about ignoring people. His upbringing had instilled certain manners in him that he found difficult to shake off. Surely it was common courtesy to at least shake one's head, or to wave a negative, when someone called out to you? Not even acknowledging someone's presence seemed the height of ignorance and bad manners.

It suddenly occurred to Reynik that if he were having problems with the simple matter of manners, then how much harder would it be to change more critical inbuilt habits? Femke was right, he decided. He would need a lot of help to make his disguise believable.

When they arrived at Femke's chosen destination, Reynik was thrown off guard again. The house that they approached was not at all what he was expecting. Femke's assertion that the swordsman he was to meet was in need of work did not fit with the large, plush-looking residence at which they were knocking. The house could not belong to a poor man.

A servant answered and Femke spoke to him in such hushed tones that Reynik could not make out what they said. The servant did not look happy, but after a moment of indecision, he ushered them inside. The hallway to the house was spacious and grand in appearance. A polished marble floor boasted a complex mosaic depicting two fighters locked in combat, and there were several wall hangings and beautiful paintings with similar themes. A life-sized statue of a swordsman in arena style protective gear stood menacingly on guard to the left of the sweeping staircase that climbed in a majestic arc to the upper floor. The wrought iron banisters were beautifully crafted with many swirling patterns, gleaming black against the creamy marble.

'This way, my Lady. Sir.' The servant did not look to see them follow. He simply set off across the hall to one of several impressive solid oak doors set again with wrought iron hinges and handles. The room they entered was a large living area; tastefully decorated, but again with the underlying tones of someone obsessed with fighting. Even the little drinks tables had legs in the shape of swords, embedded point down into small spheres of iron.

They did not stop in the living room, but crossed to another door that opened into the strangest room Reynik had ever seen. It was about ten paces square, with no furnishings or decorations other than two walls that were covered with mirrored glass. In the centre of the room was a man whose gaunt face seemed hauntingly familiar. He was aware of them the moment they entered, but continued in his pose for a few seconds before relaxing and turning to greet them.

'What's this, Aneki? Did I not tell you I wasn't to be disturbed?'

'Yes, Master, but the Lady here has a proposition that I think you would be interested to hear.'

'Indeed. Well, let us retire back into the lounge then. Bring us some drinks, please, Aneki. Would you good people prefer dahl or water? I'm afraid I don't keep any stronger beverages in the house. I find that removing temptation makes it easier to resist its draw.'

'Two glasses of water would be wonderful, thank you,' Femke assured him. Aneki bowed and withdrew to fetch the drinks.

'Please excuse me changing my shirt, but it will quickly become uncomfortable if I do not,' the man apologised, indicating his sweat-soaked garment. He crossed the room to a small cupboard and removed a clean white shirt. As he raised the garment he was wearing over his head, Reynik gave a gasp of shock at the horrific wound in the man's back that glared at him like an accusing red eye. He turned, and to Reynik's further shock, there was a matching wound in the man's stomach. Someone had run this man through with a sword.

Suddenly, Reynik recognised the reason for the familiarity of the man's face. The man was a legend – a gladiator who had built his reputation in the arena as the deadliest swordsman alive. He had killed dozens of men during his rise through the ranking system. The killing was his trademark. Gladiators normally fought until one yielded. Not so with this man. With him, every fight was to the death. During his three years in the arena, he had never left an opponent alive to face him a second time. It was said that he had faced up to five trained gladiators simultaneously in a single confrontation, and not one had survived to fight another day. At least, none had done so until his final bout.

The man watched with amusement as recognition dawned in Reynik's eyes, together with a look of disbelief. 'Serrius!' Reynik mouthed silently.

Serrius gave a small nod of admission and then turned to Femke. 'I take it this young fellow didn't know you were bringing him to see me today,' he observed casually. 'It's good to know that you're not spreading word of my survival all over the city, Femke. Now, what brings you here today to disturb my recovery?'

'Serrius, this is Reynik. I want you to train him in some of the more advanced arts of swordplay.'

'You know I don't teach. Why would I teach a man the skills he might one day use to kill me?'

'So you intend to return to the arena then? I thought you would quit after . . .'

'After I was run through by that young Thrandorian?' he finished. Serrius laughed aloud, his mirth looking strange on his normally impassive face. 'Your thinking is correct. I have quit. I would be a fool to return to the arena now; I would be diced on my first bout. My former skill and fitness levels are gone for ever; the Thrandorian's blade through my gut ensured that, but it does not do to have too many men who can better you with a sword when you have spent your life killing others in order to prove you are the best.'

Aneki entered the room with three tall glasses of water, which they each took from the tray with polite words of thanks. Reynik took a long draught, but despite sweating profusely, Serrius was more restrained. He took only small sips from his glass, unconsciously demonstrating his control over the thirst Reynik felt sure the gladiator must feel. The servant left again, bowing as he exited the room.

'Reynik has never been a gladiator and has no intentions of becoming one. What makes you think he might one day wish to kill you?' Femke asked curiously.

Serrius laughed again. 'Don't try to play your games with me, Femke. I've observed men: their posture, their movement and their fighting styles, for years. I knew the moment you entered that Reynik was a Legionnaire. His whole bearing screams "military". So why do you want me to teach him, and what makes you think I will do for him what I have steadfastly refused to do for any other?'

'You didn't answer my question, but I suppose it is only fair to give you an explanation. The Emperor needs him to possess certain skills for a mission he is to undertake. One of those skills is to wield a sword in a credible fashion. His military training has been adequate. He knows the basics, but he will need to be better than average if he is to complete his mission. If all goes well, he should not have to wield a sword in anger, but if called upon to demonstrate sword play, then it's essential that his fighting style be different from that of a regular soldier.'

Serrius fell silent for a moment, looking first at Femke, then at Reynik and finally back to Femke again. Reynik held his breath. To be taught sword skills by the deadliest gladiator the Shandrim arena had ever seen was a dream that many young swordsmen harboured. It would be an amazing opportunity.

'I sense there's much that you're not telling me here, Femke. Your secrecy does you no favours. I feel no more inclined to teach him than I have any other who has approached me. What makes you think I'll teach now, when I've always refused to teach in the past?'

'You'll do it because you need a reason to exist, Serrius. If you don't take this job, or another like it, the temptation to return to the arena will be too great. You'll go back and you will die at the hands of some unknown fighter, who will gain brief status by killing you. Someone more skilled will then kill him, further reducing the perception of your ability. The legend you created will die. Strangely, your reputation was dented little by your loss to the Thrandorian fighter. The fact that you ran each other through was viewed by most as an honourable draw. He only "won" because he remained standing longer than you did. The public have seen nothing of either of you since that day. Most think you both died after the bout, but if you were to go out in public, then you would be seen as the survivor. The official announcement that the Thrandorian had died was necessary to hide his disappearance. Any public appearance by you would cause your reputation to soar once more.'

'You don't pull any punches, do you?' Serrius said with a sad smile. 'Your words ring with a truth I cannot deny.

It's madness, but the draw is already growing in me to return to the arena. Despite knowing I would die there, and telling myself over and over that it would be sheer folly to return, I can feel the pull strengthening in my heart. If I accept your proposal, how long will I have to work with Reynik?'

'Three weeks.'

'Three weeks! That's preposterous! Nobody could learn to be a swordsman in that time.'

'I'm not asking you to make a swordsman of him. I simply want you to change his fighting style sufficiently that it does not instantly brand him as military. Also, you won't have him all day, every day, as he will have other lessons to attend.'

Serrius sighed. 'Perhaps it is good that it's only three weeks. I should know by then whether I'm up to this change. There is a suitable fee, I presume?'

'I will ensure the Imperial Treasury is generous,' Femke replied, allowing none of her inner elation to show. 'The mission is important, so the Emperor will be sure to throw resources at it.'

'Very well. We had better begin then, Reynik. Come with me.' Serrius beckoned Reynik towards the door to the empty, mirrored room.

'I'll collect him at the second bell this afternoon, Serrius. I'll then bring him back again at the seventh bell for another session. Is that all right?'

'Do I have a choice?'

'No,' Femke grinned, 'but I thought I'd be polite about it.'

Serrius gave a snort of amusement and led Reynik through the door. Femke watched the door close behind them. She raised her glass in silent salute towards the closed door before turning and making her way back through to the hall. Aneki was waiting. He led her to the door and politely thanked her for visiting.

She strode purposefully back towards the city centre. There was much to organise and little time in which to do it.

Her first visit was to the seamstress, Rikala. The dumpy little woman was as businesslike as ever. Rikala had only ever met Femke when she was in the guise of the self-centred Lady Alyssa, yet it was clear from her expression that the seamstress recognised her straight away. Femke was impressed. There were not many who would have looked at a young woman in a mid-thigh length leather skirt, matching leather boots and a plain, collarless shirt and seen a spoilt young Lady hiding underneath. Rikala was clearly one who noticed fine detail. Femke stored away that snippet of knowledge. If she were to deal with the dressmaker in future, then it was clear that she could only do so as Lady Alyssa, or her occupation would quickly become obvious.

If the dressmaker was surprised by Femke's appearance, or the manner of her request, she did not show it. She did, however, raise one eyebrow in a quizzical manner as she eyed Femke up and down.

'Where did you get those clothes, Lady Alyssa?' she asked, making no attempt to hide her contempt for the tailoring as she fingered the seam on Femke's sleeve. 'I'll make you the clothes you require for the young gentleman, but it seems that I'd better make you some more clothes at the same time. No matter how you want to look, there's no excuse for poor stitching, and by the look of the needle-work on that top, the seamstress does not deserve the title. Bring him in tomorrow at the eighth bell for measuring. I should be able to complete the work by the end of the week.'

'Thank you, Rikala. Oh, and I'd prefer it if you didn't mention anything about this,' Femke replied, looking around in an exaggeratedly conspiratal fashion. 'It wouldn't be good for my image if it were known that I sometimes walked through town dressed as a commoner.'

'Your secret is safe with me, Lady Alyssa. Actually, despite the appalling quality of that shirt, I think I prefer you dressed this way. You're much easier to communicate with when you're not acting all high and mighty.'

Femke smiled and left.

Arranging a good set of throwing knives for Reynik was easy enough. As the Legions did not train their soldiers to throw knives, it would take some considerable effort to make Reynik sufficiently adept at this skill in such a short time period, but she knew that it would be essential to his overall persona. Femke was excellent at throwing knives, but not the best. A visit to see her friend, Derryn, gained her another instructor.

Derryn was an ageing, highly talented street entertainer who had made his living throwing knives and juggling all manner of objects for many years. He had performed all over the Shandese Empire, amazing folk with his dexterity and accuracy wherever he went. These days he preferred to remain in Shandrim. However, as with any show, people were not so generous once they had seen it a few times. Extra money from any source was always welcome, so he was delighted to gain a temporary teaching job that would pay well. Femke arranged for him to give Reynik a lesson every day.

There were so many skills that an effective assassin should master, it was impossible to address them all. Ideally, Reynik should be a marksman with a crossbow. Not all assassins used this weapon, but it was universally accepted that for a heavily guarded target, it was sometimes necessary to kill from a distance. Femke was realistic enough to accept that the degree of skill required at this discipline for Reynik to be convincing was not achievable in the timescale. Having acknowledged this, she was left with the debate of whether to even attempt to improve his skill with the weapon. He would have used one before, as all Legionnaires were given training in their use. Crossbows were issued to those on guard duty, so they needed to have a modicum of skill with it.

In the end, Femke decided that the crossbow would have to be abandoned in favour of the more important skills of stealthy movement, picking locks and poisoning. She was expert in all three skills and initially concluded that in order to limit the number of people involved in Reynik's training, it might be better if she conducted his training in these areas. After considerable thought on the matter, she changed her mind and brought in one final tutor.

There was a troupe of players currently in the city with

whom she had performed during a past mission. Her cover name during that time had been Dana and she had initially been accepted into the troupe as a personal favour to her old Master, Lord Ferdand. The leader of the troupe was a flamboyant man called Devarusso, who was widely recognised for his loud verbosity and extravagant body language. It had been a while since Femke had last seen him, but they had parted on friendly terms and Devarusso was a long-term friend of Ferdand. This gave Femke confidence that the man would help her again.

What most did not know was that underneath the actor's colourful public façade, his private persona was one of understatement and subtlety. Femke knew from personal experience that Devarusso would prove an excellent movement tutor for Reynik. Learning how to move with the subtlety of an actor would help the Legionnaire both to gain stealth skills, and to conceal his military background.

Lord Ferdand had professed the greatest of respect for Devarusso's acting skills, but had also been quick to tell Femke never to trust him with secrets. Femke had long known that Ferdand was an excellent judge of character and, having spent several months with Devarusso's troupe, discovered that her Master's assessment had once again been sound. Devarusso could be a terrible gossip. There were ways to prevent this being a problem, but it did complicate the situation.

'Dana! What a delight to see you, my dear! Come in. Come in. Here, I'm just pouring some dahl. Do have a cup. Please tell me you've decided to come and join us again.

I have a role that would be perfect for you. Ah! This is wonderful! You will make the perfect Camille!'

Devarusso's expressive face beamed with pleasure as he recognised Femke. He poured a second cup of the steaming fluid and handed it to her with a flourish. For a moment her heart leaped at the thought of being back on the stage with Devarusso and the other players, but she knew that it could not be.

'I'm sorry, Devarusso,' she said with no need to feign her disappointed tone. 'I've not come to rejoin the company. I'm here on behalf of a friend.'

His face dropped momentarily, but he recovered his composure quickly. 'Of course, my dear. Tell me of your friend. Does she want to act?'

Femke smiled fondly at him. 'No, *he* doesn't want to act, but he does need to be able to disguise certain habits.' She dropped her voice to a conspiratorial whisper. 'He has . . . um . . . left his Legion a little before he was due to, and he needs to learn to hide his military background for a while. I can't think of a better person to teach him how to alter his gait and bearing than you.'

'Dana, just *how* early is your friend leaving his Legion?' Devarusso asked, raising one of his sharply angled, black eyebrows quizzically.

'Oh, about twenty-five to thirty . . . years, I'd say,' she replied with an embarrassed shrug and an apologetic grin.

Devarusso coughed, choking on his dahl as he realised exactly what she was asking him to do. Femke did not shy away from his stare. His striking blue eyes were almost purple in colour, and his square-cut features and sweeping, jet-black hair made him the perfect swashbuckling hero for any play. He was broad-shouldered and rakishly handsome enough to set any girl's heart racing, yet Femke knew his secret: the real Devarusso was a man who liked to be with other men. Devarusso was the consummate actor, but where he had concealed his inclination from the rest of the troupe, he had not been able to keep his secret from her. Femke had been trained to observe behaviour and to see beneath the surface.

'Dana, you know how busy a schedule I run. You, more than most, know how much effort goes into making our productions polished,' Devarusso said, the words tumbling out of his mouth in a spluttering stream. 'Besides, the authorities would hang me and shut down the company if they found out. All of my hard work would crumble to dust in a matter of moments – and for what? No, I couldn't countenance it. It's impossible, Dana. I'm sorry.'

Femke gave him her best puppy dog, begging look. Her eyes filled with tears to order and she clenched her knees with her fingers until her knuckles whitened. To judge by the effect it had on him, she had lost none of her acting skill.

'And this man is . . . *special*, is he?' Devarusso asked, flexing his fingers uncomfortably.

'More than you could imagine, Devarusso,' she answered fervently. 'Please. I'd really appreciate your help for a little while in tutoring my friend. I'm not expecting you to take him in and hide him. I just want you to teach him to move in a way that will conceal his military manner. He has three weeks to become convincing. Could you help him in that time? He would only be able to visit you for about two hours a day. I can pay. We have some money saved. I can pay four senna per day. What do you think?'

Devarusso frowned thoughtfully. He took a deep breath.

'Three weeks is not long, and yet it could feel like a lifetime if trying to keep a secret like this. I suppose I should be grateful that you're not asking me for more. Dana, if your friend is planning to run away from the military, or if he has already done so, you know I would be risking everything in becoming involved. Aiding someone to desert from the Legions is a serious crime.'

'I know, but I don't know who else to turn to,' she said, squeezing out a single tear so that it trickled down her right cheek. 'You were always so kind to me whilst I was in the troupe. I came to you because I knew I could trust you. You're also the best teacher I know. I'm sure you could do it with no one the wiser.'

Flattery had always worked well with Devarusso. Femke played him like an instrument, plucking at each string with such skill that he was sure to sing her tune. If she had to, she could resort to blackmail. She suspected that Devarusso would do anything to conceal his secret, but using that information would destroy her friendship with him, and she wanted to avoid that if possible. He was a soft touch. He would give in very quickly now.

'If I were to do it, then it would be best to conduct his lessons early in the morning,' he said, as if thinking aloud.

Here it comes, she thought – right on cue.

'The troupe rarely rises early after the late night performances, so I could make some time then. So long as we didn't attract attention to ourselves, then I suppose there would not be too much danger of being caught. Would your friend be available in the early mornings?'

'He would.'

'Very well, Dana. I'll do it, but I don't want to rob you of all your silver. I'll teach your friend for two senna per day. Please, though, don't breathe a word of this to anyone. Have your friend come to me at the dawn call each morning. I'll do what I can for him. I'm a sucker for a sob story, but then I'm sure you knew that all along, didn't you?'

Femke did not answer, she just smiled gratefully and dabbed at her eyes with a handkerchief.

'Now that we have that settled, tell me what you've been doing with yourself. How's my old friend, Ferdand? I haven't seen him in ages. He used to be such a regular attendee at our performances. Have I lost favour in his eyes for some reason?'

Femke had been prepared for questions about her old mentor, but she did not need to use her acting abilities to demonstrate her emotions on the subject. Even the thought of Ferdand, whom she considered more of a parental figure than her own father, brought the threat of more tears to her eyes. He had given her so much: not in material things, for she had never been one for hoarding treasures. His gifts to her had been knowledge, skills and experience, taught with a gentleness that she had never known from her natural parents.

Ferdand had shown her what it meant to be a spy. He had led her through the ethical labyrinth of the profession in such a way that she had gained an unshakeable surety of place and purpose. He had laid the foundations in her life on which she had built her career, her sense of morality and her personality. It was still hard to come to terms with his loss. Femke had felt that she could find anything, or anyone if given enough time, but in trying to unravel the mystery surrounding Ferdand's disappearance she had drawn a total blank.

'He's gone, Devarusso. He hasn't been seen for over two years now. Nobody knows what became of him, but he disappeared one night and hasn't returned. I suspect he's dead, for I feel sure I'd have heard from him otherwise.'

'Ah, that is sad!' the actor replied, his voice full of compassion. 'He was always a great supporter of the arts. It's hard to believe that he has departed this world. He was the sort of fellow that one felt would live for ever. But if he's gone, what are you doing these days? Are you working? You know you are always welcome to come back and work here with us.'

Femke nodded and mumbled her thanks. He was a generous soul, though she knew that his offer wasn't totally an offer of charity. Acting was something she did well. Devarusso always had parts for good actors.

Time was ticking away. It was already time to go and move Reynik on to his next activity. After a further short exchange of pleasantries with Devarusso, she made her excuses and went back to the gladiator's home. Aneki met her at the door with a polite smile and led her through to the mirrored room where Serrius and Reynik were quietly completing a set of callisthenics.

It was interesting to watch them finish. Where Serrius

was smooth and graceful, Reynik looked awkward and stiff, yet competent. The perfect balance and poise of the gladiator contrasted markedly with the slight wobbles and shakes of the young Legionnaire. However, Femke noted that Reynik looked remarkably composed considering he was just finishing a four-hour training session.

'I shall see you again this evening, Reynik. Think on the patterns I showed you and don't be late. I don't appreciate being kept waiting.'

Reynik thanked him for his time and followed Femke out of the house. She did not talk to him about his training, but led him silently through the streets into the city centre. The street vendors had lost some of their earlier verve. The voices calling out to passers by still had the volume, but had lost the interest and vitality they had possessed earlier in the day.

'Hungry?' Femke asked, as Reynik's stomach growled audibly.

'Starved.'

'What would you like?'

'Anything hot that's not too spicy.'

Femke led him to a food vendor and ordered him a large portion of hot meat in gravy, wrapped in unleavened bread. Reynik muttered his thanks and bit into the tasty wrap, leaning forwards to avoid dripping the hot juices down the front of his clothes.

'Mmm!' he mumbled through a mouthful of food. 'Wonderful.'

They moved away from the food vendor and down one of the side streets. A few minutes later Femke stopped in front of a bare wooden door. Reynik was still licking his fingers, having eaten his food in short order. He looked at her enquiringly.

'In you go,' she said, gesturing for him to precede her.

'Shouldn't we knock?'

'You can if you like, but no one will answer. This is one of my safe houses.'

Reynik grinned and went to open the door. It was locked. He turned and looked questioningly at Femke.

'It seems you remembered to lock up. So where's the key?' he asked.

'I don't know. I don't remember ever having one for this place.'

'So how do we get in?'

Femke grinned mischievously. 'Use your initiative,' she replied. 'But don't make any noise. We don't want to upset the neighbours.'

Reynik nodded. Femke watched with amusement as he gave a furtive look around to see if anyone was watching before he began a quick, but thorough search of the area around the door to see if there was a key concealed there. Clearly he was aware that this was a test and he didn't trust her to be telling him the truth. 'Good,' she thought. 'That's one lesson I don't have to teach him.'

His search was fruitless, so he moved on to the windows. After a few moments, he discovered that one of the window catches was loose and began gently rattling it to try to work the catch free. When this didn't work, he took his belt knife out and tried to prise the window open. The latch was stubborn. No matter how much leverage Reynik applied, it did not give. After a few minutes of effort it loosened enough for Reynik to work the tip of the knife through and raise the latch. With a look of triumph, he turned to Femke and gestured for her to enter.

'Oh, please, after you,' Femke said sweetly.

'Very well,' he replied. With another quick look up and down the street to see that no one was going to see him, he placed his hands on the chest-height windowsill and jumped up, allowing his body to pivot forwards over his hands until he was draped head first, half inside the house. Resting on his stomach, he eased his hands inside to clear the inside window ledge of breakables, then he wriggled forwards, legs kicking to help his forward momentum until he started to slide in through the window.

He was past the point of no return when he realised that the distance from the inside window ledge to the ground was such that he would not be able to lower his body totally under control all the way to the floor. It was too late for thoughts of backing out, so he allowed his bodyweight to pull his legs through the window and he hit the floor, tucking his body into an untidy roll.

As Reynik climbed to his feet, a slow clap sounded from the internal door on the other side of the room. Femke was standing there with a huge grin on her face.

'Very impressive. Well done,' she said, voice dripping with sarcasm. 'At least you didn't break any of my ornaments.'

'I thought you said you didn't have a key!'

'I don't.'

'Then how . . .'

'There are other ways of opening locked doors, you know. Come on. Shut that window and I'll teach you how to pick a lock. Given your remarkable display of grace and agility, it might save you from being caught in a compromising position.'

CHAPTER SIX

'Where have you been? The File Leader is spitting feathers. You were expected back hours ago.'

Reynik looked at Tymm wearily. His fellow Legionnaire had clearly been waiting for him, and kept his voice low to prevent it from travelling to the tent a few yards away. Reynik shrugged his shoulders. 'I can't tell you. I've been doing the Emperor's bidding. That's all I can say.'

'Well, I hope for your sake you'll be allowed to tell Sidis more than that, or you'll be back on jacks duty for a month. It's clear he's got a grudge against you, so you'd better be ready to answer to him.'

Reynik nodded. It was not what he needed after an exhausting day of training, but he knew this was a confrontation that would not go away. No matter what he said, Sidis would not be happy. The File Leader seemed set on making his life in the Legion a misery. It was unlikely this new mission would help improve their relationship.

His personality clash with Sidis was not Reynik's biggest

101

worry. Where his previous special escort assignment had caused some resentment amongst his fellow soldiers, it was likely that a second special assignment would cause outright animosity. Had they known the deadly nature of his task, some might have been more tolerant, but he knew the nature of the other men. Despite not knowing what he was doing, secretly, each would harbour thoughts that they should have been selected.

The extreme covert nature of his task meant he could not tell anyone, not even the Commander, what he was doing. This would not make it easy to deal with the Legion hierarchy. All he could hope was for the orders from the Emperor to come down through the chain of command quickly enough for him not to miss his next appointment with Femke in the morning. The training programme she had instigated was fascinating. He had learned more in his single session with Serrius about the importance of poise, balance and stance in sword fighting than he had learned in two years of training to be a Legionnaire.

'Thanks for the warning, Tymm. It would be best if I go and talk with Sidis now, I think. I'll be away again in the morning, so I'd better get this over and done with.'

'Listen, Reynik, I don't know what you're doing, but if you need help, you can count on me.'

'That's good to know. I'm sorry I can't tell you any more right now, Tymm. Maybe one day . . .' He gripped Tymm's upper arm, and looked into his eyes, trying with all his heart to express gratitude for his friend's understanding in that look. Tymm patted him back.

'I'll try to keep the wolves from your back here, Reynik,

but if you're going to be accepted into the pack, you're going to have to run with them. With Nelek and Sidis already alienated, it is only going to get harder for you to fit into the ranks with the more time you spend away.'

Reynik nodded again. With a sigh of resolve, he walked past the tent that housed his file, and continued up the path in search of the File Leaders' tents.

As he expected, Sidis was not impressed.

'Secret!' he exploded. 'What do you mean, secret?'

Reynik winced. The ears of any spy within half a mile would be burning after that outburst. No doubt they would be flocking to find out what Sidis was talking about.

'Begging your pardon, File Leader, but there may be spies . . .'

'There are no spies here!' he hissed, lowering his voice despite his statement. Sidis' eyes were burning with fury. 'So you're intent on playing the Emperor's "golden boy", are you? Well it cuts no ice with me, Reynik. If you think you're going to get special treatment in this Legion because you're in the Emperor's eye, then you're sadly mistaken. Until I receive orders from the Commander, then you're to drill with the others. I'll not take orders from a young upstart like you, and I'll not allow any insubordination either. You *will* parade with the others in the morning, or I'll have your guts to bait the rat traps with.'

Reynik met the File Leader's venomous stare with resolve. 'No,' he said simply. 'I won't.' For a moment, Reynik thought that the File Leader's eyes would pop out of his head. If the situation had not been so lamentable, it would have been comic. He had not wanted it to come to this, but he now had no choice. 'I must ask you to come with me to see the Commander, File Leader. My orders are directly from the Emperor. He wants me in the city at first light tomorrow. The night is already passing and I need to be in a fit state to function tomorrow. This must be resolved now.'

'Oh, we'll go to see the Commander,' he spluttered, 'but it is you who will accompany me, you cheeky young whoreson.'

Reynik ignored the insult. It was not worth responding to. Instead, he stepped aside and allowed the File Leader to lead the way to the Commander's tent. It was late to be disturbing the Commander, but Sidis was so incensed he was clearly oblivious to protocol. Reynik remained outside while the File Leader conversed with the Commander, but he could hear every word.

'Yes, Sidis, I am aware of the orders pertaining to Legionnaire Reynik. I received them late this evening. However, unlike you, it seems, I have some regard for the rest periods of others. I had intended to inform you of the authorisation for his absence in the morning, but as you're here, you can take it as read that, until further notice, Legionnaire Reynik is released to come and go as required in order to fulfil his duties to the Emperor. Now go and get some sleep, File Leader.'

Reynik winced at the Commander's tone. He would not have liked to face that acid dismissal. If there had ever been any hope for reconciliation with Sidis, it was now gone. The File Leader would not forget this moment.

He would be sure to lay the blame for it squarely on Reynik's head.

Sidis did not even look at Reynik as he stomped away. 'You heard what the Commander said,' he hissed in a venomous snarl as he disappeared into the night. 'Go!'

Reynik went to his bed with a heavy heart. When he crept into the tent, most of the men were already asleep. Tymm raised himself up on one elbow, giving Reynik an enquiring look, but Reynik raised a finger to his lips and shook his head. He did not want to risk waking any of the others. It was heartening to know that he still had a friend nearby, but he knew this latest mission would turn the majority against him.

Lying in his bunk, he wondered what on earth he had done. All he had ever wanted was a place in the Legions and a chance to emulate his forebears. His lifelong dream was to have a fulfilling career as a soldier. He so wanted to make his father proud. Now, somehow, he had become embroiled in events that were dragging him away from his hard-earned place in the most prestigious of Legions. If he were not careful, it would soon become impossible for him to return. What would his family think if the authorities captured him and accused him of being an assassin? Or if he turned up dead in a river, killed by the Guild? Would the Emperor ever tell them the truth? He doubted it. He was in up to his neck – that much was sure.

It was not a good night. His sleep was shallow and fitful, with broken dreams of chasing and being chased, killing and being killed. Throughout the dreams was the sense of a sea of watching, accusing faces.

He awoke before dawn and rose. He felt stiff and more tired than he had when he had gone to bed. Dressing silently, he left for the Palace. The Imperial Palace guards admitted him without question when he supplied the password Femke had told him. He made his way quickly to Femke's quarters. She answered immediately at his discreet tap on her door and indicated for him to change back into a set of clothes she had laid out on the bed for him. They fit perfectly.

'Where are the clothes I wore yesterday?' he asked once he was dressed.

'The Palace Staff are cleaning them for you. You worked up a bit of a sweat with Serrius yesterday, so I thought you'd appreciate a clean set for today. I got these from stores, but you're to be measured for fitted clothing at the eighth bell.'

Femke noted the dark rings under Reynik's eyes and wondered for a moment if she should suggest he be detached from the Legion altogether while he was involved in this mission. It would shorten his days if he did not have to walk to and from the camp every day. She knew how dedicated a soldier he was and she had no wish to make this any more difficult for him than it had to be. Some fatigue was inevitable for a few days until his body settled into the new routine. She decided not to say anything for the time being, but to monitor his health to be sure it did not degrade. He would have to be at the peak of fitness for his coming mission.

'So what are we doing until then?' Reynik asked.

'You're going to learn one of the key elements of

disguise. We're going to visit an old friend of mine, who is going to attempt to teach you something of the art of acting.'

'Play acting? Like make believe?'

'If that's how you wish to think of it,' Femke replied, clearly amused by his childish reference. 'Just don't let Devarusso hear you say so. To him, acting is the finest of the arts. He is a master at it, so be sure to observe him closely and listen to what he has to tell you. It's going to be a short lesson this morning due to your fitting at the tailor's, but for the immediate future you'll be taking lessons from Devarusso in the morning from the dawn call until the ninth, then you'll be with Serrius from the tenth call until the second afternoon call. You'll have lessons on knife-throwing with a man named Derryn from the third call until the fourth, a mixture of lessons with me from the fourth until the seventh and then a shorter session with Serrius again in the evening from the seventh call until the ninth. I'll collect you from Derryn's and see you arrive with Serrius on time in the evenings.'

'When do I eat?' he asked, taken aback by the length of the daily programme.

'I suggest you grab food as and when you can on the way between lessons. You have a vast amount to learn, Reynik, but not long in which to take it all in. The programme will vary over the coming weeks. I thought it best to start with the concentration on your swordplay, but the balance will shift later in the week, as you are far more likely to use guile than outright weapons skills when you begin your mission.'

Femke led him out of the Palace and through the streets to the playhouse at which Devarusso's troupe was currently performing. At the back of the playhouse was the area for the current players to park their travelling wagons. Devarusso's was some way detached from the others, as was the tradition of the troupe leader. At the first knock, the door of the brightly decorated wagon sprung open and the actor stepped outside. He gave Reynik an appraising look and then signalled for them to follow him.

In silence, Devarusso led them to the back of the playhouse and, unlocking the back door with a brass key taken from his breast pocket, he took them inside. The backstage area was surprisingly light. Lots of windows allowed the early morning sun to flood the large area with its bright illumination. Despite its size, the room felt small, as it was cluttered with a multitude of props and costume rails laden with gaudy costumes in every hue and style.

Reynik was fascinated, hardly knowing where to look first, as one thing after another caught his eye. He was not given a chance to indulge his curiosity for more than a few seconds, though, for Devarusso led them around to the stage wings and out onto the open air stage. The semi-circle of tiered bench seating in front of the stage gave Reynik a strangely claustrophobic feeling. It was as if he were trapped with nowhere to run. He shuddered to think of how he would feel if all those rows of seats were full of watching people, all focused on him.

'I may as well wait for him for today, Devarusso. We can only stay about three quarters of an hour. He has an appointment with a seamstress at the eighth bell.'

The actor nodded. 'Very well,' he said. 'That should be long enough for me to see what I have to work with.'

Femke hopped off the stage and took a seat on one of the lower tiers to watch as Devarusso circled Reynik, looking him up and down thoughtfully.

'Hello, Devarusso, I'm—'

'No names!' the actor cut in sharply. 'What I don't know, I can't repeat. This is not an arrangement I'm comfortable with, but Dana is an old friend. I'll help you for her sake and I hope you'll be very happy together.'

Reynik glanced across at Femke, wondering just what she had told this man about him. It was likely another of her little tests, he thought. He would just have to say as little as possible, and try not to compromise her story. It did not help that he had no clue who Dana was, nor what he was supposed to be doing that would make Devarusso uncomfortable.

'Walk across the stage for me,' Devarusso ordered.

Reynik did as he was told.

'And back again.'

The actor nodded as he watched Reynik walk.

'Now let's see how observant you are. Walk across the stage again, but this time I want you to imagine you're a beggar. You've not eaten for days and you're desperate for food.'

Reynik closed his eyes for a second and tried to picture a beggar walking. It was harder than he would have thought, for most of the beggars he could picture were sitting by the road with their hands outstretched. Had he ever seen one walking? How would they walk? He tried to imagine what it would feel like to be as Devarusso had described and he stepped out across the stage.

'Holy Shand alive, man! Have you got a rod stuck up the back of your shirt? Slouch, man, slouch. A beggar doesn't stand upright. Round your shoulders. Now slump more ... more! That's it. No, don't pick your feet up – shuffle. You don't have the energy to pick your feet up. That's better.'

By the end of the short session, Reynik ached more than if he had been swinging a sword the entire time. Muscles he did not know he had were aching with a dull, persistent throb. It was hard to understand, as all he had done was to walk back and forth across the stage for less than an hour. Away from the playhouse, he quizzed Femke about what story she had fed the actor, who Dana was, and for more background on Devarusso. He did not like the idea of being considered a deserter, but then he didn't like the idea of being considered an assassin either.

Rikala was her usual businesslike self. She manhandled Reynik around whilst taking a plethora of measurements. Arms in front, arms to the side, standing and sitting – it made Reynik wonder what on earth she could possibly want with so many statistics. Surely making a few clothes could not be so complex?

The seamstress was so quick with her measurements, that within a quarter of an hour they were being ushered out of her home so she could get on with her work. This left nearly two hours until Reynik's next appointment with Serrius.

'What now?' he asked Femke.

'Now you take the opportunity to eat, but not too much. You won't want to be bloated for your session with Serrius. Whilst we walk to the market stalls, let's discuss the skills of your adopted trade. Aside from the ability to kill without compunction, what abilities should a top assassin possess?'

'Anonymity,' Reynik answered quickly. 'The ability to blend in and out of the background and strike when it's least expected.'

'Good. An excellent starting point; let's discuss camouflage and concealment.'

For the next hour and a half Femke led a detailed discussion on the art of camouflage and deception. Reynik had already seen Femke disguise herself as a young man during their recent trip to Thrandor, so he had some ideas about how to alter one's appearance. He quickly discovered, however, that this was very superficial knowledge. Femke did not limit the discussion to disguise, for she pointed out that there were some places a simple visual disguise would not get you into. Instead, they talked about how one could move undetected through the city at all times of day and night. They discussed colour, contrasting backgrounds, differences in stealthy movement by day and night, and even talked about smells.

Many of the things Femke talked about seemed so obvious when she pointed them out, but were not things he had consciously thought about. The fact that sounds are more noticeable during the hours of darkness, whereas sudden movements are more noticeable in the daytime; the fact that the human eye is attracted to movement and that

111

quick or jerky movement will be detected faster than slow movement. They talked about the three basic principles of hiding, blending and deceiving and how they applied to movement within a city. Femke also raised the subject of camouflage in the countryside: when to use blotched and striped camouflage patterns and why they work better in different terrains.

By the end of the discussion, Reynik's estimation of Femke had raised several more notches. He had realised during their trip to Thrandor that Femke was good at what she did, but had not appreciated just how much knowledge one needed to be an effective spy. There were many areas of expertise that overlapped between spies and assassins. It was easy to see that Femke had plenty to teach him.

Four hours with Serrius and Reynik was only too pleased to have an hour-long break. Femke took him to a street vendor and bought him some food before leading him to one of the poorer quarters of the city. Here she introduced him to Derryn for his knife-throwing lesson.

To look at Derryn, one would never believe he was an entertainer. His face was serious and lined, with sad eyes that looked as if they had witnessed many tragedies. Where Reynik had expected to see someone with good poise and posture, he could see only an old man with rounded shoulders and a pronounced stoop. Derryn's sad face twisted into a lopsided grin as he noted Reynik's expression. It was as if the old man could read his mind: *this* was the person he would learn knife-throwing skills from?

Derryn led them through his small terraced house into the courtyard behind. There, Reynik found a purpose-built, home-made throwing range. There were targets of all descriptions around the courtyard: static targets of various sizes, targets suspended on ropes that could be set to swing, targets that could be knocked down and even targets that would slide along taut ropes. Each target had a circular strike point marked with yellow dye. On a bench in the centre of the courtyard were three sets of gleaming knives. Each set of knives was of a different size, and each contained eight blades. Derryn gestured for Reynik to pick up a knife.

'Go ahead,' he said, his voice surprisingly clear and strong. 'Take your pick. Let's see what you know of knives to begin with.

Derryn watched intently as Reynik made his choice. He opted for the heaviest of the blades, weighing it in his hand and nodding appreciatively as he felt its balance. It was obvious that these knives had been well made.

'So you have been taught to fight with a knife,' Derryn observed. 'You hold it as a fighter would. Now let's see you throw it at that target over there,' he said, pointing at the largest of the straw bale targets.

Reynik raised the blade to throw but did not even get halfway through the motion.

'Stop!' Derryn ordered sharply. 'Hmm, you may know how to fight with a blade, young man, but you've certainly never been shown how to throw one. Come here. Look, unless you have hands the size of shovels and muscles coming out of your ears, you can't throw a knife of this size effectively with a pinch grip. You should always throw bigger knives with a hammer grip, like this.'

113

The old man picked another knife from the same set of blades, demonstrated the hammer grip and hurled it at the target. It struck the very centre, the blade driving in almost to the hilt. Reynik was impressed. Derryn had made the throw look effortless.

'Now you try it.'

Reynik adjusted his grip to match the one that Derryn had shown him and he threw the blade hard, determined to show the old man he was not without some ability. The knife hit the target, hilt first, about half a metre above and to the right of centre and dropped to the floor. Derryn's eyebrows raised slightly and he pursed his lips.

'Not bad,' he said with another of his little nods. 'If you wanted to club your target to death, you'd be off to a good start.'

Femke coughed and placed a hand over her mouth to hide her amusement. She failed. Reynik frowned at her, annoyed at the old man's sarcasm, but more so that he had been made to look a fool in front of Femke.

'How would you change your throw next time to hit it with the point?' Derryn asked.

Reynik thought for a moment. 'I'd move back about a metre,' he said. 'Or forward,' he added quickly.

'That would work,' the old man admitted. 'But let's say you don't have that option. You must throw from the same point. What else could you do?'

'Change my grip?' Reynik offered tentatively.

'Good. How?'

'Well, the blade turned over one and a half times, so I could either try to slow the rotation, or speed it up. I don't know for certain, but if I were to guess, then I'd say grip-ping nearer the end of the handle will speed up the rotation and gripping it nearer to the centre of the blade will slow it down.'

'Which would you choose?'

Reynik considered the choice carefully. 'I'd slow the rotation down, as the point would be towards the target for longer. It would have more chance of sticking.'

'Excellent! You may leave us, Femke. You might have brought me a total novice, but at least he's intelligent. I'll make something out of him. How good he will be remains to be seen, but I'm happy to work with him.'

Femke smiled openly this time, and bowed to Derryn before turning and leaving. An hour later she returned to find Reynik was already hitting static targets with some considerable accuracy. After thanking Derryn, and paying him, Femke led Reynik away. She began his next lesson even as they walked to one of her safe houses not far from where Serrius lived.

Poisons were the topic for the afternoon. Types, names, sources, effects and antidotes made for a mind-bending two hours of difficult names. Reynik knew he would not remember half of what she taught him by the following day, and he said as much.

'We'll repeat the lesson each day until you know the information by heart. I can't give you notes. It is hardly the sort of information you would want to be found about your person. Come, we have a short time left before your next session with Serrius. Let's see what you learned yesterday about picking locks.'

By the time Reynik had completed another exhausting session with the gladiator, he was fit to drop. The walk from the city out to the military encampment had never felt so long. He was of half a mind to ask Femke to arrange for him to be detached from the Legion so that he could avoid the hour of walking each morning and evening. It was a hard choice. He knew if he did it, his chances of ever being accepted as a full member of his Legion by his peers would be further impaired. Tiring as it was, he elected for the harder option. He would bear the walking as long as he was physically able. He was not ready to give up his position for the sake of a few miles a day.

It was well that he had made this decision before he reached his tent, for trouble awaited him that may have weakened his resolve. His kit was strewn around his bed space and the File Second was standing nearby with a look of stern disapproval. The File Second, a stocky, hard-faced veteran called Dikaris, was a stickler for discipline. His particular bugbear was personal hygiene and pride in one's presentation. As soon as Reynik saw the situation, he braced himself for the inevitable onslaught.

Dikaris locked eyes with Reynik, clearly watching for clues in his body language as to how the young soldier was going to react. After a moment of staring each other out, the File Second spoke.

'Outside. Now!' he ordered, his voice projecting with the staccato punch of a spear striking a shield.

Reynik obeyed without question, his heart sinking as he realised there was to be no let up in his troubles. With Sidis already set against him, having Dikaris also after his blood

116

would make his life in the Legion unbearable. They moved away from the tent until they were out of earshot of the other men.

'Are you going to tell me who did it?' Dikaris asked, his voice flat and emotionless. 'I'm no fool, Reynik. You would not have been selected to join this Legion if you showed so much as a hint of such low personal standards with regard to property and presentation during your training. The selectors are not blind. They choose only the best. Therefore, someone in the file must be out to make trouble for you. Do you know who it is?'

'No, File Second,' he answered. A warm flood of relief swept through his body as he realised someone was finally displaying signs of an unbiased attitude. 'It could have been any one of several people. I'm not flavour of the moment amongst the other men right now. Some of them have taken exception to my being selected for two special assignments in quick succession. If they could only know the nature of this assignment, then they might be more understanding. However, I'm under orders from the Emperor to tell no one: not even Commander Sateris.'

The File Second nodded and looked thoughtful for a moment.

'How long are you likely to be on this assignment, Reynik?'

'I don't know, File Second. It might be a few weeks; it might be months. I really can't say.'

'Is there any reason you should remain living in tent city during your assignment?'

'I . . . I'm not really sure. I had thought it would be better

117

to remain living here to maintain my identity as part of the unit, but I'm not sure it's going to work.'

Dikaris nodded again and looked at Reynik with a calculating expression.

'You're adding more pressure to your assignment by trying to remain living here, Reynik. I'm not blind, and I'm not stupid. Sidis has it in for you. I've been aware of his prejudice ever since you returned from Thrandor. In my book, that means you can't be all bad. The man is an ass. How he ever got promoted to File Leader is beyond my comprehension. However, if I ever hear you have quoted me as saying that, I'll split you up the middle and feed your carcass to the birds. Understand?'

'Of course, File Second,' Reynik said quickly, smiling in spite of himself.

'Good. Now, if I were you, I'd try to get lodging in the city for the duration of your assignment. The Palace will pay. They always do. Get it over with and then start with us again. I think you'll do fine in this Legion, Reynik, but you need a clear run at establishing yourself as a part of the team. You can't do that while you're running back and forth to wherever the Emperor is sending you. Clear up your bed space tonight. I don't tolerate mess, as you know. Then clear out tomorrow. There'll be a place for you in the Legion when you return. Don't worry about Sidis. Commander Sateris is sharp enough to figure him out before long. I doubt he'll last. Good luck with your mission, whatever it is.'

'Thank you, File Second.'

'Oh, and Reynik . . .'

'Yes, File Second?'

'Do me a favour and act as if I chewed you out to the others, would you? I'll keep an eye on them over the next few days to see if any of them show signs of looking smug. It's always nice to know who the snakes are.'

Reynik saluted and marched back to the tent feeling much better about life. Getting lodgings in the city would not be difficult. He would ask Femke to arrange something in the morning. When he got there, he tidied up his things in silence. He was so tired that it was not hard to keep his face long and his body language depressed. He did not even acknowledge the presence of the others as he worked, though he sensed eyes watching him. Finally, with his legs quivering with exhaustion, he climbed into his canvas bed and fell asleep.

CHAPTER SEVEN

The plaudits of Reynik's instructors still rang in his ears: 'Surprising progress ...' 'A natural throwing arm ...' 'Would make a worthy opponent in the arena ...'. It had been great to have people pat him on the back for doing well – something he had seldom seen in military training – but the question was, could he remember enough in a dynamic situation to be effective? Femke had been very positive too, and the thought brought a flush to his cheeks. Of all his teachers, he had wanted to impress her more than any other. Today was his chance.

'Come on, Reynik. Don't get distracted. Focus. Remember what Devarusso taught you. You *are* aristocracy. You have a right to be here. You have enough money to buy the ground you tread on.'

Reynik's mind was full to bursting with all the information and advice he had tried to assimilate over the previous three weeks. He was determined not to fail.

Dressed in the finery of a Nobleman, with a wig that hid his tightly-cropped, light brown hair under a mass of styled black curls, he was sure that even his fellow soldiers would not recognise him. All that remained was to prove his newfound knowledge.

He was approaching the gates to the Imperial Palace. Back straight as a pillar, and strutting forward with an air of importance, Reynik walked up to the gates and through them with a confidence he did not feel. He sauntered past the guards as if he walked into the Palace every day. When none of the guards moved to stop him his confidence was instantly boosted. 'Now that's irritating!' he thought as he walked across the Palace forecourt to the main entrance. 'Two gold pieces for decently forged papers and they didn't even ask to see them. I'll make sure the Emperor hears about this when I see him.'

Getting floor plans of the Imperial Palace had not been so easy, but he had managed to get two of the Palace servants to draw a diagram for him over a few drinks in one of the city taverns. Reynik had made it a drinking challenge memory game. He had named a room in the Palace and one servant had drawn a route to it from the main entrance. If the fellow servant verified the route as correct, then the artist won a drink. If the corroborating servant knew a quicker way, then he got one too. There were naturally some arguments over whose route was better, but Reynik didn't mind. He bought the drinks anyway and tactfully diverted them on to a new challenge. Over the space of an hour, he had gained a good idea of the layout of most of the Palace. He could not be sure of the accuracy of the information, but it was better than wandering around opening doors at random.

Careful to maintain his posture, Reynik entered the doorway and turned left along the first branch corridor. He nodded politely to anyone who was obviously not a servant, but pointedly ignored those bearing the Imperial livery. It wouldn't do to be seen acknowledging the staff. Second turning on the right, up the staircase on the left, another left at the top of the stairs, follow the corridor to the end.

'There it is,' he thought, his heart leaping with excitement. 'Just as the servants described: two steps up to a set of double doors with pictures on either side of the doorframe. This has to be the Emperor's private library.'

The corridor behind him was empty. He approached the doors. There was no noise from within. Reynik carefully tried the handle, but as expected, the door was locked. A glance at the keyhole told him all he needed to know. Restraining his urge to look around again, he drew two tools from his inside pocket. One was like a tiny chisel, whilst the other was a thinner piece of metal bent at ninety degrees at the end. Taking care not to make a sound, he slid the thin metal blade into the lock and twisted, putting tension on the lock. Then he probed it with his pick, searching for the pins he knew were there somewhere.

The click was not loud as the lock opened, but it was loud enough to make Reynik wince at the sudden sound. He was in.

With the window shutters closed, as they were now, the

library was a great place for stealthy movement. The entire room was in semi-darkness. There was just enough light seeping through the gaps in the shutters for Reynik to see the general layout. Bookcases lined every wall from floor to ceiling with the exception of the window areas. There were also three tall bookcases that protruded out from both sidewalls at regular intervals for the first ten paces, creating three deep alcoves on either side. The central area of the vast room was open with a huge table in the middle, and a single chair. Beyond the table, Reynik could just make out through the gloom that there was a mirror set of protruding bookcases at the far end, forming more alcoves.

Where would his target be? He could not afford to delay. It was a race against time now.

The floor was carpeted, which made silent movement easy. He slipped his lock picks back into his inside pocket and drew a knife from the holster under his left arm. The alcoves on either side of him as he had entered were clear. Creeping forward, he peered into the gloom of the second alcoves. They too were clear. However, when he peeped around the end of the bookcases into the third pair of alcoves, he discovered a guard in the one on the right. The dim figure had his back to Reynik, apparently searching in the gloom for a book.

Reynik took his opportunity and hurled his knife. It thudded squarely into the centre of the guard's back. Reynik did not wait to see if the guard fell. He was already in motion. Springing forwards, he discovered a second guard facing him on the left hand side of the central area of the library. Without pausing to think, Reynik drew a second blade from his sleeve and launched it at the figure. It was a good throw and struck with deadly force. There was no longer any need for stealth, so Reynik sprinted around the table and into the furthest section of library. His target was in the first of the alcoves beyond the central area. Reynik had already got a third knife in his hand, having drawn it from the holster hidden under his tunic on his lower back, before he saw his target.

There was no hesitation. The third blade found its mark with unerring accuracy, but Reynik did not stop. He drew another concealed blade and ran all the way to the far end of the library, checking every alcove as he went. It would be all too easy to expose his back to an unnoticed guard, and die before he made his escape.

The room was clear. The hit was complete. All that remained was for him to get out of the palace.

He re-holstered the blade from his hand into the underarm sheath and then ran back to the door. After a slight pause to listen for movement in the corridor outside, Reynik realised he could hear nothing other than the pounding of his heart and the quiet rasping of his breath. Delaying to allow his elevated heart rate to subside could be counter productive, so he opened the door boldly, stepped outside and closed it behind him. For a moment he con-sidered locking the door behind him, but decided again that it would achieve little. Instead, he tweaked his tunic straight and re-entered his role as a member of the aristocracy. Walking with a casual nonchalance, he made his way back through the corridors to the exit.

Back in the library, there was a sudden click of a latch

springing free and one of the bookcases on the main wall of the central area swung out into the room. Femke and Emperor Surabar stepped out from the recess.

'So, what do you think, your Majesty?'

'Impressive, Femke. You've worked wonders on the young fellow. He was very slick. Let's take a look and see how well those knives of his found their targets, shall we?'

They moved through the library quickly, opening the shutters and flooding the room with light. With the benefit of daylight, the figures dressed in Imperial guard uniforms looked far less lifelike. One by one, starting with the first guard figure, they inspected the wooden mannequins.

Femke pulled the knife from the centre of the back of the first dummy. This was not easy, as the point was buried deep within the wood. Once she had wrenched it free, she sniffed cautiously at the blade.

'Hmm, coated with quiltiss. Good choice. Fast acting and deadly – particularly when delivered anywhere near the heart,' she commented.

'A good throw as well, given the light,' observed Surabar, nodding.

'It was a strong throw, your Majesty, but hardly difficult. The second was more impressive. He was on the move then. He had to draw and throw whilst moving forward, which is far more difficult, even though he threw from slightly closer range. Look how accurately he struck.'

When they recovered the second knife it was buried just as deeply as the first, directly into the mannequin's heart area. It too was covered with the deadly poison. Femke took great care to avoid any possibility of cutting herself as

125

she drew the blade. Although she did have the antidote for quiltiss in her room, it smelled foul and was not guaranteed to work on every person. Some people reacted as badly to the antidote as they did to the poison. Femke had no desire to see if she was one of them.

The third knife had struck the target dummy lower and more centrally than the first two, hitting the region that would have equated to a person's solar plexus.

'Not his best throw,' Surabar noted thoughtfully. 'A shame, given that this was his target.'

'Actually, your Majesty, I would say that this was his safest throw. He took no chances with missing. The blade struck the target square and hard in the centre of the body. It was close enough to the target's heart that the poison would have done its work within a minute. I'd rate that a good throw under the circumstances. No, my only gripe is with his choice of knives for each target. He made life difficult for himself. A really good assassin would never do that. I'll debrief him on it later.'

The Emperor looked at her quizzically. 'What do you mean, Femke? All the knives are the same. I see no differences in them at all.'

'It's not the knives that are different, your Majesty. Can you remember where he drew each blade from?'

The Emperor thought for a moment, his eyes instinctively rising as he accessed the memory. 'I didn't see where he drew the first one from. He already had it in his hand when he came into view. The second came from a sleeve, the third from a back holster and the last from his boot.'

'Absolutely correct, your Majesty, which means that he

must have drawn his first blade from his underarm holster – the easiest to access in a hurry. Had he taken the knife, say, from his boot when he entered the room, then he would have been faster at drawing his second blade. In a dire situation, that could well mean the difference between life and death.'

'I see. I hadn't thought of it like that,' he replied thoughtfully.

'There were a few other minor points, but on the whole I think he performed well. I'll be honest – I don't think he's ready to infiltrate the Guild, but I'm satisfied that I've given him the best preparation he could have in such a short time.'

'Good. I agree that the situation is not ideal, but the Guild has killed another two Commanders this week. If the assassins continue to kill my Commanders at this rate, it's rapidly going to become difficult to find good men willing to take command. Assuming the guards do not catch him during his exit from the Palace, bring Reynik to my study this afternoon after you have debriefed. If anything has gone awry during his escape, I will doubtless hear from the Palace guards shortly.'

'Very good, your Majesty.'

Femke gave a brief, formal bow, holstered the three poisoned blades into empty leather sheaths she had brought with her, and then wrapped them in cloth before tucking the bundle under her arm and exiting the library. On quiet reflection as she walked along the corridors and out of the Palace, Femke found she had mixed emotions over Reynik passing his test.

Over recent years it had appeared that whenever she had formed a strong emotional bond to someone, whether it be romantic or platonic, the person had suffered dire consequences. First, after training her as a spy, her mentor and surrogate father figure, Lord Ferdand, had disappeared without a trace. Then, more recently, Lord Danar had died in her arms after following her to Thrandor and helping rescue her from the Royal Dungeons. It was as if she were not destined to enjoy close relationships.

Now, despite her better judgement, she found she was developing an attachment to this young Legionnaire who was so willing to tread dangerous paths in the service of the Empire. It was hard not to like him. He was so enthusiastic about everything. Femke knew he had to be feeling the pressure of all the information he had been force-fed, yet he had not once complained about the pace of his tuition, or the difficulty of the tasks she had set him. He did not appear to take exception to being made to look foolish. Indeed, he seemed to let everything wash over him in a way that gave him stature beyond his tender years.

Femke suddenly chuckled aloud. 'Who am I to think of him as being of tender years?' she thought, realising the irony of her situation. 'I can't be any more than two years his senior, yet here I am on my high horse acting as if I know everything about everything. It's time to take a step back and get real, Femke, my girl. It's his life. He has as much right to take risks with his life as you have with yours. Don't get sentimental. Just because you're teaching him does not make you responsible for what happens to him. Face it – his chances of surviving the next week are not good. If the Guild doesn't kill him for stepping on their turf, they'll kill him when he blows his cover as an infiltrator. Stay detached.'

The problem was, no matter how much she told herself not to get involved, she knew in her heart that it was too late. She had already formed a bond with him that was too strong to snap with impunity. He was a likeable young man: strong, attractive, with enough natural charisma that his boyish looks and lack of years did not detract from his overall appeal as a potential partner. This, of course, was impossible for many reasons. Not least of these was the fact that his life expectancy could be measured in days rather than years. Femke was not ready to let the hurt be any deeper than necessary when Reynik was killed.

'Cold, calm and detached,' she thought. 'It's the only way to be. You're his tutor, Femke, not his lover. Keep things in perspective.'

Later that afternoon, waiting to enter the Emperor's study with Reynik at her side, Femke felt pleased with her self-control. The iron curtain was firmly drawn around her heart and she felt that no matter what mad plan Reynik agreed to, she would accept her role was played out. She had taught him as much as she was able in the short time given. Where her skills fell short of being the best, she had found the top tutors in Shandrim to fill the gaps. It was done. She felt convinced that she could move on and leave Reynik to his fate with no regrets. No doubt the Emperor would have another task for her, so she would be too busy to worry about Reynik.

'Who will it be, do you think?' Reynik asked her in a

whisper as they waited to be called in. 'Do you know who he wants me to kill?'

Femke had a mental list of potential favourites that were high profile enough to draw the attention of the Guild. It was good that she did not have a chance to share her thoughts, for she would have been proved wildly wrong.

'Kempten!' she exploded, when the Emperor announced his intention. 'But . . . but . . . he's more loyal than anyone else you have!'

'Trust me, Femke. I know it seems like madness, but I know exactly what I'm doing. Lord Kempten must die. If we don't kill him, then the Guild will. They are hitting the Legion commanders in order to hurt me. It will only be a matter of time before they target Kempten. I'm not going to allow that to happen.'

'Dead is dead, your Majesty! I appreciate that it's not my place to question your motives, but Kempten is a good man. He did a great job as Regent while you were away. Shand, he even had some of his peers hung on your account. How will killing him further your cause?'

'Dead is only dead if you stop breathing, Femke. I have no intention of losing Lord Kempten as an ally. That is why he must be taken out of harm's way. Let me explain . . .'

The plan was simple. Walk to Lord Kempten's office door. Throw the knife. Leave without getting stopped. As Femke had taught him, the last element was the most crucial. It was all well and good to eliminate your target, but if you got caught, then it would be a life for a life. Reynik

130

had no desire to die just yet. His eighteenth birthday was only a week away. Life had only just begun.

He tried not to let emotion get in the way of what he knew he had to do. The thought that within the next few days his status would change to a level with Shalidar brought a sick feeling to his stomach. Even the thought that he would be required to kill in cold blood brought the bitter taste of bile to the back of his mouth. It would be necessary, though. He knew that. The cause was a just one. He kept telling himself over and over that unless he acted, more and more innocent people would die. The sacrifice would be worth the end result.

At least Lord Kempten was easy to reach. His office was in the City Court building, which was not a restricted area. On completion of his short spell as Regent, the Emperor had tasked Lord Kempten with collating certain information and dealing with some of Shandrim's less critical domestic issues. The old Lord had elected to do this by making himself accessible to those with the information, which worked strongly in Reynik's favour. The City Court was not far from the Palace, but security at the Court was not as tight. He could just walk in. It was highly unlikely he would be challenged. Getting out afterwards would not be so straightforward. This would be doubly true as his brief was to make sure someone witnessed his kill. The Guild of Assassins would need something to go on if they were to make contact with him, so he needed to be seen. Seen but not caught – a tricky balance to strike.

Lord Kempten's office was in the heart of the building, which meant a long escape route. This was good in that he would most certainly be seen by someone, but bad because it heightened his chances of being intercepted. Dressed in nondescript clothing, Reynik scouted the building thoroughly that afternoon. Several routes to the main exit were possible. There was also a secondary exit that opened onto one of the back streets. This was attractive, but almost too obvious. Windows offered further exit points, but, as Reynik intended to make the hit during daytime hours, leaving through a window would also stand out as unusual.

Walking around the Court building several times without raising any suspicion was easy. Like many others, he carried several rolled parchments under his arm and walked quickly. By looking busy, striding purposefully and avoiding eye contact with anyone he met, he blended in perfectly with the bureaucratic characters who infested the corridors. No one gave him a second glance.

Later, he met with Femke to discuss his options. He swiftly drew the layout of the building on a slate, marking doors, windows and corridors with confident strokes. Femke watched intently. She already knew the Civil Court building intimately, as she had worked undercover there on several occasions. His diagram was good, including more information than Femke expected of a relative novice.

Quizzing him in depth about his reconnaissance revealed that Reynik had a good eye and an excellent memory for detail. He had noted key paintings and wall hangings, which would make good markers in the event of his becoming disoriented. Colours of carpeting, specific ornamental decoration, even anomalies in the mounting of wall-mounted torch brackets had all been noted.

'That's good, Reynik, very good. Your best route of escape is this way. Not because it's the quickest, but it offers you the most options if one way appears blocked. See here,' she said, pointing at his diagram. 'If you find the way blocked, you can not only double back, but you are left with a variety of possible alternate exit routes. You could go this way, this way, or as a last resort go out through the window at the end of the corridor here.'

Reynik followed her finger and frowned.

'You wouldn't consider going back the way I'm going in?' he asked.

'No. It would be better not to. You want people to see you, but don't give them a chance to see you more than once – at least, not with the same appearance. A second look at you will allow them to fill in too many details. When seeing someone passing by, the average person will only get a very vague impression of what the passer-by looks like. If they see that person a second time, they will begin to take in detail. The more times they see that person, the more details they will mentally note. Don't give anyone more of a look at you than you have to. By doing it my way, you will minimise the chances of anyone being able to give a detailed description.'

'That makes sense. Did you manage to get any other useful information this afternoon?'

Femke grinned. 'Naturally. Information is my business.'

'Come on then. Impress me,' Reynik offered, sitting back and crossing his legs casually, as if getting comfortable to listen to a story.

'Kempten is a man of routine and habit. He schedules all

his meetings in the morning and early afternoon. His last appointment is at the first afternoon call. He never agrees to any meetings after this, as he spends the rest of his day studying and writing his reports to the Emperor. At the second afternoon call he takes his lunch break. He puts his quill down the moment the call sounds, no matter what he's doing, and heads out of his office. He takes his lunch in one of three places: The Phoenix, Korrin's or The Old Dog. Do you want to know what he has for lunch?'

'I don't think that will be necessary,' Reynik smiled. 'It appears the ideal time for the hit is moments before the second afternoon call.'

'My thoughts exactly.'

'He'll be at his desk, almost certainly alone. The building will be quieter than at most other times of the day, because the majority of people will take their lunch slightly earlier than Kempten. It's almost too good to be true. In fact, I think with a little more deception, we might be able to make this hit work for us even more. Are you able to make an appointment in the Court with one of the other Nobles?'

Femke nodded. 'I could, but please remember that I can't compromise myself for you, Reynik. If you get caught, you're on your own. You understand, don't you? The Emperor doesn't have many who are loyal to him outside of the Legions. He'll need all the help he can get over the coming months.'

Reynik shrugged his shoulders and grimaced. 'I knew it wouldn't be easy. The most worthwhile things never are. My idea should not compromise you, though. Listen. This is what I think we should do . . .'

Two days later and he was leaning against the wall in the street outside the Civil Court. He feigned a nonchalant disinterest as he picked through the bag of nuts he had purchased from a street vendor. Under his casual exterior, his heart was beating wildly. This was it. If all went well, then in a few minutes he would be a wanted man: wanted for the murder of Lord Kempten. Murder was such an ugly word. No wonder the Guild hid behind words like 'contract' and 'hit' and 'assassination', he thought grimly.

A cloud passed over the sun and he cursed softly under his breath. 'Don't hide your face now,' he muttered, looking up to the sky to see how long the sun was likely to be obscured. Timing was everything. Even a few heartbeats late or early would make all the difference.

Reynik looked across at his marker. There was no discernible shadow line. 'Come on, sun. Don't let me down.'

Anxious moments passed with excruciating slowness. There could not be long left until he should be moving, but without the movement of the shadows over his pre-noted markers, all his preparation would be in vain. As suddenly as it had dived behind the passing cloud the sun burst forth again, sending shadows leaping across the square. Reynik checked his marker. The shadow of the building was almost upon it. A minute or two more and it would have been too late.

Painfully slow seconds passed as the shadow crept silently forward. Reynik's heartbeat quickened further as he sensed another cloud approaching. Would the shadow touch his marker before the cloud concealed the sun's progress? He knew it would be a close race. The cloud won, but only just. As the line of the shadow disappeared and the warmth died from the air, Reynik decided it was so close that if he left now, it would make no difference. By his reckoning, he had something close to the count of three hundred at a medium marching pace until the first afternoon call sounded. It would take him a count of two hundred and thirty to reach Kempten's door.

He pushed away from the wall and walked across the square towards the Civil Court building. It felt good to be moving. The sick feeling that had been growing in his stomach receded as he began to stride out. With a flourish, he scattered the contents of his bag across the road. An instant flurry of wingbeats demonstrated the vigilance of dozens of pigeons, ever quick to descend from their roosts for easy pickings.

Up the steps, in through the main door and along the first corridor; his count reached one hundred and thirty. 'Slow down,' he remonstrated silently. 'There's no hurry.'

With his heart thumping like a galley drum, Reynik reached the turning into the final corridor. Three doors down on the left hand side was the entrance to Lord Kempten's office. The corridor was empty. Under normal circumstances this would make it ideal for his hit, but he needed to be seen. He slowed further. His count passed two hundred and twenty. What should he do? If he made the hit without being seen by anyone, then it would defeat the main objective. The only alternative would be to make sure he was seen during his escape. If he made it too obvious, however, he could be considered sloppy and unworthy of the Guild's attention. Two hundred and fifty: time was running out.

'Damn it!' he cursed, gritting his teeth in frustration.

He hesitated outside Lord Kempten's door, torn with indecision as the seconds crawled slowly by. His mental count passed two hundred and eighty. It was now or never. He could wait no longer. Drawing his knife from inside his jacket, he flung open Lord Kempten's door. As expected, the Lord was sitting behind his desk. The old man hardly had a chance to look up from his work before the poisoned blade drove home with deadly force. Kempten gave a loud cry and slumped forward over his desk, hands clutching at the handle of the knife protruding from his chest. A pool of dark blood was already spreading over the work surface as Reynik turned and ran down the corridor.

A sudden shout from some distance along the corridor behind him made his heart leap. He had been seen. This was excellent, as it simplified his plan. The only thing left to do was to escape cleanly. He looked over his shoulder to see who had shouted. There were two men at the far end of the corridor. They were not guards, but they were already running along the corridor towards him. They must have seen him throw the knife. Everything was working perfectly.

Outside the bugler sounded the second call. Reynik sprinted to the end of the corridor and turned left, deeper into the building. No sooner had he rounded the corner than he stopped and began dismantling his disguise. In one fluid movement he whipped off his jacket, reversing it in the process. Inside out, his previously dark-brown jacket became a rich blue with completely different styled lapels and epaulettes topped with silver buttons. A second or two later and he was wearing it again.

A door opened further along the corridor and Femke emerged wearing a dark brown jacket in the same style as the one he had just been wearing. Reynik did not spare her more than a momentary glance as he pulled off his brown wig and ripped off his false moustache, stuffing both in an inside pocket before securing the top button of his jacket. His own hair he had, with Femke's help, dyed blonde the night before.

The pounding footsteps of his pursuers were approaching the corner as Reynik ruffled his hair with his fingers and dropped silently to the floor to assume a sprawled position. The two men rounded the corner to see him writhing on the floor, apparently winded, and a figure in a brown jacket disappearing around a corner some distance ahead.

'Are you hurt?' one of the men asked, pausing briefly to kneel next to Reynik.

'Just winded,' he wheezed, chest heaving in apparent protest. 'That way,' he added, pointing down the corridor in the direction Femke had gone. The men needed no further encouragement. They left at a run.

It took them more than a minute to catch up with Femke, who was jogging along the corridors in the general direction of the main exit. She deliberately ignored their calls to stop until they were all but upon her. When she did stop and turn to face them, Femke regarded them with an expression of frustration and anger.

'Look, I'm in a hurry. What is it? Spit it out and make it fast. I'm already late for my next appointment.'

'Next appointment! I don't think so, lady. The only place you're going is to the gallows if Lord Kempten is dead.'

'Lord Kempten? What are you talking about? I've just come from an interview with the Chief Clerk for a job here. I have another interview at the Palace for a different position very shortly. Please don't delay me. I need to get a job or my landlady is going to throw me out on the streets. I don't think my interview went well with the Chief Clerk, so I really need to get to my next one on time.'

Femke argued with them for a couple of minutes before leading them back to the Chief Clerk's office who confirmed her story, and that she had left in a hurry at the sound of the second afternoon call. At the mention of the second call, the two men looked at one another as it dawned on them that they had been fooled. Not surprisingly, there was no sign of the blonde man they had seen sprawled in the corridor. Reynik was long gone.

CHAPTER EIGHT

The Guildmaster looked around the chamber from his podium. The dying echoes of the traditional recitation of the Assassins' creed were still ringing around the chamber as he checked who was present. A second meeting of this magnitude in as many months was highly unusual, but these were unusual times. Nearly every alcove was full. The notable exceptions were those of Brothers Falcon and Wolf Spider, both of whom had lost their lives recently. Even Brother Dragon was back in his alcove. It was as complete a meeting of the Guild as had been held during his tenure as Guildmaster. He took a deep breath.

'My first point of order is to find out which of you accepted the contract on Lord Kempten. Can the Brother please explain why they took on the hit without informing me?' he asked, keeping his voice mellifluous and devoid of condemnation.

A pregnant silence formed in the gloomy half-light of the chamber. The Guildmaster turned slowly full circle, his eyes seeking out each of the shadowy figures, only to see them shaking their heads in denial. When he had completed a full sweep, he gave a thoughtful 'Hmm' and raised a forefinger to stroke his lips.

'If none of you claim responsibility, then who carried out the strike? Does anyone know anything about the killing of Lord Kempten this afternoon?'

There was another pause, but this time a voice spoke into the stillness. It was the soft voice of the woman known as the Fox.

'I heard that it was a young man who made the hit, though he may have had a young woman accomplice. Rumour has it they staged a clever switch to fool their pursuers. Whoever did this was professional and well organised. It was a slick operation.'

'Yes, I heard something similar. It was the involvement of the woman that intrigued me. It is possible, of course, that she really was an innocent bystander who happened to get swept into the assassin's escape by chance, but it does sound unlikely, more so because no one can now locate her. I confess that initially I thought the woman was you, Brother Fox. I see now, however, that I was wrong.'

The woman assassin bowed low in her alcove and the Guildmaster bowed in return. He looked around the chamber and asked if anyone else knew anything about the killing. There were no further speakers.

'Very well,' the Guildmaster said decisively. 'Please bend all your efforts over the next few days towards finding this mystery hit duo. It does not do to have unaffiliated assassins on the streets of Shandrim. It has always been accepted that the Emperor's spy network occasionally kills at his bidding, but this did not have the look of their work. For a start, Surabar is well-known for his dislike of assassinations and those who perform them. The Emperor is unlikely to have ordered a hit while in the process of trying to purge us from the city. If such hypocrisy were ever discovered, he would be ruined for life. Also, Kempten was Surabar's biggest advocate. Why would the Emperor order him killed? No. This was someone operating on the outside – on our side of the Palace walls. Therefore, it is down to us to do something about it. The Emperor is sure to cast the blame for Kempten's death in our direction. We must be ready. We must find the culprits. If they are as good as they appear to be, then we could offer them a chance to join us. If they refuse, we will kill them and send their bodies to the Emperor as a demonstration that we were not responsible. Either way the Guild wins. What do you say?'

There was a chorus of 'ayes'. The Guildmaster smiled under his hood. He hoped they would join. It was never good to be down on numbers in a time of crisis, and he was keenly aware of the losses of Falcon and Wolf Spider. If it did transpire that this was a hit team rather than a solo killer, what should he do? It was policy to keep junior members from learning each other's identities in order to ensure the safety of the Guild. The only person who knew all of the true identities of the assassins was the Guildmaster. Would it hurt for two of the junior members to know one another well? Or would it spark secret meetings between others in the Guild looking to team up? Being an assassin was a lonely life in many ways. The possibility of working in a team of two or more might be an attractive proposition for some.

The Guildmaster instinctively glanced across at the booth where Shalidar sat cloaked in shadow. What had Brother Dragon done with Brother Falcon in Thrandor? How had they linked up? Had they known one another's true identities for long? He felt it unlikely that he would ever find out the whole truth. That Brother Falcon was dead was not in question, for his icon had returned. The silver cufflink in the shape of a soaring falcon was one of the more subtle icons, but the central chamber's magical alarm had rung every bit as loud at its ownerless return as it had for the wolf spider pendant.

Shalidar had not killed Kempten. The Guildmaster was certain of this, for Shalidar had not left the Guild complex in days. The city was a dangerous place for him at the moment. There were too many people looking for him in Shandrim just itching to claim the handsome reward that the Emperor had placed on the assassin's head. The Guildmaster was also having him watched. For once, he knew for certain that Shalidar was telling the truth. It was hard to see how the man could have any involvement in this latest development, but the Guildmaster found himself reflecting that, given Shalidar's recent history, he could not be ruled out of involvement immediately. Brother Dragon had managed to stir up so many hornets' nests over the last couple of years that it was hard to ignore his ability to create trouble.

'Good. That is settled. Commence the search

immediately after the meeting please. Next on my agenda is to congratulate Brothers Viper and Firedrake for their recent successful hits . . .'

'Excellent, Femke! I'm glad the Kempten operation went without a hitch. I will miss having him around. He was a useful person to have in Court, but he is more useful to me where he is now. The bait is laid, but now we have to decide on another target so the Guild can intercept Reynik. Have you any thoughts?'

Femke felt queasy. Taking responsibility for the deaths of others had always made her feel this way. It was without doubt the most unpleasant part of her job.

'Plenty, your Majesty, but I don't think you'll like any of them.'

'Probably not,' the Emperor admitted with a grimace. 'I abhor this entire business, but I accept it's necessary if we're to locate and destroy the Guild. It helps a little for me to regard it as a tactic of war, but no matter how I dress it up, I cannot make the taking of lives in this fashion feel any less wrong. Make up a shortlist of five for me and then bring Reynik into the Palace tonight. I'll meet you in my library. We'll finalise his next assignment then.'

Femke bowed and turned to leave. As she exited the Emperor's study, a servant was about to knock on the door outside. A trolley, loaded with the Emperor's lunch, blocked her way. She squeezed past, nodding and smiling at the servant. He returned the nod, but not the smile. He looked nervous, she thought as she strode away down the corridor. One would think that the Palace servants got used to seeing the Emperor, but some never did.

As she reached the turn at the end of the corridor, she paused. Something was wrong. The servant had looked familiar, but then she knew most of the Palace staff, so that in itself was not unusual. It was the combination of his nervousness and his familiarity. Something here was not right. Then it struck her. Yes, he was familiar, but not in the guise of a servant. The last time she had seen the man, he had been involved in spying. He was not one of the Imperial spies, though. The last time she had seen him, he was working for one of the Shandese Lords. Which one, she could not remember, but recalling the memory was not a priority.

The man emerged from the Emperor's study without the trolley and closed the door behind him. As he looked around and saw her watching him, she distinctly noted a flash of panic cross his face. It was enough.

'Stop right there!' she yelled, pointing at him with an accusing finger.

He did not hesitate. He turned and ran off down the corridor in a flat-out sprint away from her. Femke leaped forward and raced after him. It took a few seconds for her to cover the ground to the Emperor's study door. She burst through it to find Surabar lifting a forkful of food towards his mouth. He paused at the unexpected and explosive entrance, looking at Femke with genuine surprise.

'It's poisoned! Don't eat it!' Femke gasped. She paused just long enough to see that Emperor Surabar put the fork down before she was off again, running for all she was worth in the direction that the infiltrator had taken.

Her ribs already burned and she had not run much more than a few dozen paces. She was clearly in no condition for a long chase. If she were to catch him, she would have to do so quickly, and without too much of a fight. Her best chance was to intercept him, rather than chase him, but that required her to anticipate where he was going.

So where would he be going? Out of the Palace, that much was sure. If he had planned thoroughly, then he would have a pre-prepared route to follow. How well would he know the Palace, though?

Femke knew the Palace intimately. She had made it her business to know every nook and cranny. There were no secret passages or hiding places that she had not explored, and she had long ago worked out all the most efficient routes to the exits. Her quarry was most likely to be heading for the servant's gate exit, particularly given his dress, but would he continue in that direction if he realised Femke was no longer directly chasing him? It was a gamble she had to take.

The shortest way to the servants' exit was to make for the central corridor to the great staircase down into the main entrance hall. From there she would cut through the servants' corridor system, through the kitchens and out to the back exit. Gritting her teeth against the pain ballooning in her side, she zigzagged through the Palace until she reached the main first floor corridor. There was a steady flow of people moving to and fro along the corridor, but it was wide enough that Femke could continue to run unhindered. When she reached the top of the great staircase, she did not hesitate. Ever since she had first come to the

146

Palace, she had always wanted to slide down the great polished banisters and this was the perfect excuse.

With a yell of 'Look out! Coming through!' she leaped onto the left hand rail and started to accelerate. It was well that she had a cat-like sense of balance. If she had over-balanced and fallen from the rail, the impact with the marble floor below would not have been pretty.

'Shand alive!' she exclaimed, as her velocity down the long, straight banister reached a peak well beyond anything she could control. The banister rail flattened out at the bottom, but she did not wait that long to disembark. She pushed clear from her breakneck ride a few stairs up from the ground floor, her momentum carrying her beyond the last of the stairs and onto the thick walkway of carpet that led from the main doors up to the staircase.

Despite the thick pile of the carpet, Femke landed hard, but she absorbed much of the momentum by tucking into a roll that spun her fully halfway across the great entrance hall. People watched in amazement as she regained her feet with the agility of an acrobat, but she did not wait for a round of applause. She ran swiftly across to one of the side exits, barging the door open with her shoulder and clutching at her side as she went.

The side corridor that she entered led straight to the Palace kitchens, which had saloon style swing doors. In agony, she crashed through them and careered through the kitchen, causing one chef to drop a great tray of food and another to burn his hand on the top of his stove. She could not pause to apologise, and she did not have the breath to do so anyway. At the far end of the kitchen, she grabbed a large metal meat fork from a wall hook as she shouldered through the opposite doors. Cries of anguish and pain followed her, but they faded quickly as she disappeared down the corridor and around the corner towards the servants' exit.

Femke's breathing was coming in ragged gasps as she staggered the final few paces. Gripping the meat fork tightly in her right hand, she opened the door and looked across the courtyard outside. There was no sign of her adversary. She had beaten him to the exit. The pain in her side was excruciating, lancing through her as if a spear had just been driven into her chest. With an iron discipline, she calmed her breathing and concentrated on blocking out the pain. There was an alcove to the side of the door. Femke ducked into it and flattened herself against the wall to prevent anyone approaching along the corridor from seeing her until the last second. She did so in the nick of time.

No sooner had she concealed herself than the would-be assassin came racing along the corridor. He grabbed at the door handle only to find the cold metal prongs of the meat fork pressing at his jugular.

'Move and I'll stick you like a pig,' Femke rasped.

The man clearly did not think she would follow through with her threat and he whipped up his hand to try to sweep aside the vicious kitchen implement. He was not fast enough. Femke jabbed the prongs of the fork into his neck even as his hand struck her wrist. As a result, the man caused the fork to tear through his own flesh, opening the main jugular artery and spraying blood in a bright red fountain across the corridor.

He screamed in horror and clasped at his neck to try to staunch the spurting flow.

'Who sent you?' Femke asked, holding the fork in front of her threateningly. 'Tell me and I'll help you.'

The man did not answer. Femke was not sure that he had heard her in his panic.

'Who sent you?' she repeated firmly. 'You need a medic, or you will die. The main artery must be stitched, or you will not last more than a few minutes. I will help you get to a medic if you tell me who sent you.'

'No! He'll have me killed if I tell.'

'And I'll let you die here if you don't. Do you want to die now, or have a chance of escaping your master's wrath? Choose quickly. You don't have long to decide.'

The man looked at her with wild eyes. She met his gaze with an icy stare.

'Lacedian,' he spat. 'Lord Lacedian sent me. Now take me to a medic. Quickly!'

It was some time later when Femke returned to the Emperor's study. The guard on the door had doubled. She smiled as she noted it. A little late, maybe, but at least the Emperor was now treating his personal safety as a matter of more import again. It was so easy to relax in familiar surroundings. It had been some time since the old-school Lords had tried to kill him, so it was only natural that he should suffer from a little complacency.

Femke asked the guards to announce her, and she was immediately called inside. Emperor Surabar's eyes were like those of a falcon when she entered: alert and taking everything in. She bowed gently, bending more at the neck than the waist, to avoid increasing the discomfort in her side. How long would her ribs take to heal? She had certainly not sped up the healing process today, she thought grimly. It was frustrating to be so limited in what she could do, but she knew that if she did not take her healing seriously, her ribs might become a permanent restriction. That was something she could not afford.

'Did you catch him?'

'I did, your Majesty. He is no longer a threat.'

'Did you kill him? I hoped to question him.' Surabar frowned, staring at Femke's injured side. 'You're hurt again, aren't you?'

'My ribs are not yet fully healed,' Femke admitted with a grimace. 'I'll be more careful with them in future.'

'You're not fit to be doing anything but rest, young lady. If I weren't so stuck for good operatives, I'd have the medics lock you in their emporium until you were fully recovered. Sadly, I don't have that option. Tell me, where is he and what did you learn from him?'

'He's locked up. He's lost a lot of blood, but the medics are tending him. I think he'll live. I can tell you that he's not a member of the Guild of Assassins. I've seen him before, but I don't know his true name. I would have considered him a spy rather than a killer, but he was offered enough money that he decided to branch out. It seems we have found Reynik's next assignment.'

The carriage approached the large rectangular country house at a stately pace. Lord Kempten peeped out through

150

the closed curtains of the carriage windows. The stone building looked cold and grey. In some ways it would be nice to spend some time here again. It had been some months since he had last visited. Of course, Izzie had been with him then. It would not be the same here without her.

Izzie had dominated his thoughts during the journey. How would she react to his 'death'? The Emperor had promised that he would send her out here to the country house at the earliest opportunity, but to send her immediately would look suspicious. His heart ached at the thought of what she would be feeling right now. At least he could count on the children to look after her. They were reliable and sensible. They would help her through it.

'I can't tell her,' Surabar had told him. 'It's too risky. I need her to react with authentic grief if the deception is to feel real. I know it will be hard on her and your children. You can be sure that I'll apologise to them all at the first opportunity afterwards, but I'm sure they'll see I've done this for the best of reasons. You have become a legitimate target for the Guild. I'm not going to let them get to you. This deception has a double benefit. It will instantly give Reynik the sort of profile he needs if he is to infiltrate the Guild, but it will also put you out of harm's way for a while.'

The carriage stopped in front of the main doors. The driver, who was actually a member of the Imperial spy network, jumped down and opened the door.

'All clear, my Lord. Don't dawdle outside, though. There's always the chance of a watcher.'

Kempten stepped out of the carriage. His back was stiff

151

after the long ride, but he did not wait to stretch. He climbed the few steps to the front doors as quickly as he could and slipped inside.

The house staff was minimal; just enough to keep the place clean and tidy whilst the Lord and Lady were not in residence. Izzie would bring the bulk of the house staff with her from the town house in Shandrim when she came. There was no one around. He went to the kitchens and rummaged through the cupboards until he found the dahl. The embers of the kitchen fire were still warm. A little fuel and some gentle encouragement with the bellows soon revived it to a healthy blaze.

A short while later Kempten sat in his favourite chair in the study with his feet on a footstool and a large cup of steaming dahl in his hands. He looked out of the windows at the green trees and open fields. It was so peaceful here. He closed his eyes and his mind suddenly raced back to the moments before his 'death' in the Court office in Shandrim. The scene was vivid in his mind. He could remember every detail:

What would it be like to die? The thought would not leave.

He fiddled with the papers on his desk, first tidying them and then messing them up again. The bag of pig's blood felt awkward and obvious. Would the fake dagger hilt that Femke had given him fool anyone? He ran his fingers through his silver-grey hair. A moment later he ruffled it again.

'This is ridiculous!' he muttered aloud.

How best to look for one's own assassination was not a thought that had ever crossed his mind before. There were so many little details that could give him away. Was his hair

152

normally combed this neatly? Was his desk usually this tidy? Where should he put his quill and inkpot? Should he be holding his quill? Should he die in a dramatic pose across the desk, or just collapse like a bag of turnips on the floor? The questions flooded his mind, increasing his tension and nervousness with every passing minute.

How long to go? It must be soon.

A new thought crossed his mind. What if I'm being set up? What if this assassination is for real? Did Emperor Surabar really forgive me for intending to kill him at his coronation? Reynik's training as an assassin was real enough. Would the Emperor now test his protégé's resolve by having him make a real kill? What could be easier than to throw a knife at a target who had been ordered to sit still?

His agitation increased still further.

What a fool he would look if he were found with a fake knife sticking from his chest alongside a real one. What would people make of it? Would anyone put together the pieces of the puzzle? Would anyone care to? He had made a lot of enemies amongst his fellow Noblemen recently. He had never been a popular man, but supporting the Emperor had done little for his reputation amongst his peers. To them he was a traitor. In their view, one who upheld a commoner's right to wear the Mantle of the Emperor had resigned his right to be called a Lord. Could the contract be real?

He moved to get up from his chair, paused, and then sat down again with a sigh. 'Oh, Izzie! What have I done? What am I doing? I hate to hurt you like this, but it won't be for long. It'll all work out. You'll see.'

For a moment, every minute of his sixty-six years weighed

down on him. He felt old, yet he knew he had many more years of life left in him – assuming, of course, he was spared a violent death. He drew his fingers under his eyes and across his face, feeling the slack skin tighten as he stretched it over his cheeks. 'You're a wrinkled old fool, Kempten,' he thought sadly. 'Surabar is only five years younger, but despite his silver hair, he looks and acts as if he's still in his late forties. What do you think you're doing? You're no Surabar. One way, or another, this mess is going to be the death of you.'

There was no warning. The door burst open. It was Reynik. He registered the blade already in flight and his mind, despite working at high speed, found yet another gear. He froze. The knife passed over his shoulder at a blistering velocity, striking the target inside the cupboard behind him with a frightening thud. He was not hit. His worries had all been nonsense. Surabar was protecting him as he had promised. Relief flooded him with a warm glow, spreading from the pit of his stomach to flush his face.

Reynik paused in the doorway for a moment. His boyish face was intent, his balance perfect. 'Shand! Was I ever that young?' he thought in a bizarre mental aside.

He knew what he had to do. Easing his jacket aside to reveal the fake knife hilt protruding from his chest, he punched the bag under his tunic, causing a flood of pig's blood to release. Then he grabbed the false knife with both hands and sank forward onto the desk, allowing a pool of dark red blood to spread from under him.

Reynik was gone. The sound of his feet retreating at a run down the corridor was getting softer. As the young man's running footfall faded, so more feet approached – also at a pace. The new arrivals paused at the doorway.

154

'That man just killed Lord Kempten. Hey, you! Stop!'

The voice belonged to Jeremus, one of Femke's fellow spies. He recognised the man's tones from the planning meeting they had held the previous day. Without pause, Jeremus led his unwitting accomplice away in rapid pursuit of Reynik. The noise of their retreat faded quickly. It was all going perfectly. Could it really be this easy to fool everyone into believing he was dead?

He remained where he was, still and silent. He knew that if he moved, he would disturb the blood on the desk. All he could do now was wait. If all went well, he would not have to wait long.

The next phase was to get him swiftly out of the building with the minimum of fuss. The less people saw, the more they would speculate. Rumour would spread like wildfire. It would only be a matter of hours before news of his murder would be all over the city. It would help, of course, that the rumour and speculation would be fuelled and amplified by Femke's network of agents and tattle touts. The whole process from beginning to end would take less than a day. Within a week, talk of the assassination would die down to become yesterday's news and the name, Lord Kempten, would be consigned to a footnote of Shandrim's bloody history.

A minute went by – then another. There was a noise at the door. He did not flinch. To look would be to potentially ruin everything.

'OK, my Lord, the stretcher bearers are on their way.'

It was Reynik. His quick return meant he had successfully fooled the man accompanying Jeremus. Everything was running to plan. No wonder the Emperor was well informed if his intelligence service was this effective, he mused.

The sounds of further approaching feet became apparent. He

155

remained unmoving, determined not to inadvertently give the game away. As the new arrivals entered, Reynik began directing them.

'Put the stretcher down there. Have you got the jacket? Great. You spread this jacket on the stretcher. We'll put Lord Kempten on top of it. Give me that one. Thanks. Right, you and you, grab his shoulders. We'll take his legs. On three . . . one, two, three.'

He relaxed totally, allowing the men to lift him from his chair and place him on the stretcher. Reynik was very precise in his instructions. The lift was clean, efficient, and did not bump him in the slightest. It must come from the military training, he mused. Inside a minute of them arriving, he was being carried out of his office and along the corridor towards the main entrance foyer. It was incredibly tempting to crack his eyes open a little to see how people were reacting to this sudden dramatic turn of events. He knew, however, that this was no joke. He could not afford to give people the slightest reason to doubt that what they were seeing was real. He did not give in to temptation.

A sudden change in temperature and acoustics told him they had exited through the main doors. The street noises in the square outside the building included the usual bustle of carriages, pedestrians and horsemen that characterised the centre of Shandrim. The exception was the scream of a woman who could not have been more than a few paces from where he was being carried. His heart leaped in his chest at the sudden, piercing shriek. How he restrained the rest of his body from jumping at the alarming noise, he was not sure. Maybe he didn't.

The stretcher was lifted into a carriage, which pulled up even as they left the building. Reynik climbed inside with him and closed the door. He felt the light dim as the young man drew the *window curtains. The carriage lurched forward and they set off at a trot away from the scene of his murder. They had done it — or had they? Everything had happened so quickly that someone would surely question the circumstances. From the assassin's strike to the body leaving the building had been a matter of just a few minutes. Would the illusion be undone by its sheer efficiency? Only time would tell.*

'It's all right, Lord Kempten. You can sit up now. We're unlikely to be stopped. Congratulations, my Lord. You may now consider yourself as one of the dear departed.'

He sat up, feeling strangely detached and vacant. From the look on Reynik's face, he judged his appearance was none too healthy. The young Legionnaire's expression was grave and worried, as if watching a man on the verge of collapse.

The noise of the carriage wheels clattering along the cobbled streets was loud. 'Poor Izzie!' he muttered under his breath. 'I wonder if she'll ever forgive me for this.'

'It's said you offer money for information,' she croaked.

'That depends on the information, crone. What is it you would sell me?'

Toomas looked at the filthy old woman at his door. Her clothes were poor and ragged, her muddy cloak drawn tightly around her in an effort to hide the tatty garments beneath, and she stank. The smell radiating from her was that of the stale unwashed filth of months. It was hard to comprehend how even the poorest person could sink so low.

Her hood was drawn low to hide her face, but that was not unusual. Many who sold him information wanted to remain anonymous. She need not have bothered, though. He had no desire to seek out the identities of ragged old beggar women.

'I'm told you would like to know about the man who killed Lord Kempten.'

That got his attention. The old woman cackled. He had tried to conceal the flash of hunger in his eyes, but he was too slow. She had seen it, and she knew he would pay dearly to learn what she had to say.

'How much?' he asked.

'Five gold sen,' she replied with another cackle.

'That's ridiculous!' he said quickly. 'No one would pay that much for your information, woman. I'll give you two silver senna, and not a sennut more.'

The old woman turned and started to shuffle away.

'Wait! Where are you going?'

'I may be old and poor, Toomas, but I'm not a fool,' she replied over her shoulder. 'The information I have is worth five gold sen. If you won't pay me for it, I know there are others who will.'

Toomas ground his teeth in annoyance. He did not want to part with so much gold, but he knew there were those in the city who would be willing to pay much, much more for information about this particular man.

'OK, old woman, five gold sen. Wait there a moment and I'll fetch your money.'

Toomas closed the door, closed the bolt and raced upstairs to where he kept his secret stash of money. He had always done well at his little sideline. It was well that he did, for his legitimate business was not so lucrative. He would have had several lean winters if it had not been for his ability to make a profit from trading snippets of information here and there. His network across the city had become quite extensive over the last few years. It was not as big as some, but he had stolen the march on several of the more established tattle touts recently. This might be his chance to make a serious coup.

He opened the door again with the small stack of gold coins in his hand. The old woman was still there, shuffling her feet and seemingly staring at the ground.

'I want an idea of what you're going to tell me before I hand this sort of money over, crone. What do you know? Is it just a name? I'm not parting with five gold sen for a name that could be false.'

'I have a name, but not his. I know who his next target is.'

Toomas nearly choked. His mind raced. Did she understand what she had? He doubted it.

'His next target? You're sure? If you're wrong, old woman, I'll have you found and gutted. This is dangerous information.'

'But worth five sen,' the woman pointed out.

'Very well – who is it?'

'Lord Lacedian,' Femke whispered dramatically from beneath her stinking disguise. 'He's going to kill Lord Lacedian.'

'Damn it! I wish I'd never started this,' Surabar muttered, scattering the papers on his desk with an irritated flick of his hand. 'I can't concentrate. I can't think. It's ridiculous!' He got up and began pacing back and forth across his study. 'As decisions go, declaring war on the Guild of Assassins has to rate highly on my all time poor judgement list.'

His eyes were distant as he paced and his mind churned back over the same old ground that had haunted him during the past few weeks.

'None of this should have happened. I should have stepped down as Emperor when I got back from Mantor,' he thought, his face grim. 'I could have gone back to the Legions. The ethics there are so much more straightforward. If it hadn't been for that blasted Shalidar's meddling, I could have bestowed the Mantle on someone more suitable. None of these moral issues would then have surfaced. Hindsight is a wonderful thing, Surabar, but it's too late for a change of heart.

'It should have been so simple: find the Guild headquarters and flush out the enemy. The tactics would have worked on a guerrilla group, or a dissident faction, but the Guild is like nothing I ever tackled with the Legions. Instead of scouts, I have spies. Instead of Legions, I have the city militia; and a fat lot of good they are! Of course I can call on the Legions to supplement the militiamen, but this is not a traditional war zone. There are the implications of my actions on the civilian population to consider.

'Femke and her colleagues in the Imperial spy network are great, but they have their limitations. The Kempten ruse worked because with all the Guild assassinations of military commanders, no one had any reason to suspect that this hit was any different. There was no one watching closely enough to see through the deception. But for Reynik to get into the Guild, they will want to see a body. Someone must die for real.'

He stopped in his tracks.

'Why should the death of one man – one traitorous man – make me feel so dirty of spirit? As a Commander I laid ambushes that led to the slaughter of hundreds of men, yet this feels repugnant in comparison.'

There are no unfair tactics in war, only winning tactics and losing tactics. The trick to being a good Commander is making sure that you use winning tactics.'

The quote from his old mentor rang in his mind. 'So why is this different?' The question hung in the air. He had been talking to himself more and more recently. He would have preferred to discuss his problems with someone, but it was a matter of trust. He had considered discussing them with Femke, but did not feel it appropriate.

The answer had been there all along. He began pacing again, this time striding back and forth with even more purpose.

'The person who has to die is not a part of the same fight,' he realised. 'Lacedian might be a traitor, but he's not linked with the Guild of Assassins. That's why it feels wrong. It's like mounting an assault on a nation with whom you're not at war to get to your enemies. That nation might not be friendly, but they are not a part of the current fight. It contravenes the military codes of conduct.

'There may be no unfair tactics in war, but that assumes the only parties involved in the conflict are those at war. I thought to do the unexpected; to fool the Guild by ordering something they would never expect. Even if it were to succeed in the long run, I cannot deny my nature. I have to abide by ethics I can justify. I thought I could justify this, but I can't. It's inherently wrong.'

It was too late to stop Reynik. Surabar had no way of contacting him now. If the young Legionnaire did kill Lord Lacedian, then Surabar would have to live with the consequences. Reynik might be the arrow that killed the Lord, but it was his hand that had released the arrow from the bow. There would be no further attempts of this sort. If Reynik were not contacted by the Guild after this hit, Surabar would put a stop to the mission. He knew what he had to do now. He had to get back on ground that he understood. It was time to call in the Legions. Causing discomfort to the civilian population was one thing. Killing them was another. He would have the Legions dismantle the city stone by stone if he had to, but he would find the Guild headquarters.

'I can't help you this time, Reynik. You'll have to make the hit alone. The Guild will have a constant watch on Lacedian, and I wouldn't be surprised to find that your target knows you're coming as well. If I were seen, then you would be compromised.'

Reynik nodded and smiled at Femke. He hoped that the nauseous feeling in his gut was not transmitting through to his face. He did not want to give her the wrong impression of him. It was hard to imagine how someone like Shalidar could live with killing again and again in cold blood. He did not want to be like his uncle's killer in any way, but given the circumstances it was hard not to envy the cold detachment of the man.

Just the thought of killing Lacedian turned Reynik's stomach, but he did not want to show his weakness to Femke. He knew that she had coped with having to make kills in cold blood in the past, yet she had found ways of coping with the feelings. Even knowing that she had killed, he did not think of her as a murderer. Why was that? What made her any different from Shalidar? Perhaps it was that she had feelings about it. Shalidar would not think twice about killing someone if it furthered his interests. Femke had killed when ordered, but he knew from his discussions with her during his training that she still struggled with her conscience over what she had done.

'I know,' he replied, trying to block the negative, distracting thoughts from his mind. 'I anticipated as much. I'd appreciate your thoughts on a strategy for how to make the hit, though. You're so good at this, I feel like I'm still a bumbling amateur.'

Femke gave him a hard stare. He had progressed beyond the amateur level so fast it was frightening, but he needed a strong dose of self-belief. There were times when she wanted to hit him, and others when she just wanted to kiss him. Damn it! Why did he have to be so likeable? What was it about him? He was young, but his features were already strong and handsome. Was it her imagination that he was attracted to her? He had never shown any outward signs, yet she sensed if she initiated a relationship, he would respond. Her feelings for Reynik were growing, and there appeared little she could do to stop them.

'Reynik, you're constantly putting yourself down. You cannot afford to do that. The more you tell yourself you're no good, the more you'll convince yourself it's true. Listen to me – you've picked up the skills you need to do this mission faster than I would ever have believed possible. You're a natural at this. You can do it, Reynik. You must believe in yourself. I believe in you. I really do. You *can* do it.'

'Thank you. It feels good to hear you say so, but the proof will be in the head count, as they say. Where do you think I should make the hit? Shall I go for another daylight job, or should I do this after dark?'

'My initial instinct is to make this hit at night. He will have all his defences arrayed against you, but he'll feel safe in his home. No matter how good his defences, there will always be a weak spot. Also, it should be quiet enough that it will give the Guild a chance to contact you without worrying about getting the wrong person, or being seen. The trick will be to circumnavigate Lord Lacedian's defences and get out again with minimum conflict. Do you know where he lives?'

'No.'

'It's not far from the centre of the city. It's quite a big house, but not the biggest. From memory it looks like this.'

Femke walked across to her dresser and took out a piece of parchment from the top drawer. Placing the parchment on the top, she dipped her quill in the inkwell and started to sketch the outline of a house. Reynik moved alongside her and watched with interest as her diagram took shape. Within moments, Reynik began to get a feel for the style in which the house was built. He had seen several of a similar design in the richer parts of the city. The style was not uncommon. He did not know the history of the architecture of Shandrim, but he guessed the houses had all been built around the same period, most likely by the same builder.

'Lacedian is a widower,' Femke stated, her voice slipping into her teacher tone. 'He has no children, so if there are others inside his house, they are most likely either guards or servants. Ideally, you don't want to hurt any of these: the cleaner the hit, the better. But how to do it?' Femke paused, running her right index finger from her lips down to her chin, clearly lost in thought.

The motion attracted Reynik's attention and his concentration on the problem of how to kill Lacedian evaporated as he became aware of her proximity. They were shoulder to shoulder, hunched over the parchment. 'Shand, but she's lovely,' he thought, watching with fascination as her fingertip drew her bottom lip down just fractionally with each stroke. The movement electrified him. All of his awareness focused in on her lips. How he wished he could kiss them, and have that kiss returned with passion. His body tensed and his heart began to beat faster as her closeness threatened to overwhelm him. The fresh scent of her filled his nostrils, its effect dizzying.

Suddenly, she pursed her lips. Reynik's heart skipped a beat.

'Hmm ... it won't be easy, but if I were you, then I would ...'

'How can I be thinking of such things now,' he wondered. 'We're discussing how I'm to kill an old man in cold blood, for Shand's sake! This is surreal. Damn but you're so professional, Femke! How do you do it?' Somehow she managed to keep her feelings about the mission detached from the business at hand. He wished he knew how.

The moment had passed. Business called. This was life or death – *his* life or death. He knew he had to concentrate on the job at hand, or his fanciful daydreams would never have a chance of seeing fruition. With a silent sigh, he forced his attention back to Femke's sketch.

'The Fox wishes to see you, my Lord Guildmaster.'

'Now?' he replied wearily. 'What time is it?'

'It is shortly after the second bell, my Lord.'

The Guildmaster sighed heavily. It had to be important for her to disturb his rest at this time. Shantella was one of the most intelligent women he had ever known. His mind was fogged with sleep, but he knew he could not ignore her request.

'Very well. Please inform Brother Fox that I'll be along to see her in a few minutes,' he said, unable to control a yawn as he spoke.

He stretched briefly and swung his legs over the side of his bed. It only took him a few moments to dress, but before he left his chambers to climb up to the main level of the Guild complex he took time to splash his face thoroughly with cold water. Drying it with a soft towel, he felt much more alert. His body still protested its tiredness, but at least he felt fully awake now.

The Guildmaster climbed the spiral staircase into the Guild meeting chamber. As he walked he pondered what news Shantella bore. He traversed the chamber and entered through the gate sporting the fox emblem. It must be news of the mystery assassins. Had she found them? Were there two, or just the one?

He knocked at the door to her private chamber and her melodious voice called out for him to enter. He opened the door and found her reclined on a small couch, glass of red wine in hand. There was another on the table, clearly meant for him. He would not touch it, of course. One did not accept food or drink lightly from a known assassin – even if you were their Guildmaster. In some cases he did not accept it *because* he was the Guildmaster. There was very little chance that any of the other assassins would know who was in line to be the next leader of the Guild, so the odds were always against a person killing the Guildmaster to take his place.

The Fox was quite a woman. She teased him mercilessly with her body. Her long, slim legs were clearly visible through the split in her casual robe.

'Welcome, Guildmaster. Have a seat,' she purred, shaking her head slightly to settle her auburn curls on her shoulders.

'Thank you, no, Shantella. You didn't call me here to talk pleasantries at this time of night, so what do you have for me?' he asked, keeping his tone businesslike. 'Have you found the mystery assassins?'

'Assassin, singular, apparently – though I've not confirmed the fact beyond doubt,' she corrected.

'Well, that's a start. Who is he . . . she?'

Shantella pouted slightly at the Guildmaster's cold

manner, though her voice remained silky smooth as she answered.

'I don't know who *he* is . . . yet,' she admitted. 'But I do know that he's accepted another contract.'

'Another contract? Who? And who employed him?' the Guildmaster asked, his voice betraying his eagerness for the information.

'The employer remains a mystery. As to who he is going to kill, word on the street is he has a contract on Lord Lacedian.'

'Lacedian! An interesting character. I wonder who wants him dead. He's old school, but not really in the race to become Emperor should they manage to get rid of Surabar. Thank you, Shantella. You've done well. I'll arrange to have a team of our people watch Lacedian night and day. I don't want to miss the opportunity of catching this mystery man and bringing him here for a chat. I'll arrange the surveillance. In the meantime, I'd like you to find out who employed him. This man is clearly operating in the upper echelons of society here in Shandrim, but who trained him? Where did he come from? I need to know more about this man, and fast.'

CHAPTER NINE

'Tremarle! Tremarle! He's coming for me. It's all over town. He's coming for me.'

Lord Lacedian burst into Lord Tremarle's drawing room with none of his normal decorum. Tremarle looked up at his friend, taking in his pallor and trembling hands without allowing his own cool, unruffled demeanour to crack. Inside, however, his heart leaped. What was his friend talking about? Who had frightened Lacedian enough to get him into this state?

'Calm down, old friend. Calm down,' Tremarle replied, keeping his voice low and soothing. He rose smoothly from his chair and crossed the room to a drinks cabinet. Taking out two glasses, he poured generous measures of brandy from a crystal decanter into each and handed the fuller of the two to Lacedian. The old Lord accepted it with both hands, gripping the glass tightly in an effort to prevent his shaking from spilling the spirit on the expensive carpet.

'Take a seat, Lacedian. Calm down and tell me what has you in such a fluster.'

Lacedian took a large pull at the brandy and closed his eyes for a second as he attempted to regain his composure. He made a move as if to sit down, but changed his mind at the last second. Instead he began pacing up and down the drawing room, his mind clearly racing as he organised his thoughts to speak.

'The man who killed Kempten is coming for me next. A tattle tout came to me this morning and sold me the information. I was tempted to ignore it as scaremongering, but another came this afternoon. The second was annoyed that he was not the first to reach me with the news. Someone has deliberately fed the news to the touts. The only thing I can think is the killer *wants* me to know he's coming. What sort of sick sadist is he? Did he torment Kempten like this?'

'Don't be too hasty, Lacedian. I doubt that Kempten knew he was the planned target of an assassin, or he would have increased his personal security. From what I hear, the man walked into the Civil Court and threw a knife at him. There were no guards on Kempten's door. He was not wearing any sort of protective armour. Nothing. Also, this may just be a hoax. Have you annoyed anyone enough recently to warrant them putting out a contract on you?'

Lacedian stopped pacing and looked pointedly at Tremarle.

'No one apart from the obvious,' he answered.

'Surabar! Ridiculous! He's in the middle of purging the city of assassins. Can you imagine what it would do to his image if he were found to have contracted a killer during such a campaign? Such hypocrisy would see him handing over the Mantle before he could blink twice. The man is too strait-laced for such an action. No, I would forget any idea of it being Surabar. If the killer you hired to kill the Emperor had talked, you would be hanging from the gallows now – with me alongside you, most likely.'

'But the assassin I hired was caught. Surabar must know that I tried to have him killed. The man was not of the Guild. He would not feel the same constraints about revealing his employer that a Guild member would.'

'That still doesn't make it any more likely that Surabar would order you assassinated, Lacedian. You're being irrational.'

Lord Lacedian started pacing again. 'But if it's not Surabar, then who's hired him? I'm not in the running to take over if Surabar steps down as Emperor. I've not done anything to annoy, or insult, anyone sufficiently to warrant sending an assassin after me. Is it all a hoax? Or is someone really going to try to kill me?'

Lord Tremarle did not answer for a moment or two. He watched as Lacedian paced restlessly back and forth along the drawing room carpet.

The Guild of Assassins was a strange organisation. They had been hitting Surabar where it hurt most over the last few weeks. A contract on Lord Lacedian made no sense whatsoever in the light of their recent targets. First they had killed several of the Legion Commanders, then Lord Kempten; the Guild appeared set on removing those on whom Surabar relied the most. Lacedian could hardly be counted in this category, so they would not have accepted a hit on him on those grounds? So who had placed the hit, and why? It was strange timing.

'Listen, old friend,' Tremarle said eventually. 'I have a contact in the Guild of Assassins. I'll get in touch with him and find out if there's a hit out on you. In the meantime, I'll send you four of my men to supplement your personal guards. I suggest you have them patrol around the house night and day until I get an answer from the Guild. You might want to get some guard dogs for your garden as well. Assassins don't like dogs.'

'Oh, thank you, my friend. Thank you. I cannot tell you how much your help means. I'll sleep a lot more soundly for the extra protection. I intend to hire more men as well. If this assassin does come after me, then he's going to have to face a small army if he's to earn his contract money.'

Rain sheeted down. The rattling impact of the large droplets driving onto the slate roof was loud, hiding any slight noises made by the crouching figure dressed in black. The footing was treacherous, the visibility abysmal. Lightning flickered, momentarily lighting up the skyline with its harsh, blue-white light. From his vantage point on the high rooftop, Reynik squinted out from under his hood at the distance to the lower roof of Lord Lacedian's house. During the brief, flickering flash of lightning it looked closer than it had during his daytime reconnoitre. It was an illusion, of course. He knew how far it was. He just hoped his crossbow had not become damp inside its canvas wrapping.

A slow count of three, and a crackling rumble of thunder

172

growled its angry complaint at the passage of the lightning. The heart of the storm was not far away, and closing fast. He would have to move quickly. In these conditions, the moment he removed his equipment from the waxed canvas, the sand would be trickling through the hourglass. He would only have a few seconds before the cord became too heavy with water for the bolt to carry it across to the neighbouring rooftop. If the bowstring became wet, then it would stretch, losing tension and power.

There was one good thing about the storm: Lacedian's guards were all heads down and miserable. The chances of one of them looking up and seeing him in this weather were very slim. However, this was the only good point amongst a host of bad. Getting into Lacedian's house would be more than doubly dangerous in this weather. He would inevitably leave tracks once inside, and getting away after the hit could prove every bit as dangerous as getting in.

Reynik realised he would only get one chance tonight. His first shot must be perfect. Taking off his backpack, he wedged it by his feet in the 'V' between the chimney-stack and the roof. Once ready, he worked swiftly. First he removed the canvas-wrapped bundle from the pack and began to unwrap it. It was not easy, but crouching down against the brickwork, he managed to keep the crossbow sheltered by the canvas as he first unwrapped it, then cocked and loaded it with the grappling hook attached to the thin rope. Rain hissed around him, swirling on the gusty wind. The drumming patter on the canvas sounded loud and obvious to his ears, but was lost amongst the background white noise outside of a very small radius.

It still seemed incredible that such a thin cord would hold his weight, but Femke had demonstrated it to his satisfaction during their training sessions. She had assured him rain would not affect its load-bearing properties. He hoped she was right, as he had never tested it in these conditions. If the rope broke, it was unlikely he would survive the fall.

'OK, lightning, do your stuff,' he murmured, the words lost in the wind.

On cue, another jagged spear of fire lit up the foul night sky. The timing was so uncannily perfect that Reynik's face twisted into a smile of amusement as he angled the crossbow and squeezed the trigger. There was a 'thunk' and the grappling hook shot off in a low, arcing trajectory towards Lord Lacedian's rooftop, the cord-like rope snaking out behind it as it whistled out of its neat coil. A wicked gust of wind buffeted the rooftop, turning the flight path of the grappling hook subtly to the left.

'. . . two, thr . . .'

An ear-splitting crash of thunder rattled shutters and doors, with after-rumbles continuing for some seconds as the fury of the storm came closer. Reynik followed the flight path of the rope anxiously, but it was impossible to see where it had landed. The rain lashed even harder on the wind, reducing visibility still further. He knew that a deflection left was less critical than one to the right, for it was likely the grappling hook would simply impact higher up the sloping rooftop, allowing it to slide down and around the chimney-stack he was hoping to hook against. Too far left, however, and it would go over the top of the roof crest. There was nothing there for the grapple to hook against.

The uncoiling of the rope slowed. The energy given by the crossbow was spent. Reynik grabbed the remaining coil and peered across at Lord Lacedian's rooftop in a further effort to see where the hook had come to rest. It was impossible to tell. All he could do was to slowly pull on the cord and hope the grappling hook caught on something solid.

With infinite care, he pulled the rope towards him, gathering it back into a neat coil as he went. He had marked it with a splash of white at the length he thought would be needed to reach the Lord's chimney-stack. The white mark reached his hands, but the line had not pulled tight. He paused for a second and took a deep breath.

'Hold,' he prayed silently. 'Come on. Catch the chimney-stack and hold.'

Hand over hand he carefully drew more of the cord into the coil. Five arm lengths past the white mark, the cord tightened. The grapple had caught on something. The question was what? Would it hold his weight? There was only one way to find out. Using the chimney-stack as a safeguard against falling, Reynik gradually increased the tension on the cord until he was leaning against it with all his weight. The line held fast. 'Thank Shand for that!' he murmured with a sigh of relief.

Taking care to maintain some tension and not to jerk the rope in any way, he gathered some coils from the spare and threw a large loop over the chimney-stack against which he was leaning. Then, with the ease of much recent

175

practice, he increased the tension on the rope around the chimney, tied a self-tightening knot, cut off the spare coils and stowed them in the pack.

Out of the pack he pulled a rope-tensioning device that Femke had introduced him to a few days before. It took a moment to attach, then he was twisting the device round and round, watching as the angle of the rope climbed until it pointed away from his position in a straight line at Lord Lacedian's rooftop. Ideally, he would have liked to tension the rope further, but without knowing for certain how much grip the grapple had, he was reluctant to risk increasing the load too much.

With the tension as great as he dared, he secured the tensioning device and took out yet another of Femke's gadgets. This time it was a strange contraption: a narrow central drum that freely rotated around a thick circular axle of iron, which protruded two hand spans from either side of the drum's axis of rotation. Cloth handgrips had been bound around the outer hand span of each end of the metal rod, and loops of strong cord were attached at the inner end of each of the handgrips. Reynik put the device down carefully into the 'V' between roof and chimney, then secured the top of the pack with the toggles and slung it onto his back.

He picked up Femke's contraption, placed his right hand through one of the loops, twisted the loop until it tightened against his wrist, and settled his fingers around the hand-grip. Satisfied that the grip was secure, he lifted the device, placing the narrow drum on top of the tensioned cord. He looped his left hand through the remaining safety loop, again twisting it tightly around his wrist, and worked his fingers into a secure grip. All that remained to begin his slide was to lift his feet and suspend his weight totally on the iron bar. This was it – the moment of truth.

'Shand help me! I must be mad,' he whispered, gritting his teeth and narrowing his eyes against the driving rain. He knew if he procrastinated, he would look for excuses not to make the blind leap of faith, so, before he could change his mind, he straightened his arms and lifted his feet to begin his descent.

The rope dipped markedly under his weight, but never-theless he accelerated away from the higher rooftop. Lightning split the sky again in a spectacular double fork. Gusts of wind caused him to swing wildly from side to side as he raced across the void. A particularly strong gust whipped his hood from his head. The rain soaked his hair instantly. The rest of his cloak billowed behind him with an alarmingly loud flapping noise, while the deluge plastered his other clothing against his skin.

Rain blinded him. Blinking and squinting against the barrage of wind-driven water, Reynik did not see the problem until it was almost too late. At the last second, he realised what had happened and braced his body for impact. He had not tensioned the rope sufficiently to allow him to glide onto the rooftop. Instead, the rope had dipped under his weight such that as he approached the house, the rope was almost parallel to the surface of the roof, and little more than a hand span above it.

With little time to react, Reynik crashed into the side wall of Lord Lacedian's house at high speed. Despite having done his best to brace against the impact, his collision with the wall was not pretty. All the air was driven from his lungs, which prevented him from crying out more than an 'oof' of pain. What sound he did make was whipped away by the wind. It was well that he had twisted his hands tightly into the safety loops for they saved him from a long fall. His left hand slipped from the cloth grip, causing the device to tilt rapidly to the right. His right hand then lost grip too, leaving him dangling by the safety loops.

Winded and bruised, he hung against the wall for a moment, the gusts of wind swinging him on the line and scraping him back and forth against the rough surface. His arms felt stretched beyond their normal length. Pain spiked in his armpits and the whole of the front of his body felt mashed and bruised from the high-speed impact.

A noise from below drew his attention. There were two guards directly beneath him, trudging around the house on one of their regular patrols. His vulnerability spurred him back into action. Using the wall as a brace, he walked his feet upwards until he was almost inverted, hooking first one foot, then the other, over the rope. Then, pulling simultaneously with both arms, Reynik pulled his torso up towards the rope and made a grab for it with his right hand. It was awkward, as both of his hands were twisted into the safety loops of the sliding device, but there was just enough flex for him to get his fingers over the top. Untwisting his left hand from the safety loop took a scant few seconds, whereupon his left hand joined his right on the rope, leaving the drum device dangling from his right wrist.

With an inverted crawling motion, Reynik shuffled his

body forward onto the roof until he felt it safe to unhook his feet and lay flat against the surface. As he took weight off the rope, so it rose under tension away from the surface. Without letting go, he regained his feet and traversed the slippery slates to the chimney-stack.

He crouched in the lee of the narrow brick tower for a moment, luxuriating in the break from the elements. Taking off his backpack he removed another, pre-measured, coil of rope from one of the inside pockets. After the near disastrous crossing from the nearby building, it would have been nice to take a rest, but Reynik knew he could not afford to stop here. He must get in and out of the house swiftly if he were to limit the danger of being caught. He did not dare to cast loose the grappling hook, so the high-wire would have to remain, leaving an obvious indicator and trail for anyone who saw it. Although the storm had proved a blessing for masking the noise he had made during the crossing, the lightning could yet betray him with its flickering light. The elements were a fickle ally at best.

Throwing a loop over the chimney, he tied off the rope in a self-tightening knot. Then, as Femke had taught him, Reynik pinched a 'U' in the rope and fed it through the figure-of-eight-shaped, cast iron accessory on his belt. He put on his pack once more and, bracing himself with the rope, he stepped tentatively around the chimney-stack and started to back down the steeply pitched roof.

As he descended and the rope settled around chimney, he gained in confidence. His worst moment was the transition from the roof to going down the side of the house, but once past this hurdle, Reynik progressed smoothly down the wall until he reached the upper floor window shutters. As Femke had predicted, they were only held shut with simple internal lift latches, which were easily opened with his knife. Once open, however, it became a bit of a juggle to stow his knife and open the shutters without allowing them to rattle or bang in the gusty wind.

He latched the left hand shutter open and looked inside. Through the window, Reynik could see that the room inside was empty and the internal door was shut. Within a few seconds, he had opened the window. He was in.

Reynik swung silently inside, drawing the remaining free rope into the room with him. He took a quick look around to memorise the layout of the furniture, then, wedging the loose rope on the window ledge between the shutter and the window, he shut everything behind him. The sudden drop in noise level was marked. With the wind and rain shut out, the silence in the house was profound. Had anyone heard the increase in storm noise as he had opened the window? He could hear no signs of movement, but that could be because men were waiting for him on the other side of the door.

Cat-like, he crept through the dark room to the door. If Femke's information were accurate, then when he left this room, Lord Lacedian's bedroom would be to his left, two doors along the upper hallway on the right hand side. He found the door by touch and then paused to listen – still no sound. Reynik drew the knife from his back holster. With extreme care to avoid making any noise, he squeezed the door handle to the open position.

A single torch burned in its bracket at the top of the

stairs to his right. The orange flicker chased shadows with leaping tongues that weaved and danced their stuttering patterns. Reynik peered cautiously around the door at the landing area. A shadowy figure not two paces away caused his breath to catch in his throat. It took only a moment to realise it was an empty suit of armour. His breath released in a silent sigh. There was no sign of anyone else about.

The door creaked slightly as he inched it open far enough for him to squeeze through. He paused again, his breath catching in his throat at the sound, but nothing stirred. Having got inside, could it really be this easy?

Working hard to move as Devarusso had taught him, light-footed and stealthy, Reynik slipped along the upper hallway to the door to Lord Lacedian's bedroom. The next few seconds would be crucial. He must not allow the old fellow to attract attention to his presence.

Even as he placed his hand on the door handle, a low growl sounded inside Lacedian's room. Reynik froze. The growl was not that of a human. It sounded like a large dog. Was it a pet? Did Lacedian sleep with a guard dog in his room? If so, the hit had just increased in difficulty.

Reynik backed away silently from the door and the growling subsided. 'Damn!' he thought. 'What do I do now?'

Femke had known nothing of dogs in the house, or she would have mentioned it. The Lord obviously knew someone was out to kill him and had taken extra precautions. The additions to his house guards had made that much obvious, but the use of dogs was not something Femke and Reynik had anticipated.

181

'If I were Lacedian, and I knew someone was coming to kill me, would I sleep in my own room? Unlikely. So where would I sleep?' he thought, looking back and forth nervously along the upper landing. 'I would certainly leave a trap in my normal room – hence the dog, but would I even sleep in my own house? Probably not – but Lacedian is. I'm sure he's here somewhere. He came in. I didn't see him leave. He *must* be here, but where?'

Time was running out. Turning back towards the top of the staircase, Reynik noticed the trail of footprints he was leaving on the carpet. Not surprisingly, the wet moss from the roofs he had traversed had caught in the tread of his boots. The upper hall carpet was pale beige and his tracks were painfully obvious. He had to move swiftly.

Reynik peered over the gallery banister to the lower hallway. A guard was sitting at the base of the stairs. He looked bored, and not very alert. Reynik moved away from the banister rail and edged along the upper hall until he was as far as he could get without potentially exposing his presence to the guard at the foot of the stairs. He needed to cross the top of the stairs, but he was not sure how best to do it without drawing attention to himself. His mind raced through the possibilities, but before he had come to any conclusions, the front door to the house opened and two of the guards who had been patrolling outside stepped into the hallway.

The distraction was perfect. He raced across the top of the stairs, stooping to avoid casting a long shadow as he passed the bracketed torch. None of the guards noticed the movement. The two from outside were too busy shaking water from their cloaks and complaining about the weather. The one seated at the base of the stairs was watching them.

There were three doors on this side of the landing. Femke had drawn the layout of the house for him. If he remembered correctly, the middle of the three was the most likely, as it led to the guest suite. Lacedian was an older man. By Reynik's reasoning, the Lord would not give up comforts unnecessarily. Reynik did not pause. Knife in hand, he tried the door. The noise of the chatting guards masked any slight sound he made.

The door would not budge. What now? It looked as though Lacedian had barred the door from the inside. This was getting more and more difficult. Should he give up and try to make the hit somewhere away from his home?

Suddenly, an idea began to form. He could still make the hit, but getting away afterwards might prove a bit more troublesome than he had originally hoped. The guards were all still chatting away in the lower hall, so Reynik darted back across the top of the stairway. Again he managed it without being seen. Sliding silently back along to the room where he had entered through the window, he cracked open the door and slipped back inside, pulling the door to behind him.

His memory of the room did not fail him. By touch, he found the wall torch nearest to the door. A flint and steel hung on a string beneath the wall bracket. Some noise was inevitable, but he was far enough from the guards that he did not expect to be heard.

Reynik lit the torch. The scratch of the flint on the steel sounded loud in the quiet of the room, but the instant shower of sparks fell just right, lighting the torch at the first attempt. Taking the torch from the bracket, Reynik fanned the flame of the torch until it had a good hold and then moved to inspect the furniture. A nicely upholstered chaise longue appeared perfect for his purpose. He held the torch to one end of the seat, working the flame back and forth across its width until the whole end was burning with a substantial flame. Smoke belched from it, quickly filling the upper half of the room with a thick black cloud. This presented a new danger, but Reynik was committed to his impromptu plan now.

He threw the torch into the corner of the room, where it set light to a rug. The room would be an inferno within the next few minutes. The chaise longue was not as heavy as Reynik had anticipated, but having not shut the door completely, it did not matter. He picked it up by the end that was not alight and charged the door, using the flaming piece of furniture as a battering ram. The crash as he smashed the door open certainly drew attention from the guards, but they did not have more than a second to react before the burning piece of furniture launched over the gallery side and descended like a flaming meteor at the guard seated at the base of the stairs.

'FIRE! FIRE!' Reynik yelled at the top of his voice, drawing a knife with each hand.

'What in Shand's name!'

The guard at the base of the stairwell had managed to dive out of the way of the incoming missile, but the impact scattered burning pieces of wood all over the lower hallway.

184

'Put out that fire. Quick, before the whole place goes up. Jarron, Dakreas, get upstairs and kill him before he torches the entire house,' ordered another voice.

There was the sound of running feet and the dog in Lord Lacedian's bedroom started barking at the top of its voice. Footsteps also sounded on the stairs. Reynik impaled both knives point down in the banister rail, turned and grabbed the nearby suit of armour. Surprisingly, it was heavier than the chaise longue, but he managed to heave it over the banister rail. The resulting clatter, yells and cursing yielded exactly the result he had been hoping for. On the other side of the upper landing, the door handle moved.

'FIRE! FIRE! RUN FOR YOUR LIVES!' Reynik yelled again, determined to encourage Lacedian out into the open.

It worked. Reynik snatched his knives from where he had stuck them in the wooden banister rail and was perfectly poised as Lord Lacedian's door opened and the old Lord looked out tentatively to see what was going on. The throw was longer than Reynik would have liked, but it was a clean shot. He took it, hurling the blade with all his strength. The blade flew straight and true, burying itself in the old Lord's chest before he had a chance to react. The image of the old man's shocked face burned into his retinas. It was a moment Reynik would never forget: a moment that would leave a stain on his soul that he knew could never be totally cleansed.

Reynik did not wait around. It was all about getting away now. He turned and ran back into the smoke-filled room, retching at the wave of nausea that gripped his gut. It was

185

easy to blame the smoke for emptying the contents of his stomach on the floor, but he could not deny the truth. What he had just done was wrong – terribly, irrevocably wrong. Every fibre of his body knew it. Nobody would ever know the truth of how much this mission was costing him. All anyone else would see was the killer – the man who had first killed Lord Kempten, and now Lord Lacedian.

Crouching to stay below the worst of the smoke, he realised that the torch had now set light to the floorboards. Unless someone got the fire under control soon, the entire house would go up in flames very quickly.

He raced across to the window and opened it. His hands were shaking as he grabbed the rope from the window ledge. He kicked open the shutters. The wind slammed them shut again, but he had broken the latch. He shouldered the shutters apart, climbed out through the window, and proceeded to descend the rope hand over hand as far as it went. His gloves gave him extra purchase on the water-soaked rope, for which he was very grateful.

From what he could see below him, all the guards were now inside the building, either dealing with the fire in the hallway or looking for him. His stomach threatened to heave again, but he fought the sensation by tipping his head back and allowing the rain to wash over him for a moment. The feeling of the rain battering against his face was strangely cleansing.

He looked down. The ground was about two body lengths drop from the end of the rope. He let go, landing lightly and drawing another knife as he launched into a sprint away from the house.

The dark night closed around him as he ran, the thick curtain of rain adding a further veil of concealment. There was no sign of immediate pursuit, but he did not slow just yet. Around the first corner, Reynik shucked off his pack and dropped it into a dark, shadowy alleyway. He did not want to be caught by the militia carrying such equipment.

He began running again, taking his pre-planned escape route through the side streets and alleys until he had put a good distance between him and his victim. At least he had only had to kill his target, he thought, grateful for this mercy. The assignment would have been many times worse if he had been forced to kill one of the innocent guards. Lord Lacedian had been proved a traitor. That fact did give some small consolation for his actions.

Reynik prayed the men fighting the fire would have enough sense to save themselves if the blaze became too fierce. The elements were on their side to contain the fire. The torrential rain would have a cooling effect, though he doubted it would be enough without some swift and positive fire fighting from within the building.

Despite the pouring rain damping down the smell, Reynik realised that he probably stank of smoke. Having inhaled a fair amount of the acrid stuff, he could not smell anything, but the odour of burning was sure to be creating a miasma around him that could prove incriminating. He needed to change and dispose of his clothes quickly.

Where would be the best place to go? A slight sound in the alleyway behind him gave an instant of warning. His knife was already in his hand as he spun to face the person behind him.

'Hold! I don't want a fight. I only want to talk,' said a man's voice from the shadows of the alley.

'Who are you, and what do you want to talk about?' Reynik replied calmly, his stance perfectly balanced for maximum flexibility.

'Names are not important. I bring a message from the Guildmaster of the Guild of Assassins. He offers you a simple choice. You can apply for membership of the Guild, or he will have you killed.'

'That's it?' Reynik asked, fighting to keep all emotion from his voice. 'What if I apply for membership of the Guild and am not accepted?'

'Then you won't leave the Guild alive.'

'Doesn't sound like much of a choice to me.'

'It isn't meant to.'

CHAPTER TEN

Reynik paused for a moment, as if considering what he should do. Inside, his heart was racing. It was all working perfectly. The man in the alleyway would lead him to the Guild. Once accepted, he would be able to give the location of their headquarters to the Emperor and the Guild would be wiped out for ever. The sticking point was the 'once accepted'. Would he be accepted? How would they decide if he were acceptable to join? Did they suspect what he was really trying to do?

'Don't be negative,' he told himself silently. 'You must convey cautious strength. If you get this wrong now, you will have bloodied your hands for nothing.'

'Well?' the man asked. 'Will you come with me, or must I give the order for you to die?'

'I will come,' Reynik replied with a firm, controlled tone.

A dark figure stepped out of the shadows. Like Reynik, he was hooded and cloaked in black. Reynik could see nothing of the man's face, but then he doubted the man could see his either.

'Follow me,' the man ordered, and he set off down the street, flowing effortlessly through the rain and darkness without making a sound. Reynik followed, feeling clumsy in comparison. Dark puddles lurked at every step, yet his guide seemed to glide past them without making the slightest splash. With grim determination, Reynik drew on every ounce of skill he had absorbed from his lessons over the previous month. Devarusso and Serrius had both concentrated much of their effort on improving his balance and movement. Now Reynik began to appreciate why it was so important. This man was clearly a master in the art of moving silently in all conditions. It seemed likely that he was an experienced member of the Guild. If all assassins in the Guild moved as smoothly, then Reynik would have a lot to prove if he were to be allowed to join. Suddenly his feelings of inadequacy returned tenfold.

It was hard to keep track of their position. The man wove a complex path through the city. It felt as if he was making random turns for much of the way, yet Reynik doubted this was the case. It was only when he heard a slight sound behind him that he realised what the man was doing. He was not alone. Those following would doubtless be checking to see if Reynik was working alone before they led him to the Guild. They were taking no chances.

They were in one of the poorer areas of the north west quarter of the city when they finally stopped. Reynik was not familiar with this part of the city, but he had enough mental references that he would be able to find it again when he needed to.

'Remove your hood,' the man ordered.

'Remove yours and I'll remove mine,' Reynik replied firmly, planting his feet in a strong stance.

'That is not allowed.'

'Then why should I remove mine?'

'Because I told you to. In case you hadn't noticed, a team of assassins currently surrounds us. They will pepper you with arrows before you can move two paces if I give the signal. I don't want to have you killed, but if you leave me no choice I will not hesitate. Now, remove your hood. I must blindfold you from here.'

'A team of assassins!' The thought shot through Reynik as if he had been struck by one of the flashes of lightning that were still drilling their fiery paths through the black night sky. He could not resist a swift glance around to see if he could see any of them. He could not. All he could see was teaming rain in empty streets, yet he had heard at least one of them moving along behind them. It was pleasing that he had not made such a noticeable noise as he had moved along the streets to this point.

'Very well,' Reynik agreed, and he lowered his hood to reveal his short-cropped black hair. Black was not its natural colour, but Femke had insisted he change the colour to help disassociate him from his real past. She had also dyed his eyebrows and insisted he shave carefully every day to conceal the lighter colour of his facial hair.

The assassin stepped forward, drawing a dark strip of cloth from beneath his cloak. Reynik stood defiantly still, with his eyes wide open and staring straight ahead as the man placed the cloth across his eyes and tied it securely behind his head. He had hoped he might be able to see something through the cloth, or by angling his eyes down as low as possible he might see through any slight gap that might occur around his nose area, but there was none. He was totally blinded.

'Trust me. I will lead you carefully. It is not far from here,' the man said quietly.

Reynik sensed the man move behind him and he felt hands settle on his shoulders, gently pushing him forward. They moved slowly, but steadily, the man's hands guiding him with subtle changes of pressure to turn him left and right as required. Although Reynik tried to keep a mental plot of where he was going, he quickly realised it was a pointless exercise. All he could really do was to try to keep track of time, so he could work out a possible radius from the point he had been blindfolded to their final destination.

The man had said they were not going far, but Reynik was very surprised when the pressure on his shoulders stopped him in his tracks. Surely they could not be at the Guild headquarters already? If they were, then Reynik would easily be able to narrow down the possible locations from his knowledge of where they had started. Did the man take him for a fool?

'Put out your right hand,' ordered the voice of the assassin. 'Good,' he said as Reynik did so without hesitation. 'Now hold this between your thumb and forefinger.'

Reynik felt something metallic touch his hand and he

gripped it as directed, trying as he did so to discern what he was holding. The object was about the thickness of an arrow shaft, but curved and slightly textured. He wanted to move his fingers to explore the object, but his guide placed his own hand over Reynik's and lifted it up to shoulder height, pulling him forward slightly at the same time.

The object touched something. Reynik was certain there was the slightest of jars through the metal as it made contact, but the sensation that followed was unlike anything he had ever felt before. It did not hurt exactly, but it was not comfortable either. A tingling sensation raced through his body, making him feel as if a strange energy were sparkling and popping from the tips of his fingers to the very depths of his chest. Then there was a wrench and for a moment it felt as if every part of his body was exploding painlessly into a million pieces before coalescing again with another wrenching snap of force.

Reynik collapsed. He could not help it. The strength in his legs had apparently disintegrated with the weird rush of energy, and he fell to the floor with all the grace of a dropped sack of grain. His head began spinning as if he had drunk too much strong ale and he rolled over onto his back, placing his palms flat on the ground to help recover from this loss of orientation and balance.

New sensations began to register. It took a second for his brain to comprehend what he was feeling through his fingertips, but then his other senses began to confirm what his fingers were telling him. He was no longer on a wet street. There was no rain beating on his face, nor wind tugging at his clothing. The air was still. He was indoors.

What he was feeling was the cold, dry, dusty surface of a stone floor. But how could that be?

He had been on the street. His feet had not moved a step before he fell here. The strange sensation he had felt through the metal object he had been holding had not involved any feeling of falling. The fall had happened afterwards. Had he fallen down some sort of chute? No. He would have remembered, and the landing would have involved more momentum. Whatever had just happened was beyond his mind's ability to understand and yet he could not deny the evidence of his senses. He was definitely no longer in the open air.

Concentrating hard, Reynik listened intently for any sounds that might give him a clue as to where he might be. There was nothing. The only sound he could hear was that of his guide stepping lightly around him. Then it struck him – there *was* nothing! No sound of wind, or rain. There was not even the slightest hint that there was a storm raging outside. Where in Shand's name was he?

'When you have recovered sufficiently, you may remove your blindfold,' his guide said suddenly. 'The transfer takes a bit of getting used to, but the effects will wear off in a few minutes.'

Even the man's voice sounded different now they were inside. There was just the faintest hint of an echo. Could they be underground? Reynik reached up to his face and eased off the blindfold.

The sight that met Reynik's eyes filled him with an even greater sense of wonder. He was in a good-sized living chamber, about six paces long by five paces across. Most of the furniture in the chamber was old – very old, and of beautiful craftsmanship. There were also some wonderful hangings on the wall that looked to date back several dynasties. A single newer hanging covered the wall next to the larger of the two doors out of the chamber. It appeared to display an image of the Imperial Palace floor plan in great detail, which would no doubt be of considerable use to an assassin who moved in high circles.

The central wall hanging, flanked by bracketed wall torches on either side, depicted a striking viper. It was a chilling picture, but somehow apt. As Reynik pushed his body up into a sitting position, he noticed that the motif of the viper was duplicated on small wooden shields over each of the doorways.

'Welcome to my humble abode.'

The man who had brought Reynik to this place was still hooded and cloaked, but in the flickering light of the torches Reynik could just make out the lower part of his face. The man wore a dark, trimmed beard and moustache in a style common amongst the wealthier men of Shandrim's high society. A hint of amusement quirked the man's lips slightly, but Reynik could see nothing else except the tip of his nose, which told him nothing more of his features.

'I thought we were going to meet the Guildmaster,' Reynik said, croaking slightly. His throat was dry. This could have been a result of having inhaled smoke earlier, but he suspected it was more to do with his method of getting here.

'All in good time. First, you will probably need a drink.

Would you like a mug of ale, a glass of wine, or would you prefer water?'

'Water will be fine, thanks.'

There were no windows in the chamber, despite it having the squared feel of a room in a house. This did not surprise Reynik, for he felt sure they were not in a building. There was something about the feel of the air in the room that increased his sensation of being underground. Both doors out of the chamber were shut, but he would bet every last copper sennut he had that no matter which door he exited through, he would find no windows there either.

The hooded man went to a cabinet and poured clear fluid from a crystal jug into a glass. Reynik wondered briefly if he should be wary of drinking, but it made no sense that the man would bring him here only to poison him. If the man had wanted him dead, Reynik suspected his method of attack would have been more direct.

Reynik took the glass and drank without hesitation when it was offered. He felt better immediately. His senses sharpened and he felt more alert. The hooded assassin watched on with interest.

'I remember my first time entering the Guild. It was not pleasant. Water is a good restorative. Help yourself to more from the jug, but do not leave the room. Wait here and I'll return shortly.'

The man went out through the larger of the two doors. Reynik glimpsed a dim corridor outside before the door shut with a firm thud. He got to his feet and began to prowl around the chamber. Where in Shand's name could he be? He could not have travelled far from the rain-soaked street in the north west quarter, or could he? The sensation he had experienced had been most unusual. Could it have been magical?

Even as the thought occurred to Reynik, the image of the silver wolf spider talisman leaped to the forefront of his mind. His hand had tingled uncomfortably when he had touched the spider necklace taken from the assassin a month before. The tingling had not been the same as he had felt today, but the fact that the spider had dissolved with a strange sparkle of magical energy gave him cause to wonder again what had happened to it. Were the two events linked? Had the spider simply melted away to nothing, or was there more to the incident than he had cared to think at the time?

'Yes, Brother Viper? Did you get him?'

'We did, Guildmaster. He is in my quarters.'

'Excellent! Advise him to remain there if you would. I would appreciate it if you would stay in Brother Falcon's quarters tonight. They have been cleared of his belongings. Place guards in the corridor outside your own quarters. I will see our potential recruit tomorrow morning. Assuming he elects to join us, I'd like to gather those of the Guild who are in the complex to witness the induction ceremony. Do we know any more about his background?'

'Nothing, Guildmaster. His hit was ... spectacular, if flawed. I doubt that much will remain of Lord Lacedian's residence by morning. The last I saw, the fire he set during his escape had a firm hold. He made mistakes, but he improvised well. He has much to learn if he is to become a master, but he clearly plans well and can think on his feet. If he is not a plant, then he should do well.'

'You remain unconvinced, then, that he is a genuine assassin? He's made two high-profile hits in two weeks on targets that are at opposite ends of the political spectrum. I have had people working on a possible link between Lords Kempten and Lacedian, but our best people have drawn a blank. The only connection between them appears to be their deaths. What is it that makes you suspect him?'

Viper looked at the Guildmaster, pursed his lips and shrugged. 'I don't know,' he admitted. 'It's a gut feeling. I've been wrong before.'

'Yes, but you've also been right. I'll bear your hunch in mind when I speak to him in the morning. Thank you, Brother Viper. Please pass on my thanks to the rest of the team too. You've all done a good job tonight.'

'Ah, Femke! Good. I was hoping you would get my message.'

'Message, your Imperial Majesty? I got no message,' Femke replied, as she entered Surabar's bleak study. 'I came to inform you that Reynik was successful last night. At least, he was successful in the first part of his mission. Tattle touts all over the city are talking of nothing but the killing of Lord Lacedian. The fact that Reynik has subsequently disappeared without trace leads me to believe he has also made contact with the Guild.'

'I'd like to say excellent, but I don't feel very excellent about this affair at all. I allowed my determination to outweigh my morality. Let's pray the Guild accept him. I'd hate to see him turn up dead in a back alley somewhere, and I'm not ready to sanction any more killing of this nature.'

Surabar's words echoed Femke's worst fear. She had thought of nothing else since she had parted with Reynik the previous afternoon. Sleep had not come easy. Even when her body had finally succumbed to the need for rest in the early hours, bad dreams had tormented her through what was left of the night. Her ribs ached terribly today, more than they had since the early days after her fight with Shalidar. She knew it was due to nervous tension, but also realised there was little she could do to alleviate it until she knew Reynik was safe.

The Emperor looked at the dark rings beneath her eyes and smiled sympathetically. He had lived for years with decisions that had sent men to their deaths. As a spy, Femke would have made similar decisions when sending out her agents, but it was always different when you had worked closely with the people whose lives you were risking. The sense of responsibility was heightened above the importance of the actual mission. He had suffered sleepless nights on many occasions in his days as a junior officer in the Legions. Even now he could remember what it was like to worry oneself sick over a particular plan. He knew there was nothing he could say to make it better for Femke. She would have to deal with the emotions in her own way. If anything, what he had to tell her would only make matters worse.

'Femke, I've decided to call in the Legions,' he said softly.

'Which Legions, your Majesty? You have most of them here at the city already. You're not planning to break your agreement with King Malo, are you? I'm not sure it would be a good idea.'

'No, Femke, you misunderstand me. I've decided to call the Legions into the city to search for the Guild. I'm going to have them take Shandrim apart – literally if necessary. One way or another, I *will* find the Guild and destroy them once and for all.'

'But what about Reynik, your Majesty? Are you not going to give him a chance? If he's been accepted by the Guild, you could have the location of their headquarters within the next few days.'

'That's true, but I might also save lives if I begin the search now. Another Legion Commander was murdered last night. This time they went too far.'

'Commander Sateris?' Femke asked, noting the deep hurt in the Emperor's expression.

General Surabar nodded. 'He has been a good friend for many years. The Guild chose the wrong man to kill if they think this will persuade me to let them be. I have sworn an oath over the body of my old friend that I will hunt every last one of those murderers down if it's the last thing I do. I take such oaths very seriously. If I achieve nothing more in my short reign as Emperor, then ridding Shandar of this outdated abomination shall be my personal legacy. I intend to purge the streets of Shandrim, driving them out of whatever dark holes they live in. One way or another, they will answer for their crimes.'

'Your Majesty, I know you want to act swiftly, but we

have worked so hard to get Reynik where he is. Will you not give him a chance? Lord Lacedian was killed last night on your orders. Reynik killed him in cold blood, just as one of the Guild killed Sateris. I know what Reynik is feeling at the moment, your Majesty, for I abhor killing as he does. Reynik wants to be a soldier like you. He would like nothing more than to be back with his unit, marching and drilling against the day he would be called to action for the Empire. Instead, he is carrying out a dangerous secret mission for you that goes against his philosophy. Why is he doing it? Because he respects and trusts you, your Majesty. Your reputation for fairness and fighting for just causes has won his loyalty. Does loyalty not work both ways? Will you not let him finish what you had him start?'

Emperor Surabar's expression during Femke's impassioned plea changed from cold and dispassionate to angry. Femke stood her ground defiantly and looked him in the eye as she asked her final questions.

'You dare to lecture *me* on loyalty, young lady? I respect you for your skills, and I value your support and your ideas, but I will *not* have you lecture me. Do I make myself clear?'

Femke nodded, but her eyes smouldered with an inner fire.

'Yes, it was *my* idea to infiltrate the Guild,' Surabar continued. 'Reynik was *my* choice of agent. *I* will therefore take responsibility for his actions. I will also take responsibility for his death if he should die in the course of his mission. However, I also have wider responsibilities to the citizens of Shandrim. Do you think I like making decisions

201

like this? All my life I have made decisions that have resulted in good men losing their lives so that my plans, or those of my superiors, will be fulfilled. Well, Femke, I no longer have a chain of command above me that I can blame for these decisions. *I* carry the full weight of responsibility for *all* the deaths.'

He paused for a moment and took a deep breath. When he continued, much of the anger had gone from his voice. His face looked more lined with age than Femke had ever seen it. The weight of the Mantle was clearly taking a heavy toll.

'The Guild of Assassins has been blatantly flaunting their illegitimate trade under my nose for the last month. Last night they went one step too far. I'm not blind to the advantages Reynik's information would bring. It was my plan to put him there in the first place, damn it! However, this is a very fluid situation. Plans change. I'll give him his chance, but I'm not willing to wait long, Femke. He has two days. No more. After that time, I *will* begin taking the city apart. I suggest that if you have any strings left to pull, you pull them now. I'm sick of the killing. I intend to put a final end to the Guild of Assassins this week.'

'Send out messengers, Sasso. Contact the tattle touts. I want to speak with someone in the Guild of Assassins – today if possible. I want to place a contract, and I'll pay a thousand gold sen to the man who completes it.'

Lord Tremarle's personal manservant bowed and left the room. His face was pale as he left. One of the other house servants was hovering outside the door as he emerged.

'How did he take it? Not well from the look on your face.'

Sasso shook his head. 'I've never seen him like this,' he said, cringing as he thought of his master's expression. 'I thought when he lost his son that he was as low as any man could be, but I was wrong. He's hurt. He's shocked. But more than anything, he's angry. I've never seen a man so angry. It's scary. I'm not sure he's entirely sane any more.'

'What makes you think so?'

'He's ready to spend every last sennut he has to gain revenge, yet I don't think he really knows who is responsible. I think he'll strike out at whoever he feels to be the obvious enemy. I think we both know what that means.'

'I'll start enquiring about jobs with other Lords right away, Sasso. We don't want to get caught up in anything treasonous.'

'Good idea. In the meantime, though, I'd better do as Lord Tremarle says. In his current mood, he'd have anyone flogged for the least deviation from his orders. Where are the messenger boys?'

'One's down in the basement, the other two are running errands for the cook.'

'Thanks. I'll see you later.'

Reynik woke with a start. What time was it? How long had he slept? It was impossible to tell in this underground prison.

When the assassin had returned and told him he was to remain in his quarters until the following morning to await an audience with the Guildmaster, Reynik had not known

203

what to think. Was this normal? Were they deciding what to do with him in his absence? What had they found out about him? Did they know the Emperor had sent him?

'Don't be a fool, Reynik,' he had told himself. 'If they knew what you were doing, you would be dead already. Do as you're told and ride out the uncertainty.'

It had not been easy. The living quarters were not small by any stretch of the imagination, but they had not taken long to explore. There was a sleeping area, a separate dining area, a bathing area and a small toilet chamber. Indeed, the complex was luxurious, with more than enough living space for several people. Where the man who normally lived here had gone for the night, Reynik had no idea, but given the size of his underground apartment, Reynik did not think living space was something the Guild lacked.

The man had told him not to exit the room through the larger of the two doors on pain of death. He had not, though he had been sorely tempted. The temptation teased him again now. There was a corridor there. Where did it lead? When would the Guildmaster come? If only he knew what the time was.

He paced up and down the room a few times before stopping next to the exit to listen. Was there anyone out there? Did he dare peek around the door? Would it be such a crime to look?

'Patience, Reynik,' he muttered. 'He'll come when he's ready.'

While he was waiting, he decided to have yet another look around the living chamber. It was a fascinating room, with lots of interesting things to look at. The image which most intrigued him, though, was the hanging depicting the viper. The fact that the image was repeated on the wooden shields above the two doors was clearly significant. Was it the Guild emblem? It would make some sort of sense. Snakes struck with venom, and assassins often did the same. But if the viper was the Guild emblem, then why had this never been discovered before?

Reynik was still standing and contemplating the picture when the door opened and two figures entered. One was the man who had led him here. The other was shorter, but also dressed in a cloak and hood that was so deep he could not see the face under its shadow. Although the man did not stoop, Reynik instantly recognised the man as being advanced in years. It might have been the way he stepped, or some other subtle body language sign Reynik had subconsciously picked up on, but he was pleased when the man spoke, for his voice had the slight rasp of age in it that confirmed his instinct.

'Welcome, young man, to the headquarters of the Guild of Assassins. Judging by your expression, I gather you have deduced I'm the Guildmaster here. Has Brother Viper told you why you were brought to us?'

Brother Viper! That explained the snake emblem, he thought. 'He has, Guildmaster. I understand I'm being considered for membership of the Guild. May I ask if a decision has been made yet?'

'You may ask what you like. That's why I'm here – to answer your questions, and for you to answer mine. You will be inducted into the Guild shortly, but you will not become a full member until your first contract for the

Guild has been successfully carried out. Until then, you'll be on probation. Most members keep secrets – it goes with our profession. However, if you join us and do not follow our creed, or your presence prejudices the future of the Guild in any way, then you should know that you will die at the hand of one of the Brothers. That is no idle threat. I have had to order such deaths in the past. I will have no hesitation in doing so again.'

'I understand,' Reynik replied solemnly.

'Good. Brother Viper, please leave us for a few minutes. I don't think our friend here will be foolish enough to try to harm me. He does not have the look of a suicide killer to me.'

'Very well, Guildmaster. The guards will remain within earshot, should you need assistance.'

The assassin bowed and left, his feet once again making no sound as he moved. Reynik watched him leave with a sense of fascination at the man's smooth, flowing movements. He would begin practising again as soon as he got a chance. Devarusso had been able to move with cat-like grace when he wanted to, but the assassin known as Brother Viper took the art to a whole new level.

'Now, young man, I will only ask you this question once. It will be for my information only. No other member of the Guild will learn of your answer unless you choose to reveal the answer for your own purposes. What is your true name?'

'Reynik,' he replied, looking straight at the Guildmaster's shadowed eyes as he did so. Reynik knew enough about reading body language to know that he could not lie easily to a man who could read others well. His was a fairly common name in central Shandar, so when Femke had built his false identity for him, she had decided not to alter his birth name. For someone inexperienced in the art of maintaining the façade of a false identity, it would reduce the chances of his making a mistake from which he could not recover.

'It is good to meet you, Reynik. I would tell you my name, but the fewer people who know that information, the better. I'll not lie to you. Some in the Guild do know my real name, but this is because they knew me before I took over as Guildmaster. It is tradition that when being inducted into the Guild, the newcomer bares his face to the assembled assassins. This is the only time the others will see your face, and you will never see theirs unless they choose to reveal it to you. This, I feel, is one of the wisest of the Guild traditions, as it means only the very senior, most trusted, members of the Guild will have ever seen the faces of the majority of the other members. By the time they become senior members, it will often have been many years since they last caught their one glimpse of many of the others. In the event that a member is captured and tortured for information, none of them can reveal much current information about the others. It works well.'

The Guildmaster watched Reynik's face intently as he explained this aspect of Guild life. He was always interested to see how the new members reacted to information about the Guild. The young man was thoughtful and listening intently to his every word. Most did to begin with. If they were going to stray, it normally took a year or more for their baser instincts to tempt them into ignoring rules for personal gain. When members did stray from the creed, there were no second chances. However, they had to be caught for the Guild to exact its harsh justice. The Guild-master was more than aware that not all infringements were discovered. There were certain members, even now, who lived life precariously – constantly straining at the boundaries of the creed.

'I can see the logic behind such precautions,' Reynik said carefully. 'But surely someone must know what everyone else looks like, or how would you guard against impostors?'

'A good question, Reynik. The answer is two-fold. Firstly, it is impossible for someone to enter here as an impostor. The founders of the Guild made robust security plans when they had this complex built over six hundred years ago. Some of the most powerful magicians of their time created a series of magical icons. Each new member accepts one when inducted into the Guild. It is this icon that allows access to and from the Guild complex. It cannot be stolen, for it is magically bonded to the life force of the Guild member. If it is taken more than a few paces from the person it is bonded to, then the person will die and the icon will magically return here to the complex.

The second part to your answer is that there are a select few who do know all the faces. I am one. The others are selected from the serving staff. Of the assassins, only I know which of the staff serve all members.'

Lots of things were beginning to fall into place for Reynik now. The silver spider talisman worn by the assassin who he had fought in the street that night must be one of the icons. By walking over to the street lamp to view it in a clearer light, Reynik had inadvertently taken it too far from its bonded owner. It was horrible to think he had killed the man by such an innocent act, but it must be true. The talisman had dematerialised before his eyes. It all fitted.

If the man who had brought him here were 'Brother Viper', then Reynik would expect the man's icon would be in the shape of a snake. The metal thing he had been asked to hold whilst blindfolded had been curved and almost tubular like the body of a snake. Yes, that made sense too. One thing that did not make sense was the serving staff.

'But how do the serving staff get here, and how do you know they are trustworthy? Do you not worry about infiltrators amongst them?' Reynik asked, puzzled.

The Guildmaster smiled. 'No,' he said, clearly amused. 'When men come here to serve, they do so for life. Members bring them here, but once they're in, they cannot leave. There is no conventional way in and out of this complex. As you've probably worked out by now, it is totally subterranean. This complex was tunnelled out over six hundred years ago. No one knows exactly where it is, not even the Guild members. It is one of the greatest secrets of our time.'

CHAPTER ELEVEN

'No one knows . . .'

The phrase echoed in Reynik's mind like the ringing toll of the death bell. Even if he were accepted as a member of the Guild he would not learn the location of the head-quarters. How could he have ever anticipated this? What was more, he was about to be life-bonded to a magical icon that would tie him to the Guild for ever. Could things get any worse? Then he remembered something his father had once told him:

'*Son, no matter how bad things look, they could always be worse. Never let despair overtake your ability to look for the positive.*'

The positive – he had to look for the positive in this situation. The Guildmaster was here and willing to answer questions. This was an opportunity that may not arise again for some time. He had better make the most of it and look to pass on as much information as he could to Femke when he next saw her.

'Guildmaster . . . Sir? I'm not sure what form of address you prefer.'

'Guildmaster is fine.'

'Guildmaster, my mind is full of questions. Your answers each fill in a small piece of the enigma that makes up this Guild, but every one you put in place makes me aware of ten more pieces I didn't know were missing. For example, you say there is no conventional way in and out of the Guild, yet you have servants living here. To live here would require regular supplies of food and drink, along with many other small necessities of life. How does the Guild maintain such supplies without anyone in the supply chain knowing where the goods are going? Also, if this is a subterranean complex with no way in, or out, how is it that the air is still fresh after centuries of use?'

'It's good that you're thinking of such things. It shows a sound understanding of logistics. Many of the other Guild members take such things for granted. Suffice it to say for now that the designers of this place thought of such things. When you have settled in and become established as a member, then, if you're still curious, I'll show you how these things are achieved.'

'Thank you, Guildmaster. I've always been interested in how things work. I'm also curious about these magical icons. Magic is not something I've encountered very often, so I know little about it. In this case, though, the magical process does not interest me as much as the practicalities. The place where Brother Viper used his icon to bring me here – is this the only such place from which he can transport into the Guild, or are there others? And the

211

reverse – can he transport anywhere with this icon, or are there limitations?'

The Guildmaster laughed. 'Your questions are both understandable and intelligent. I'll answer them, but then we must move on. I called for the ceremony to begin soon, as the Guild is in the middle of a very busy time.'

'Yes, I imagine so. The Emperor has not made life easy for you recently. The Emperor's declaration of *anaethus drax* was a major reason for not seeking involvement with you, but now I see how impossible it will be for the Emperor to touch us here, I'm glad your people came to me.'

'Indeed. Well, as you will soon see, the icons do have limitations. They are the moving parts in a citywide network of magical items that have been in place for centuries. Each icon is magically linked to four other objects: the binding stone, the home stone and two city destination stones. The binding stone is used to bond each member with his icon. When a member dies, his icon transports to its appropriate place on the binding stone. The next person to touch that icon is bound to it. Some of the icons have had literally hundreds of bondings since they were first made. Others have had only a few dozen.'

The Guildmaster paused for a second as if pondering why such differences had occurred. When he continued, Reynik wondered if the pause had been to consider the history of his own icon, if indeed he had one.

'To use the icon to travel, the bearer must touch it to his home stone, or to one of the destination stones. If the icon touches a destination stone, the bearer will always be brought to his quarters here in the Guild complex. If the icon is touched against the home stone, then where the bearer is transported to depends on which side of the home stone the icon touches. There are thirty destination stones in all. Each icon has one unique destination stone and one that is shared with another. You will quickly learn the location of yours.'

'Fascinating,' Reynik said with genuine enthusiasm. 'And you, Guildmaster, do you have a separate icon?'

'That is a question I'm not willing to answer at this time. Come. We need to go to the central chamber. It's nearly time for your induction. We don't want to keep the others waiting.'

'Lords and Ladies of Shandar, I appreciate you all coming here today. I know you all have busy schedules to attend to, so I'll not keep you long. I've called you together to ask your help with a most important matter.' Emperor Surabar paused and scanned the sea of hostile faces. It was plain that the last thing the majority of these people wanted to do was to help him, but what they wanted was irrelevant. If there was even one among them who would give him information that could save further bloodshed, then this meeting would have been worthwhile.

'As you know, I declared the Guild of Assassins *anaethus drax* a short while ago. I firmly believe this organisation to be an abomination from another age. It should not be allowed to exist in a civilised society. There may be those of you who have reason to disagree with this view – that is your prerogative. However, I would implore those of you

213

who are sympathetic to my beliefs on this one issue, if you have any information that could help me in my quest to stamp out this organisation once and for all, then please arrange an audience as soon as possible. If no information is forthcoming within a day, I will initiate drastic measures to commence the destruction of the Guild by other means. I'm merely attempting to minimise the pain for everyone with this appeal.'

A buzz of speculation fizzed in the Court at what the 'drastic measures' might be.

'Your Majesty.'

Silence fell. Expectation hung in the air like an aroma. Was someone going to give support to the Emperor in public? Who had spoken?

'Yes, Lord Merrik?'

'With all due respect, what you ask is nonsense, your Majesty.'

'Really, Lord Merrik? Why do you say so?'

'Because no one with even the slightest sense of self preservation would consider giving such information even if they had it, your Majesty. The Guild of Assassins is not an organisation to be trifled with. They have existed here for centuries . . .'

'Leeching off foolish Lords with more money than sense of honour, or decency,' Surabar interrupted. 'Don't give me any tripe about them having a creed, as if that justifies their murders. There is a justice system in this city. It is not always perfect, but it is here for a reason. I want the days when people seek to circumvent the justice of the Empire to come to an end. The Assassins' creed is an excuse for them to make money from murder – nothing more.'

'I was not going to endorse their existence, your Majesty. I was going to point out that they have enjoyed hundreds of years in which to establish information-gathering networks that put the Imperial spy network to shame. They have people everywhere, your Majesty. You cannot protect your people from them. Lord Kempten spoke up on your behalf and he paid for it with his life. Legion Commanders are now falling like flies because they're loyal to you. As the Emperor, however, you remain safe from their attentions. They cannot kill you because of their creed, your Majesty. You did know that, didn't you? That's why everyone around you dies, while you live on. That's why no assassin has come knocking at your door.'

'An assassin was caught whilst making an attempt on my life only last week . . .'

'Then I would bet my last coin he was not a member of the Guild, your Majesty. If he had been, then it is highly likely you would now be dead.'

The Emperor paused to contemplate Lord Merrik's words for a moment. Surabar knew he had lost the initiative. Merrik was right. The Guild did have an excellent intelligence network. They had also been killing one after another of the military commanders who were loyal to him, and he had been able to do nothing to stop them. Anyone who did give him information would be in extreme danger of a visit from one of the Guild. However, he had one last card to play and he decided to use it now.

'I accept, Lord Merrik, that what I ask of you today could bring danger to your door. However, think of the benefits: a society where justice was served in the court-room rather than the back alleys; life in a society where an impartial mediator settled disputes rather than the first side to hire a talented assassin – some ends are worth the means. There are those who would sacrifice everything to make those ends a reality. Lady Kempten, would you join me a moment?'

All eyes in the Court shifted to watch the demure figure wearing a sombre black dress who rose from her seat in the front row and gracefully ascended the steps to the Emperor's dais. She stopped at the Emperor's right side and turned to address the Court.

'My husband ...' she began, her voice strong and true. 'My *late* husband believed passionately in Emperor Surabar's abilities to reform the Empire. He believed Emperor Surabar's reforms would benefit every citizen of Shandar, from the most powerful Lord to the poorest beggar on the street. If he were here today, he would have volunteered any information he had despite the possibility of reprisal from the Guild. Why?' She paused for effect. 'Because he believed it was right. Because he believed it was the way forward. Because he believed that society as a whole would benefit. My husband was willing to give his life for those beliefs. Do not let fear hold you back. The Guild's days are numbered. Emperor Surabar's new Shandar will be a stronger and better place to live for everyone.'

Lady Kempten had got to them. Surabar could see it. Not all of them, of course, but a few. The Emperor had not expected miracles. But, looking around the Court at the faces of the Nobles, he felt the result had been worth the effort, even if no one came forward with information afterwards.

'Thank you, Lady Kempten. I believe I speak for the majority present in offering sincerest condolences at your loss. I understand that you are retiring to your country house for a time, which is most understandable. My warmest wishes go with you and your family.'

Lady Kempten curtsied to Surabar and descended from the dais, a picture of elegance and fortitude in the face of great tragedy. Surabar waited until she had taken her seat before concluding his short address.

'Lords and Ladies of the Imperial Court, thank you for your time. I will not keep you any longer from your day. My door will be open to any who wish to speak with me on this matter.'

Reynik felt a sense of dread building inside him as the Guildmaster led him down the corridor away from Brother Viper's quarters. At the end of the corridor was a door. It opened into a dark, stable-like booth in which Brother Viper was standing next to a solitary chair. The booth looked out into a large chamber with a central podium.

The Guildmaster acknowledged Viper's bow with a nod as he passed through the booth. Without pausing, he opened the gate out into the chamber and led Reynik out towards the podium. As he walked forward, Reynik noted the other booths around the outer wall of the chamber. There seemed to be lots of them, each with a different animal symbol on its gate and on the wall above it.

Reynik turned around to look at the symbols. A cougar, a wolf, a bear, a firedrake, a falcon, an eagle, an owl, a fox – they were all predators. Finally it made sense. His eyes settled for a moment on the dragon motif on one of the gates and he shivered. Alarm bells sounded in his head as he looked at the dragon. He had seen that symbol before. 'Shalidar!' he thought, the sense of impending doom momentarily shattering, as a wave of hatred surged through him. His mind flashed back to Mantor and the house Shalidar had owned there. The house had sported many pictures, images and ornaments featuring dragons. The reason for the assassin's interest in them was suddenly clear. The dragon was his symbol.

The slightest of movements in the darkness of the dragon booth brought Reynik back to the present. Had he been staring? He hoped not. He should have realised the booths would be occupied. If Shalidar recognised him, he was as good as dead. Would Shalidar recognise him, though? It was unlikely. They had only met properly once, when Reynik had been pretending to be the representative of a wealthy client for Shalidar's services. Reynik did not believe their encounter on the Palace rooftop counted, as Shalidar had barely glanced at him before running away. No. The link was too tenuous. They were hundreds of leagues from their last meeting, and Reynik had since changed his appearance. There was little likelihood of Shalidar linking him to their brief encounter in Mantor.

The Guildmaster had climbed up onto his pulpit-like podium. Reynik remained at the base of the steps. He tried not to look nervous, though his apprehension was building again. It was hard to know where to look, as he did not want to be seen to be staring at anything in particular. Also, there was the difficulty of what to do with his hands. It felt wrong to have them by his sides, but if he put them behind his back it might be seen to be a military stance, which was something to be avoided. If he clasped them together, he knew he would fiddle with his fingers. His palms were already slick with nervous sweat. What was to happen next? The Guildmaster had not primed him with any details.

The Guildmaster's voice suddenly punched out into the dim hall. 'I accept . . .' There was a slight pause, then a number of voices joined together in a ritualistic chant that Reynik realised must be the infamous Assassins' creed. He listened to the words, fascinated by some of the phrasing. If the assassins were bound by these words, then it was clear that Shalidar had been treading a dangerous path over recent months.

'I state this creed in the full knowledge that should
  I break it,
My life will be forfeit.'

The final words rang around the chamber. Reynik's chest tightened, his nervousness heightening by the second. Where was the binding stone the Guildmaster had spoken of? It did not appear to be in this chamber. How did it work? Would the binding be painful, or disorienting, like his first magical transfer into the Guild headquarters?

'Brothers, this is a good day. We welcome in a new

219

Brother to our Guild. Please, walk around the central podium, young friend.'

Reynik did as he was told. He walked slowly, keeping his face impassive and his eyes straight ahead. He did not allow his eyes to linger on the dragon emblem this time, but swept past it as he did all the others until he was back where he had started.

'You have all had a chance to see his face. Does anyone know of any reason why this man should not be acceptable as a member of our Guild?'

Reynik's heart thumped in his chest. Would Shalidar say anything? Had his uncle's killer recognised him? Precious seconds of silence passed unbroken. Apparently he had not.

'Very well.' The Guildmaster looked down at Reynik. 'You may raise your hood,' he said solemnly. 'Do not lower it again in this chamber. Step forward, Brothers, and we will proceed to the naming room.'

The Guildmaster stepped down from his podium and led Reynik over to the wall between the bear and the griffin alcoves. The wall looked to be solid rock. Reynik could see no sign of a way forward, but he was not about to make a fool of himself by saying anything aloud. The Guildmaster drew something from beneath his cloak and waved his hand in a peculiar gesture at the wall. Reynik itched to see what it was that the Guildmaster held, but there were a dozen assassins standing close behind him. He did not want to do anything that might be misinterpreted.

In the blink of an eye, a section of the wall vanished, leaving a dark, door-shaped hole. Reynik had gone beyond being astonished. It appeared there was a lot to this complex that defied everyday understanding. What had happened to the wall? Had it been an illusion all along? Had a section of it been transported away using the same sort of magic as the talismans possessed? The question was irrelevant, he decided. The Guildmaster was leading him forward into the dark passageway. His concern was what awaited him at the far end.

As they entered the blackness of the stone passageway, Reynik realised that it was not totally dark. There was a dim glow emanating from somewhere ahead that lit their way sufficiently for them to see where they were going.

When they entered the chamber at the far end of the passage, the contrast from the meeting chamber was startling. Where the meeting chamber had been clearly dug out and fashioned with the tools of man, this chamber looked as if it were a naturally formed cave. Irregular walls glowed with an eerie green light that Reynik took to be either natural, chemically made, or magical in nature. No fire he had ever seen burned with such a colour, but then there were no flames. It almost seemed as if the rocks themselves were glowing.

For a moment, Reynik's mind wandered back to the Royal Court in Thrandor and Femke's trial. Alchemist Pennold had used a rock that gave off an invisible influence to demonstrate Shalidar's guilt. Was this the sort of reaction happening here? Reynik would love to have time to study the place in more depth, but events were pressing him forwards with unrelenting pace.

In the centre of the chamber there was a large, flat block

of stone that looked suspiciously like an altar. As he drew nearer, Reynik could see that there were deep engravings in the top surface. Pictures matching the predator symbols in the meeting hall had been carved into the stone. Some were tiny. Others were larger. However, each predator symbol on this rock had something in common – there was an identical circle of runes carved around each one.

The language of magic was written in runes like this, Reynik realised. The hairs on the back of his neck prickled at the thought. It was one of the few things he knew about the magical arts. Until now, he had questioned in the depths of his mind whether the magical transfer to the Guild headquarters could have been an elaborate hoax. Any last doubts he had harboured dissolved in an instant at the sight of the runes. This was real.

The Guildmaster led Reynik right up to the stone, whilst the rest of the hooded assassins formed a circle around it. The cave was large, but Reynik was suddenly overwhelmed by a sense of claustrophobia. He was hemmed in on all sides by deadly killers and sealed in solid rock. There was no way out. Panic welled inside, but once again his father's calming words filled his mind.

'*Panic is death. Do not give in to it. Breathe deeply and slowly. Relax your shoulders and be ready. The best way out of a bad situation will only become apparent when you're thinking clearly.*'

'Brothers, we gather again around the binding stone faced with a decision. Our new Brother here needs a name. There are three available. What say you, Brothers? With which icon should our new Brother be bound? The Falcon, the Sea Serpent, or the Wolf Spider? You have all heard the tales of his most recent kills. Which would you say suits him most?'

Reynik glanced again at the top of the binding stone and saw the three silver icons nestled in their respective carvings. 'Oh, Shand, please not the spider!' he prayed silently.

The Guildmaster turned to the nearest assassin. 'What say you, Firedrake?'

'Wolf Spider.'

'What say you, Bear?'

'Falcon.'

And so it went on around the circle.

'What say you, Dragon?'

'Wolf Spider,' the hooded figure answered. An involuntary shudder ran down Reynik's back. The voice was distinctive. It was Shalidar. Definitely. His uncle's killer was the Dragon.

A woman's voice, low and purring answered when the Guildmaster addressed 'Fox'. She named him 'Falcon'. Reynik was surprised. The Guildmaster never referred to 'Sisters', only 'Brothers'. How had a woman gained membership of the Guild if it were so gender-biased as to not even recognise her as female?

The last member was asked.

'Two say "Sea Serpent", five say "Falcon", and five say "Wolf Spider". The casting vote is mine,' the Guildmaster announced solemnly. 'I have considered the approach you took to your last kill and, to me, your naming seemed self-evident. I name you ... Brother Wolf Spider. Take up your icon, Brother, and bind your soul with ours.'

Reynik's heart sank. The silver wolf spider icon gave him the creeps. It was not pleasant to think he would have to live with it close to him for the rest of his life. But this was not a time to show hesitation. With jaw clenched in anticipation, he reached out and lifted the silver spider from its underlying carved image. For the briefest of instants, the world reeled under him, but then . . . nothing. He felt completely normal. No unusual sensations, no magical tingling, no sense of anything out of the ordinary at all.

He had thought he would feel different somehow. The link that the Guildmaster had described between icon and the life force of an individual had made him expect to be consciously aware of it. He was not. It was a complete anticlimax.

'Now, Brother Wolf Spider, you are required to repeat the creed. By this creed you will live and be judged. No matter what the present Emperor may believe, this brother-hood has stood the test of time because of the integrity of its members. We have a proud tradition of loyalty and respect that spans centuries. For better, or for worse, you have become a Brother to us. As long as you uphold the creed, you shall enjoy the protection and support of this Guild. Do not seek to twist its words, or bend it to your will, for it will destroy you. Repeat after me, please: *I accept that as a member of this Guild . . .*'

Reynik did as he was told, repeating each clause of the creed with as near identical inflections to those of the Guildmaster as he could manage. The final lines threatened to stick in his throat, but he forced them out.

'I state this creed in the full knowledge that should
   I break it,
   My life will be forfeit.'

It was done. He had successfully infiltrated the Guild
of Assassins. But at what price? Was the information he
had gained worth his life? Maybe the Emperor would feel
it was a small price to pay: the life of one Legionnaire
for information that could possibly bring down the Guild
of Assassins. Yes, to the Emperor this might well appear
a reasonable exchange, Reynik mused. A General will cal-
culate and analyse attrition rates carefully before, during
and after any campaign. A good Commander will do the
same. Sometimes sacrifices are needed to win the day.
There is no place for guilt in the minds of such men.
Reynik knew this all too well. It ran in his blood. If a
Commander allowed feelings for individuals to interfere
with his decisions, then how could he possibly expect to
win the day?

Reynik had so much to tell Femke and the Emperor.
Despite not learning where this secret headquarters was,
he had plenty of hitherto unknown information about
the Guild and how it worked. With what he knew about
the organisation, it would become much easier to identify
members of the Guild. This information would be invalu-
able to them. All he had to do now was to survive long
enough to ensure he passed it on.

'Welcome, Brother,' the Guildmaster announced, his
voice sounding genuinely warm. He put a friendly arm
across Reynik's shoulders. 'There will be a short period

225

during which you will be on probation, and you will have to make your first kill for the Guild before you're truly a full Brother. However, I don't anticipate either will offer you any great problems. Come now. I will get one of the servants to show you to your quarters. Please do not attempt to use your icon to transport out of the headquarters until I give you my permission. It would not be advisable to risk travelling alone until your body has adapted to the transfer sickness. On your first foray back into Shandrim, your stone Brother will accompany you. Brother Cougar is your stone Brother.'

One of the other assassins bowed. 'Welcome, stone Brother,' he said. 'It will be my pleasure to shepherd you.'

The Guildmaster led Reynik out of the naming room and back through the dark corridor to the main meeting chamber. They were met there by a servant in plain brown robes who, in turn, led Reynik onwards through the wolf spider alcove and into the corridor and chambers beyond. Shalidar watched him go, following his every step through narrowed eyes. The rest of the assassins were dispersing to their relative alcoves, but Shalidar held back.

'Guildmaster. A moment, please,' he called softly.

'Yes, Brother Dragon? What is it?'

'There is something about Brother Wolf Spider that bothers me,' he said, his voice hesitant.

'And what is that?'

'I don't know, Guildmaster. A feeling. An instinct that tells me he will be trouble.'

'That's rather rich coming from you,' the Guildmaster chuckled. 'But Brother Viper indicated a similar feeling.

226

Fear not, Brother Dragon. He will be watched carefully. On second thoughts, given your feelings about him, I'd like you to be one of those to watch him. Be careful, Brother. From Viper's report, he's lacking in experience, but he's got a lot of raw talent. Don't underestimate him. If he is here to betray us, then he may have more abilities than he has let us see.'

'If the Guild have him, then you'll never find him.'

'The Guild must be based *somewhere*, Shedrick. It's got to be here in Shandrim, because they react so damned quickly to events. Surely someone must know. No organisation can keep their headquarters totally secret for ever.'

Femke's frustration was building. She had tried to find the headquarters of the Guild of Assassins before, but had never taken the search seriously. Her previous search had been purely to satisfy her personal curiosity. Information was her business, and it never hurt to anticipate the market. People were always looking to uncover secrets. The Guild of Assassins was one of the most secretive societies ever formed. It stood to reason someone would want to know about it eventually.

'Ah, but they can, Miss,' Shedrick replied softly, his face twisting into a conspiratorial grin. He looked around nervously and lowered his voice still further. 'They magic away somewhere. They can . . . disappear.'

Femke almost laughed aloud at his dramatic conclusion, but she restrained herself. Shedrick was a good source. He was clearly serious about his statement. If he thought she was mocking him, he might decide to take his information

227

elsewhere. She needed Shedrick too much to lose him over such a trifle.

'Disappear, Shedrick? Are you sure? I don't want to doubt you, but if the assassins can disappear at will, then why are they ever caught?'

'I don't know, Miss, but I know it's true. I've seen it, Miss. One minute he was there, the next there were some sparkly lights and he was gone. I've never seen the like before, nor since, Miss. It was eerie – made all the hairs on my head stand on end.'

'Who, Shedrick? Who did you see disappear and when?'

'One of them assassins, Miss. I can't say I've ever heard his name, but I saw him sneaking out from the camp of the Legions last week. All dressed in black, he was. Black cloak and hood. Looked like death, he did. One of the Legion Commanders was killed that night. It doesn't take deep thought to work out this man in black was the killer.'

'So you saw him out near the military camp. Is that where he disappeared?'

'No, Miss. He led me a merry path through the city first. We were almost to the inner city when it happened. I'm wondering now if he caught on to my following him. I was being extra careful, 'cause you don't want to upset a member of the Guild. I could have sworn he hadn't seen me, but then, all of a sudden he paused at the entrance to an alleyway and looked back. He was looking straight at where I was hiding when he just faded away. All that was left were a few sparkles in the air and then they were gone too. I swear, Miss. It's Shand's own truth, it is.'

Femke looked hard at the man's face. It was hard to pin

him with her stare, as his eyes were almost constantly on the move. He was a weasel of a man: small, alert, and always quick to stick his nose in where there was trouble. However, there was no hint of fabrication in his body language. He clearly believed what he was saying to be the truth. The question was, what did he actually see? Had it been a clever illusion, something to disguise a hidden entrance? She needed to find out.

'Thank you, Shedrick, you've been most helpful.' She handed him several silver senna, which disappeared into a pocket at the speed of a striking snake. 'You can have the same again if you show me where the man disappeared,' she added.

Shedrick paused for a moment and he scratched nervously behind one ear. 'I don't know, Miss. It could be dangerous.'

'Would this help you decide then?' Femke asked, her voice becoming silky soft as she produced a gold sen and rubbed it gently between her fingers. Shedrick licked his lips and reached for the coin, but Femke was faster. 'Not until you've shown me the place,' she insisted, giving the coin a final waggle before putting it back in her pocket.

'You play a dangerous game, Miss, but I'll show you. Come with me. It's dark out there, but it's a bit early for cutthroats and thieves to be abroad yet. Let's get it over with before I change my mind.'

CHAPTER TWELVE

'At last! I thought you'd never come. Welcome. Here – sit down. Have a drink. I have a lucrative proposition for you.'

'They're always the best kind, Lord Tremarle,' Shalidar responded with a twisted smile. He strolled casually across to an armchair. Turning, sitting, and crossing his legs in one fluid movement, the assassin leaned back, steepling his fingers in front of his chest as he regarded his host with an intense gaze.

It was easy to see Lord Tremarle was in a state of emotional turmoil. Anger and grief warred with the nervousness that was common in those who dealt with members of the Guild. Shalidar eyed the thickset old Lord carefully, trying to discern if there were any specific knowledge behind Tremarle's grief and anger. Did he know that his son's killer was sitting across the room from him? It was unlikely. Lord Tremarle could be a devious power monger, but when it came to family and friends, he wore his heart on his sleeve.

Tremarle handed Shalidar a generous glass of wine. The assassin took a tiny sip and nodded his thanks.

'When I left the message requesting you to come, I did so with different intentions,' the Lord began. 'Lord Lacedian told me he had become the target of a member of your profession. It appears his information was correct. Was the assassin responsible for my friend's death a member of the Guild?'

'No . . . and yes,' Shalidar replied, taking another sip of wine. 'The person who killed your friend was not a member of the Guild when he carried out the hit, but he has since been inducted into membership. As we speak, he is settling into his new quarters. If you are looking for revenge on the killer of your friend, then I'm afraid I must leave now, for no matter how much I might wish to help you, I cannot accept a contract on one of my fellow Guild members.'

'No, it's nothing like that,' Tremarle said quickly. 'I'm the last person to want to upset the Guild by proposing such a thing. However, I'd like to take out a contract on the person who was ultimately responsible. I want you to kill the person who ordered Lacedian's death, for I'm certain it's the same person who was responsible for the death of my son.'

Shalidar raised an eyebrow in surprise. 'This should be interesting,' he thought. It was hard to imagine a connection between the two deaths, given his rather unique inside knowledge.

'Lacedian confided in me that he was certain he knew who had taken out the contract on his life,' Tremarle continued, oblivious to Shalidar's body language. 'Some time ago I heard the merest whisper of a rumour that you may have carried out a similar service in the past. It is not a rumour that ever spread far, for no one wanted to be heard repeating such a thing. I'm aware of your creed, and that such a service is not normally for sale, but my fee for making this hit may make you feel it worth the risk.'

Lights began to flicker on in the assassin's mind. Shalidar knew now what Tremarle wanted. He had killed the last Emperor for Vallaine. Somehow, Tremarle knew this. How, and who had told him, was worrying, for Shalidar was in enough trouble with the Guildmaster as it was.

Lord Tremarle's reasoning for taking out a contract on Surabar was flawed, though. He must have been badly misinformed to think this Emperor, of all people, would ever order an assassination. His reasoning for Surabar being responsible for the death of Danar was also twisted. Shalidar had killed him to further Femke's pain – how could that be Surabar's fault?

It was true that nothing would please Shalidar more than to be paid for killing the Emperor, unless maybe it were to be paid for killing the girl, Femke, but the Guildmaster was watching him. He could not break the creed so spectacularly and expect to get away with it. Still, he thought, there was nothing lost by hearing Lord Tremarle out. He could always pass on information of the Lord's offered contract to the Guildmaster as a show of loyalty.

'I'm not sure what rumour you have heard, Lord Tremarle, but I have been incorrectly attributed many kills over the years. I can only assume you are referring to the ultimate Imperial target, which is, as you have correctly stated, out of bounds to Guild members. Let's imagine for a moment, however, that such a target were fair game. What would this fee be, that would be worth my facing not only the direct danger involved, but the wrath of my Guild into the bargain?'

Lord Tremarle met his eyes with an expression full of determined passion. 'Everything I own,' he replied.

Shalidar laughed aloud, quickly putting his glass of wine on the side table to avoid spilling it. 'Everything, my Lord! How could you give me everything? Where would you live? What of your wife?'

Lord Tremarle held his gaze firm and his expression remained deadly serious. 'I will give my estate, my wealth, indeed my very name to the man who can achieve this thing,' he breathed. 'I will legally adopt him as my son, such that upon my death he shall gain full inheritance of my House.'

Femke sighed and pushed the plate away. The food on it had barely been touched. Ordering it had been a mistake. Her stomach was twisted with worry for Reynik. Even the smell of the steaming meat and potatoes repulsed her. It was too soon to give up on seeing him again. They had arranged a different rendezvous point and time for every day of the week. This was the third he had missed, but she would continue to go to the pre-arranged meeting places until all hope had gone. How long would that be, she wondered? A week? A month? It did not bear thinking about.

The Legions were already beginning their first sweep through the city. They would enter every building in the city and tear it apart in their search for the Guild. It was unlikely they would miss much. Wherever the headquarters was, it would have to be all but invisible to avoid discovery in the face of such a determined search, she thought grimly. Shand help Reynik if he was there when the Legionnaires found the place.

Femke had searched the entire area around where her source, Shedrick, had claimed he had seen an assassin disappear. There was no indication of anything unusual there. Shedrick had always been a reliable source in the past, but Femke had her suspicions that he might have been drinking on the night he claimed to have followed this 'assassin'. Nothing about his information made any real sense, but his tale did remind her of Reynik's account of the silver wolf spider talisman disappearing after he removed it from an assassin's body. One story of a magical disappearance was unusual, but two such stories about assassins and their possessions indicated more than coincidence.

It was late – too late to expect an appearance from Reynik. Femke threw a few copper sennuts on the table as a tip for the serving girl. She rose and threaded her way through the tables towards the door. There were still a few last contacts she could try. There was always a faint chance one of them might provide her with the lead she needed.

Femke was almost at the door when she noticed the man sitting at the corner table at the far side of the inn common room. Her heart skipped a beat. It was Reynik. He did not look up from the plate of food he was eating, but she could tell he was aware of her presence. A single glance at him was all she needed to get the information she required. She waved her thanks to the landlord and exited onto the street.

Reynik was using the code she had taught him. He had not contacted her because he was being followed. Instead, he had sat somewhere she was likely to see him and arranged the items on the table to convey a message. His knife had been sideways above his plate with the sharpened blade away from his body, which meant 'Do not approach'. He was eating with his right hand only. His left was casually placed on the table next to his plate with his thumb tucked underneath his palm and the four fingers extended. Femke was to meet him at the rendezvous point arranged for the fourth day.

A short while later Femke browsed a stall at one of the many open markets some distance from the inn. She saw Reynik coming this time, but again he did not approach. As he passed, Reynik straightened his cloak. It was the signal 'Check my tail'. Femke stayed at the stall and surreptitiously monitored the passers-by for any sign that someone might be following him. There was none. He seemed to have shaken any watchers. Reynik circled the market, occasionally pausing to browse stalls. When he approached the second time, Femke gave him the 'All clear' signal and he casually wandered up to her.

'Well?' she asked.

'I'm in,' he replied, 'but they don't trust me yet. I'm being followed everywhere. I'm fairly certain I've thrown them off, but they have more than one following me at any one time.'

'Are you aware of the purge by the Legions? Will they find the Guild headquarters, do you think?'

'I'm aware of it, but the Legions are wasting their time. They will never find the headquarters, as there is no conventional entrance to it. The assassins have magical icons that transport them to and from an underground complex of caverns. Where the caverns are is anyone's guess. They would do better to look for the individuals. Each of the assassins wears, or carries a silver object.'

'A wolf spider talisman by any chance?' Femke asked.

'No. The only person carrying a wolf spider talisman is me,' he replied. 'By killing the previous owner, it seems I inadvertently set myself up to become the talisman's next keeper. I'm guessing that Phagen was either carrying a silver falcon, or a sea snake, as those were also without keepers.'

'Damn!' Femke swore, biting at her lower lip. 'The Legionnaires have all been briefed to detain anyone wearing silver wolf spiders of any description. Can you get rid of it? Or avoid wearing it when you're out? Hide it somewhere and recover it when you need to transport back to the Guild headquarters?'

'No, that's not possible. If I try to do that, I'll die. The icon has been linked to my life force somehow. I don't pretend I totally understand it, but I do know that I'm bound to the Guild now. I can't just walk away.'

Femke could not totally hide her dismay.

'I'd better get a message to the Emperor quickly. I'll get

236

him to change the order,' she said. 'So there's a falcon and a sea snake – what other icons are there?'

'All of the icons are predators – real and legendary. Viper, puma, cougar, bear, fox, firedrake – you get the idea? There are twenty altogether. Shalidar carries a dragon. I'm sure of it. Femke, what am I going to do? The Guildmaster is going to tell us how the Guild will respond to this purge by the Legions later. What if I'm given a hit to carry out? Should I follow it through to maintain my cover? It made me sick to kill when the person was already condemned to death for treason. I don't know if I could kill someone in cold blood without such a justification.'

'Yes . . . no . . . I don't know. Give me some time to think. It's a difficult question,' Femke said, her voice hesitant. 'If you get given a hit, tell me. I'll think of something. Have you managed to identify anyone else in the Guild?'

'No. Whenever they meet, they remain hooded and cloaked throughout. The layout of the meeting hall is interesting. The assassins do not mix, but sit in individual booths looking in at a central room where the Guildmaster presides over the meeting. As far as I can tell, the assassins never work together unless directed to by the Guildmaster.'

'What about Shalidar and Phagen? Are you telling me the Guildmaster was behind the plot in Mantor?'

'I don't know, Femke. I can only tell you what I have seen. The Guildmaster does seem to have a tight rein on the other Guild members, but that might be due to the unusual circumstances at present. He is universally respected . . . and feared. If Shalidar was acting against the Guildmaster's wishes, then he is either very brave, or very reckless. I get the impression the Guildmaster would kill any of the members of the Guild without hesitation if they stepped over the line.'

'Shalidar has always lived on the edge,' Femke said thoughtfully. 'Look at his history. I doubt the Guildmaster was aware of how closely Shalidar was tied to Lord Vallaine. He would have claimed to know nothing of the sorcerer's deception in the Imperial Palace. Because Vallaine used arcane arts to disguise his true appearance, the Guildmaster would likely accept Shalidar's explanation. Any rational man would give the benefit of the doubt under such circumstances. No, it's my guess that Shalidar was acting outside of the remit of the Guild in Thrandor. He thrives on danger and risk.'

Reynik nodded. 'That is logical, in a twisted sort of way,' he admitted.

'Listen, Reynik, could you get me into the Guild? If I could get in, I might be able to find some sort of reference to where the complex is located. I don't know much about magic, but I do know that just like moving things conventionally, moving things magically will take more energy the further they have to move. That means the Guild is most likely under the city somewhere. If I could just find one small clue, then I might be able to tell the Emperor where to start digging. Once we dig out their nest, it will be much harder for them to survive.'

Reynik thought for a moment. His first journey into the Guild complex had been achieved through Viper's icon. There was no reason he could think of that the same should not be possible using his spider.

'It should be possible,' he said cautiously, 'but the transfer is disorientating the first couple of times you experience it. It's likely that you'll be incapacitated for some time once I've got you inside. If anyone finds you during that time, you'll be helpless.'

'Is there anywhere you can hide me while I recover?'

'Well, the only people to enter my quarters are the servants and the Guildmaster. If I get you in during the dead of night, there would be no reason for the servants to be there. It's also unlikely the Guildmaster would be there in the small hours. I could put you under my bed. I can't imagine anyone wanting to look there. We'll have to wait a few days. I'm still being watched at the moment. The fact that I've shaken off my tails today will probably result in my being monitored all the more for a while. Let's meet again in three days. If I desperately need to speak to you in the meantime, I'll come to your room in the Palace.'

'OK, Reynik. The rendezvous schedule can stay as we arranged. I'll meet you at the appropriate place. Be careful.'

Shalidar was distracted. The thought of inheriting the Tremarle estate was playing on his mind. If he were to inherit the title to the House of Tremarle, then what was there to prevent him from aspiring even further? He had put the Mantle on the shoulders of one Emperor and would have done so a second time had it not been for Femke. If he were Lord Tremarle, what was to stop him from aspiring to put the Mantle on his own shoulders?

The Guildmaster could hardly complain, as it would not breach the creed. Neither would it be detrimental to the

Guild – they would regain their status and more. To have one of their own at the helm of the Empire would put them beyond reproach. His ascension would have to appear legitimate, of course. He could not simply organise a blood bath that left him on the throne. The Guildmaster would see straight through such an obvious ploy. Therefore, he could not rise to power overnight. He would have to use all the guile and cunning he possessed to bring such a thing to pass, but it was not beyond the realms of possibility.

The first major obstacle was Surabar. He would have to kill the Emperor to become the legal heir to the Tremarle Estate. This would violate the creed. No matter how he twisted the circumstances, he could see no way around this fact. It was not the violation of the creed that made Shalidar flinch from attempting it – he had habitually circumvented the creed ever since joining the Guild. What worried Shalidar was how he could cover his tracks such that the Guildmaster would not feel bound to order his death.

'Shand's teeth!' he muttered, scanning the road ahead for signs of his mark. Brother Wolf Spider had disappeared. Where had he gone? Shalidar turned around to see if he had inadvertently overtaken the young man during the daydream. There was no sign of him.

What should he do? Cougar was out there somewhere following as well. He would have to hope that Cougar had been more attentive.

The young man had done nothing suspicious during his venture out into the city today. He had wandered through the market place, spoken to a few known tattle touts and had lunch on his own in a quiet tavern. Notably he had been buying information from the touts rather than selling. If the new boy had tried to sell information, then he and Cougar would have been forced to act.

Despite Wolf Spider's behaviour so far, Shalidar was not yet ready to give him the benefit of the doubt. His instincts still told him there was something untrustworthy about the newest member of the Guild.

He had met the young man before somewhere. He was sure of it. Shalidar was good with faces – normally he had no problems remembering where and when he had seen someone before, but this young man's face eluded him. 'It must have been recently,' he thought, 'because he's barely more than a boy. Maybe he reminds me of someone else. That could be it. But who?'

The answer was clearly not ready to leap out at him, so he decided to let his subconscious work on it. If he stopped trying to consciously work it out, his memory block might dissolve. Doubtless he would wake up suddenly in the night when inspiration struck, and it would all become clear, he thought. He hoped so.

Shalidar decided to walk back to the nearer of his two transfer stones and get back to his room in the Guild headquarters. He had not gone far when he trod on something sharp that caused a jab of pain to shoot up his leg.

'Ow!'

He stopped and inspected the sole of his right boot. The sole had worn thin. A sharp stone was still sticking out from where it had penetrated the leather, which was both annoying and painful. He plucked it free, revealing a small hole. The boots were old, but so comfortable that he was loathe to replace them.

Shalidar thought for a moment. He was not one hundred per cent certain, but he vaguely recalled a cobbler's stall on the nearby street market. He had never used the man's services before, but it was a simple job. It would not take a cobbler long to re-sole the boots. The weather was pleasant and Shalidar was not in a hurry any more. He could afford to sit and wait for the repair to be completed, which would save him the expense of buying another set.

Having made up his mind, Shalidar limped around to the street market and found the cobbler's stall. This time his memory had not failed him. It was exactly where he remembered it. The cobbler was not busy, and was delighted to pick up the trade. He bustled around, bringing a stool for Shalidar to perch on and a cup of water for him to drink while he was waiting. The assassin watched him in amused silence for a while before looking along the street to see what else was going on.

His eyes brushed past the couple casually chatting at the tanner's stall, but his focus was quick to snap back to them when he realised whom he had just seen. 'Femke!' he breathed. '*And* young Wolf Spider! Now I have you. Now I remember.'

'What news, Femke?'

Femke entered the Emperor's study, ensuring the door was firmly closed before approaching Surabar's desk. As usual, he was leafing through a large stack of parchments. The man's thirst for knowledge was unquenchable, she decided. It was a good trait for one in the ultimate seat of power, but also a dangerous one. There were times when too much knowledge served only to complicate decisions. To Surabar's credit, however, he had not shied away from making the difficult choices.

'Reynik has succeeded, your Majesty. He has been accepted into the Guild.'

'He has? That's fantastic news! Where are they hidden? I'll have an entire Legion surround the place . . .'

'Unfortunately, your Majesty,' Femke interrupted, raising a hand to indicate she had not finished, 'it's not that simple.'

Surabar gave her one of his penetrating looks. 'I've always hated the word "but". I sense one coming now. Come, Femke. What is your "but"?'

Femke smiled. 'Reynik has penetrated the Guild, *but* does not know the location of the Guild headquarters.'

'Why not? Have they not taken him there yet?'

'Yes, he has been there. The way I understand it, no one knows where the headquarters is, because it is not accessible by normal means. Even those within the Guild do not know where it is. Your Legions are wasting their time searching the city. The Guild cannot be found this way. Reynik has discovered that the Guild headquarters is a huge complex of underground caverns that are not directly accessible from the world above. The only way in and out is by using one of twenty silver icons that have been imbued with a powerful magic. When an icon is brought into contact with a particular stone, it transports any who are touching it into the Guild headquarters.'

Emperor Surabar got up from his chair and began to pace back and forth across the room. He ran his fingers through his silver hair as he stalked up and down. 'Yes,' he said. 'It does make some sort of sense. I can understand how they've remained undetected for so many years. One thing puzzles me, though. It is hard to believe that something so big could be constructed without any record being made of it. It is beyond the realms of probability that there could be a complex of caverns perfectly formed for the Guild to just move in to, so they must have been excavated at some time. If we follow that logic through, then there must once have been an entrance to the caverns. What became of those who excavated them? Did any create records of the project? Builders are often methodical men. I would not be surprised if such a record existed.'

'It may have done so in the distant past, your Majesty. However, the Guild would have sought to destroy any such records, and we may be talking centuries since the complex was constructed.'

'The air in any sealed caverns would have become stale long ago if they had no direct link to the outside world. No. I don't think Reynik has the full picture yet. The logistical practicalities of supplying such a set of caverns with everyday necessities would make the arrangement you describe unworkable. The Guild must get supplies from somewhere. That means someone is providing them with food and other provisions. This tells me two things. One – there must be an alternate entrance of a conventional nature. It may be that only a select few in the Guild are aware of it, but it must exist. And two – there must be a money trail to follow. Money and records go together. Somebody will be keeping a set of records somewhere. If not, how could suppliers keep track of what they were owed?'

Femke was not so certain. She followed the Emperor's logic. His reasoning was sound and he clearly had a head for logistics, however, Femke was more of a lateral thinker. What if there was no access big enough for a person to enter through? What if ventilation shafts circulated fresh air and the stores were supplied through a system that utilised more magic? Would the ventilation shafts alone give enough of a clue as to where the caverns were located? It seemed unlikely.

'So what do you suggest, your Majesty? Reynik has agreed to get me into the Guild headquarters using his icon. Is there anything in particular you would have me look for whilst I'm there?'

'Look for anything that might indicate how they are supplied, or who supplies them. Note the colour and texture of the rock. Get a small sample if you can. We might get lucky. There are those in the city who claim to be experts in the identification of rock types. Maybe one of them will be able to tell us where to look for more rock of the same type. Also, try to find out whom it is we're up against. If you can discover the true identity of the Guildmaster, then we may be able to better anticipate him. Don't do anything foolish, Femke. I'm sure I don't need to tell you to be careful. The danger is self-evident, but I don't want you taking unnecessary risks. I need you alive.'

Femke nodded. 'Of course, your Majesty. I'll do my best.'

'Just because Brother Wolf Spider spoke with an imperial spy does not make him a traitor. His conversation with Femke may have been totally innocent, or instigated by her. You admit you did not see who approached whom, so how can you be sure he's plotting treachery?'

Shalidar gritted his teeth as he fought the urge to shout. Why could the Guildmaster not see it? Normally he was so quick to stamp on any hint of traitorous activity. He took a deep breath and spoke again with passion.

'When I first saw Wolf Spider, I thought he looked familiar. He was in Thrandor recently – *with Femke*. The last time I saw him, he was dressed as a Legionnaire. Femke is a known spy and she's close to the Emperor. Wolf Spider *has* to be an infiltrator. He's a spy like Femke. I'm sure of it.'

'Brother Dragon, we are short of members. We're also at a time of crisis. Brother Wolf Spider has proven himself to possess raw talent as an assassin. Let's see if he's willing to employ his talents in support of the Guild before we judge him. I'll set him a hit later. Follow him. Make sure that he carries out his duty to the Guild. If he doesn't, then you have my permission to kill him.'

'The Guildmaster wishes to talk with you. Please attend him in the meeting chamber in one hour.'

'Thank you,' Reynik replied, nodding politely. 'I'll be sure to be there on time.'

The servant bowed deeply and backed out through the door, closing it behind him. Reynik looked back at the book he had been looking through. He shut it. It was no use. He could not concentrate enough to read anyway.

His quarters gave him the creeps. Reynik did not have a great love of spiders, but just as Viper's living rooms were full of images of snakes, so were his full of arachnids. The crests above the doorways bore the wolf spider insignia. Ornaments, hangings, even book spines were cast, woven, printed, or otherwise adorned with images of his predator namesake. Was there something in the magic of the icons that imbued the wearer with an obsession for the symbol he bore? If so, the silver pendant had not yet begun to work its wiles on Reynik.

The servants were another enigma of the Guild headquarters. He was at a loss as to how to address them. None of them would reveal their names; they simply ignored the question if asked. They dressed in plain, brown robes, complete with deep hoods to keep their faces hidden. Reynik had distinguished defining characteristics for a handful of them, but he could not begin to guess how many there were in total. At least seven or eight had attended him in his rooms at some point during the past few days.

Where did they live? If each of the assassins had separate quarters which were not accessible to one another except through the central meeting chamber, then did the servants' quarters form another spoke or two leading out from that central hub, or were they on a different level? Could it be that they lived above, or below, the level of the assassins? Reynik had seen no stairs, but then he had not dared to

247

venture far. Should he explore? Or should he leave the sneaking around to Femke?

Everything about his situation posed dilemmas. Even the simplest of tasks involved choices he did not want to make. Life in the Legion had been tough, but at least there he had understood the challenges.

He got up and crossed the room to where an hourglass was standing on top of one of the three bookcases along the wall. He turned the glass on its central pivot until the legs of the ugly spider-shaped top housing secured the sand-filled half of the glass in place. He watched for a moment as the sand began to trickle through. The hourglass would take half an hour to empty. If he turned it again when about three quarters of the sand had passed through the venturi, then it would give him a good idea of when to leave for his meeting with the Guildmaster. He did not want to be late.

The next three quarters of an hour passed slowly. When the last of the sand had finally trickled from the hourglass, Reynik was out through the door like a rat out of a trap.

No doubt the Guildmaster would want to know where he had been today, he thought nervously. There was no reason for him to lie. He would just omit the part about his meeting with Femke – or gloss over it. Why should he not meet with spies? He had to get information from somewhere. Why not get it from the best sources? No, there would be no reason to lie.

Reynik reached his cubicle and sat down to wait. It had taken no more than half a minute for him to walk from his room to the cubicle, so he was more than a little early. The central chamber was still and silent except for the occasional fluttering noise of a torch. Reynik leaned forward over the gate into the chamber. Was he alone? There was no way of telling. The other cubicles were all shrouded in shadow. He could see the dragon symbol off to his right. It was very tempting to hop over the gate and take a closer look, but he thought better of it. Instead he settled back on his bench and waited.

Sitting in the dark shadow within his cubicle proved extremely soporific. Before he realised he was in danger of dropping off to sleep, his chin impacted his chest as his head flopped forwards, startling him awake. He was lucky. The Guildmaster was crossing the floor of the chamber towards him. Reynik did not think his nod would have been visible, as he was sitting in such deep darkness.

When the Guildmaster spoke, his voice was as warm as it had been at their last meeting. Reynik braced himself for the questions, but they did not come.

'I hope you have settled into your quarters and find them to your satisfaction, Brother Wolf Spider. Brother Cougar tells me you've adapted fully to the transfer system now, and that you feel little discomfort when you use your icon. Is that true?'

'Yes, Guildmaster. I would not say it's a comfortable experience, but I can stand it without feeling any ill effects afterwards.'

'Good. Very good. Tonight you will plan your first service for the Guild. As this contract was actively sought by the Guild, the fee is not great. Don't worry. The nominal fee of ten gold sen is a fraction of the price you can expect to receive for normal hits. The Guild will not expect you to do many such tasks without proper recompense.'

'I understand, Guildmaster. I'll do my best.'

'Good, Brother Wolf Spider. I'm sure you will. This is your target. Good luck.'

The Guildmaster handed Reynik a slip of parchment, turned and walked across the chamber to another alcove where he began talking softly with someone else. Reynik squinted at the parchment, but could not make out the writing in the dim light, so he got up and walked back out into the passageway that led to his quarters. There was a torch not far from the alcove door. Reynik stepped forward and held out the slip of parchment again.

'No!' he breathed, a choking feeling of horror constricting his throat and squeezing his heart until he could feel it pounding with panic. 'This can't be happening!'

He read the name over and over again, willing it to change. It did not. Written in clear letters across the sheet were the words 'Lutalo, Commander of the First Legion'. With all the recent assassinations of military Commanders there must have been a lot of postings. As far as Reynik knew there was only one Commander Lutalo. His first task for the Guild was to kill his own father.

CHAPTER THIRTEEN

'Oh, Shand! What do I do now?'

Reynik fought the urge to give in to panic. His instinct was to run, but he knew he could not do it. Where would he go? He was tied to the Guild for ever by the spider icon.

A sick feeling began in his stomach and spread throughout his body. It was like a droplet of dye falling into a glass of water, permeating through the liquid until the entire volume had changed colour. His mind raced. How could he have considered carrying out a hit for the Guild in order to maintain his cover? If a twist of fate was ever destined to bring someone to his senses, this must be it.

He knew he must warn his father. The question was – how? He could hardly walk into the middle of the Legion campsite and say 'Hi, Pa. Thought I should let you know I've sold my soul to the Guild of Assassins. Oh, and by the way, they've now commissioned me to kill you.' Or could he?

He looked again at the sheet of parchment. The First

Legion – he still technically belonged to the First Legion. After nearly a month of training to be an assassin, it was difficult to imagine going back to his old unit again. Despite his derision of that first thought, the idea of just walking in was actually not a bad one. If he were to be successful, however, he must first make sure that he threw off any followers that the Guildmaster might send after him. The best way to do this would be to take them by surprise.

The constriction in his chest receded as the sense of panic ebbed away. He had a plan. With a plan, life was suddenly less complicated again. Striding along the corridor to his quarters, he did not pause, but went straight to the transfer stone. The right hand side would take him closer to where the Legion were camped, but the left would take him closer to where he had his uniform stored. Being in uniform would make getting into the campsite easy.

He touched the spider talisman to the stone. The now familiar tingling sensation as the transfer began, followed by the unnerving sense of exploding and coalescing, was almost welcome. The uncomfortable wrench, followed by his emergence in the back alley, left him feeling cleansed of the taint of his quarters. He was out of the confines of the Guild complex, and engaged in an act to save, rather than to kill. It felt good.

Evening was already giving way to night. The shadows were deep, and the stiff breeze blowing through the alley could take the blame for any small noises he made. Flitting through the alleyway to the far end, he removed his cloak. With a series of quick, precise folds, Reynik transformed it into a neat bundle, and stuffed it behind an old broken window shutter. He ran his fingers through his hair several times to get rid of the residual feeling of the hood, then stepped out of the alley and onto the back street.

Reynik was determined not to stay still. By moving swiftly, he would make it difficult for the Guild's watchers to follow him undetected. Without his cloak, the breeze sliced through his clothing, but if all went well, he would not be in the open for long. He set off along the street, striding briskly across to the far side and around a corner to the left. Two hundred paces down this street on the left hand side there was a tavern.

It was too early for any except the hardened drinkers to be in the bar, but Reynik had no intention of staying. The warmth of the log fire was inviting, but he did not pause. He nodded to the innkeeper as he made a beeline for the back door. The innkeeper nodded back, clearly disappointed that Reynik was not going to stop to spend his coin at the bar.

'Later,' Reynik mouthed.

One of the lessons Femke had taught him was how to throw off pursuit by unwanted watchers. During his period of acclimatising to the transfer experience, Reynik had utilised some of his break time between transfers to explore the area around his two emergence sites and set up specific routes away from the area. These routes built in traps and changes of appearance designed to throw off shadows. Unknown to Cougar, he had not been going into the local inns and shops out of curiosity, but to make arrangements with the proprietors. One such arrangement he had established was with the innkeeper here.

As promised, on the cloak stand adjacent to the back door of the inn, there was a blue cloak on the back peg. Reynik took it, threw it around his shoulders, pulled the hood over his head and stepped out through the back door into another street. He continued to move at pace – not running, but walking at speed, weaving through alleys and back streets with a confidence in his step that gave fair warning he was no easy prey for thieves or cutthroats.

Femke had asked him to tell her if he was given a target by the Guild, but he did not feel he had time for this. If he were to give his father a chance to escape the long arm of the Guild, then he had to act now. The Guildmaster would not expect him to go straight to the Commander's tent without any scouting. This would give him an edge; not much of one, it was true, but any edge was a bonus.

Reynik had stored his uniform in the room he had been renting whilst in training. It was a fair distance in a straight path, but with all the added twists, it took Reynik over half an hour to reach the house. By the time he got there, he was convinced he had long since thrown off any pursuers.

It did not take more than a few minutes to change into his uniform. He was surprised how good it felt. It was like coming home after a long trip away – slightly strange, but comfortable and familiar at the same time. The leather belt and boots felt stiff, but he knew they would soften once he got moving again. He checked his sword for rust spots, but this was a part of his uniform he had not neglected while it had been out of use. He had only cleaned and sharpened the blade a few days ago, so when he drew it, he was pleased to see the metal was still in perfect condition.

Donning his cloak and helmet, Reynik stepped out into the streets again. Evening had given way to night now. The street lamps cast their dim glow over the cobbled streets, and dark figments lurked in every shadow. His skin prickled with the sense of being watched. He knew the chances of someone following him here were slight, given all the precautions he had taken, but this was not a time to be taking unnecessary chances.

On the way to the house, Reynik had drawn his cloak tight about him to shield his body from the chill wind. Now he was in uniform, he could feel his posture had changed. His pride in the status his Legionnaire's uniform carried made him straighten his limbs as he walked. He did not march, but walked taller – more upright. Despite wearing no more layers than before, he did not feel the cold as much. Anyone watching him would see nothing but a proud, young soldier – sword at his side, head held high.

Reynik took a straight route through Shandrim towards tent city. Every now and then, he doubled back on himself, or waited just around a corner to see if anyone were following him. By the time he got to the guard post at the edge of the military camp, he was convinced that his imagination was playing tricks on him. The guards' fire was burning brightly to the left of the road as Reynik approached. He was not surprised to see all but one guard standing around it.

The solitary guard at the camp entry point called for him to halt. Reynik did as he was told.

'What unit are you from?' the guard asked.

'First Legion.'

'Strange. The First Legion is all accounted for. The last of their patrols came back in an hour ago. Besides, orders are that no one is to walk the streets of Shandrim alone at the moment. What's your name and who's your File Leader? I'll need to report this.'

'I'm Legionnaire Reynik. File Leader Sidis leads my file, but I need to report directly to Commander Lutalo. I've been on a special mission. The report I have for him cannot wait. If you wish to have me escorted to his tent, that will be fine.'

'Reynik, is it? Well, Reynik, you will have your escort,' he promised, though his voice was not kind. 'Tam! Get over here. I need you to escort Legionnaire Reynik to see Commander Lutalo. Says he's been on a special mission. Make sure the Commander recognises him before you leave, will you?'

Tam muttered something unintelligible. Reynik caught the words 'bloody typical' and 'warm', so it was not difficult to gather the gist of his comment. The guard stomped over with no effort to hide his disgust at this assignment.

'Come on then,' he growled. 'Let's get this over with.'

'Sorry to drag you from the fire.'

'So you should be. Only just managed to get feeling back in my toes. Don't know why we bother mounting a guard here. Any intruder who wanted to get into the camp could enter at any one of a hundred points around the perimeter. No assassin would be stupid enough to choose to come in along the road.'

Reynik grinned. 'But having guard posts isn't all about keeping the bad guys out,' he said, unable to completely disregard the irony of his situation. 'It acts as a point of contact for members of the general public. It also demonstrates our commitment to security, even if it is not as effective as we would like. The random patrols are a more effective deterrent, I agree, but the guard post does serve a purpose.'

'Have you been taking loyalty pills, or something, Reynik? Give me a break!'

They walked through the camp in silence. Tam seemed determined to enjoy his bad mood, so Reynik let him sulk in peace. As they reached the edge of the First Legion's section of the huge tented area, Reynik's sense of anticipation heightened. He was back in familiar territory, though in reality, he had spent little time here. Between the mission to Thrandor and his current mission, he had spent more time away from the camp than in it.

The tent of the Legion Commander was no bigger than the File tents. The difference was that it only housed one person instead of ten. A pennant displaying the legion insignia fluttered in the strong breeze from a flagpole just to the right of the entrance to the Commander's tent. Reynik glanced up at it as they approached. It was impossible to make out the insignia in the darkness, but he did not need to see it to know its design: a golden helm with crossed swords. The emblem was very personal to Reynik. The right to belong to the Legion it represented had been hard won. It would be difficult to return now. Would he ever be able to? It was not easy to say.

The glow of an oil lamp shone through the canvas. Tam stepped forward to the entrance flap.

'Commander Lutalo. Sorry to disturb you, sir, but there's a Legionnaire Reynik here to see you. He claims it is important, sir.'

There was a momentary pause, then the tent flap was thrown open and Lutalo stepped out. He took one look at Reynik and his face broke into a broad smile.

'Reynik! It's good to see you. Come inside. I very much want to hear your report.'

'Thank you, sir,' he replied, nodding his thanks to Tam, who saluted Lutalo before turning and setting off back towards the gate. The Commander returned the salute, before ushering Reynik inside his tent. Once inside, Reynik was surprised when Lutalo caught him in a big hug.

'Where have you been, son? I was worried sick about you. Didn't you stop to think that I might want to know where you'd gone? I didn't dare tell your mother you'd disappeared off on some secret mission. She would have been frantic. I only found out you'd gone when I took over here after Sateris was murdered, but no one could tell me where you were.'

'It's a long story, Pa. It's also very complicated. There are things I must tell you that you won't want to hear, but I have no choice. The situation is spinning out of control. The Emperor did not fully realise what he was beginning when he declared the Guild of Assassins *anaethus drax*. We're both in terrible danger – you especially. Pa, you're going to have to leave the Legion for a while. If you don't, you'll be killed. The Guild have accepted a contact on you.'

Lutalo looked at his son with a penetrating gaze. He was silent for some seconds before he replied.

'I think you'd better sit down and tell me this story, Reynik. I want to know exactly what you've got yourself into. How do you know details about what the Guild of Assassins is planning?'

Reynik sat in the chair his father indicated, took off his helm, and in a hushed voice he began to speak. He relayed the whole story, complete with a brief account of what had occurred in Thrandor. Lutalo regarded his son intently throughout. When Reynik finished the story, his father sat back in his chair with a curious smile on his face.

'Son, what can I say? I'm incredibly proud of you. You'll make a fine commander one day. I always knew you had it in you, but now I'm doubly sure. Gen . . . *Emperor* Surabar has used you, Reynik, but in the long run it will put you in a strong position to advance your own cause.'

'If I survive long enough to use it,' Reynik commented with a bitter edge to his voice.

'Yes, son, that's often the big catch. But have faith. You're here. You're still alive. You have gained a lot of critical information that you must take to the Emperor. I suspect that with what you already have, you could break the Guild of Assassins if your insights are used to best effect.'

'Femke will have already taken the majority of the information to the Emperor. I managed to pass on the critical stuff earlier today.'

'Good. From what you've told me of this spy, I'm sure she'll give credit where credit is due. You've done well. I would not have had the stomach to do some of the tasks the Emperor set you. Killing in battle is something we're trained

259

to do. There are those amongst the Legions who go out of their way to look for trouble. They itch to try out their skills. I do not believe this to be the case with you. I can see the depth of your distaste for the assassin's trade, and I can only admire you for having followed through the Emperor's plan in spite of your feelings. Consider it ended, Reynik. You've done enough. You must go to the Emperor now. When the Guild realises that you've not carried out your task, they will look to track you down and kill you. Only the Emperor has the resources to protect you properly.'

'But what about you, Pa? They sent me to kill you. They'll send others. I've seen some of these people, Pa; they're deadly. They move more silently than the mist, and kill without compunction. Commander Sateris died in this very tent. You're not safe here.'

Reynik's father looked him in the eye.

'I know, son. I admit the knowledge has struck fear in my heart, but I cannot give in to fear. If I ran away, what message would that give to the troops? A Commander is a leader, Reynik. I know you understand. I must lead by example. However, I promise you that now I know for certain they're targeting me, I'll initiate a whole host of extra security measures around the camp. I will not let them get to me easily.'

In his heart, Reynik knew that no security measures would stop a top rank assassin. Someone like Shalidar would dance past patrols as if they did not exist. But it was also clear that his father's mind was made up. Pressing harder would only serve to anger him, and Reynik did not want to part from his father on a sour note. Instead, he got to his feet, caught his father in another hug and stepped back.

'Take care then, Pa. I'd better leave. I'll go straight to the Palace. Can you give me something with your seal on it to allow me out of the camp? The guards were insistent about no one allowed out on his own tonight.'

'No problem.' Lutalo went to his small table, took a piece of parchment and carefully inked a short message on it. He lit a candle and melted some wax, dripping a small pool of it onto the bottom of the sheet. Then he pressed his seal firmly into the wax. 'Good luck, son. No matter what happens, always remember I'm proud of you.'

Reynik smiled gratefully. The sickness that he still felt from having killed for the Emperor had receded a little. He knew it would never go away, but it felt good to have his father's blessing. He rolled the parchment, tucked it into a pocket on the inside of his cloak, replaced his helm on his head and saluted. Commander Lutalo saluted back.

Outside the tent, the temperature had dropped further. The stiff breeze added a chill factor that made the air feel positively icy. Reynik settled his cloak more evenly about his shoulders and did up one further clasp, fastening it together at his upper chest in addition to his throat. He took a moment to let his eyes adjust to the darkness, then set out along the main path through the campsite back towards the guard post. Behind him a shadowy figure stepped silently from where he had been eavesdropping in the deep shadow behind Lutalo's tent.

Shalidar had not been able to hear everything, but he had heard enough. Wolf Spider was the Commander's son – an interesting development. On its own, this information might have given the Guildmaster cause to excuse the newest Guild member from completing the kill. The Guildmaster had been known to show compassion in the past. However, Shalidar had heard the Commander exhort his son to go to the Emperor. The circle was complete. The link to the Emperor had been established. Shalidar knew he could act without fear of reprisal from the Guild. As an infiltrator, Wolf Spider had to be eliminated – quickly.

The assassin trailed his prey for about a minute to be sure his talk of going back past the guard post had not been a ruse, then he doubled back. Shalidar would get a fee for killing an infiltrator, but while he was here, he intended to earn the ten gold sen for the hit on the Commander as well.

As he re-approached Commander Lutalo's tent, Shalidar could see the commander's shadow. He was standing close to the nearest sidewall of the tent and verbally running through potential security measures he could instigate to make life difficult for assassins to penetrate the camp. Shalidar grinned. He did so love irony.

Since becoming the Dragon, Shalidar had killed many times, using many different weapons. He always preferred to make kills up close, so he could watch as the life left his victims. The sense of power he gained by taking another's life made him feel god-like. Yet he was not so power-struck as to ignore the opportunity for an easy kill. Silent as the shadow he cast, he drew his sword and stole up to the tent. With a thrill that bordered on ecstasy, he drove the blade through the canvas and through the Commander's body. Lutalo's voice stopped mid-word. Shalidar twisted the blade and wrenched it free.

The body fell with a lifeless thud, but the assassin did not wait to see if it would move again. He was already on the move. The father was dead. It was time to deal with the son.

Shalidar moved through the camp like a breath of wind – silent and invisible. His form melted into the darkness, submitting to its enveloping embrace and wrapping it around him like an extra layer of clothing.

He had thought he would catch up with Reynik before reaching the guard post, but his prey was moving faster than he had anticipated. As he approached, the young man was already talking to the guards. Shalidar paused for a moment in deep shadow. He knew where Wolf Spider would be heading. The young man would go straight to the Palace. He had promised his father as much.

The quickest way to the Imperial Palace was along the central street that ran right through this quarter of the city. Shalidar decided the best thing to do would be to intercept him further into the city, where his friends would not hear him if he were to call for help. It would not take much effort to get ahead of him. The only question remaining was how to make the kill. The uniform, with its protective elements, made a killing knife-throw from any distance less easy. No, he thought. It will be far more satisfying to kill him with the same blade that still runs with his father's blood. No military brat possesses enough skill with a blade to worry me. I'll run him through, as I did his father. There's a certain poetic feel to killing both in such a fashion.

Reynik had a few problems convincing the guards to let

him back out of the camp on his own. However, the parchment with the Commander's written authority was enough to see off the most stubborn objections. With admonitions to be careful ringing in his ears, he strode along the main street towards the city centre and the Imperial Palace.

He had walked no more than four hundred paces when a shadowy figure stepped out from a side street to his left and angled across the road towards him. Reynik's hand went instinctively to his sword hilt.

'Stop where you are! Come no closer, or I'll draw my sword. I have no wish to harm you,' he warned, his voice ringing out loud and clear.

'Sorry, young master, I didn't mean any harm. I was only goin' to ask if you'd a few coppers for an old veteran.'

The stranger's voice was querulous and pitched like that of an old man, but Reynik was suspicious. Anyone out on his own after dark in the city at the moment was potentially dangerous. Reynik was too on edge to allow strangers to get close without getting a close look at them first.

'Step into the light of that lamp. Let me see what you look like,' Reynik ordered, pointing at a lamp a little further down the street.

The shadowy figure put his hands out in front of him with his palms forward in a sign of peaceful intent. He sidestepped carefully until he was standing in the pool of light under the oil lamp. As far as Reynik could see, the man was an ordinary old man dressed in poor clothing. His cloak appeared torn in several places. From what Reynik could see, his other apparel was in a similar state.

'I'm sorry, friend. I didn't mean to appear hostile, but

264

despite all the patrols, the streets of Shandrim are not safe these days. I suggest you choose better lit areas to do your begging if you want to avoid getting hurt.'

'Good advice, young sir, but the streets in the richer parts of the city are run by villains who would be quick to kill me. They don't want people like me walking their areas. They only give one warning. If seen a second time, they dispose of those who trespass on their territory. What choice do I have? I'm too old to be of use to anyone. I was once a soldier like you, but I no longer own a sword. I have nowhere to live. I'm reliant on the charity of strangers. It's not much of a life.'

Reynik felt pity for the old beggar, but he was still wary. Keeping his eyes on the old man for any sign of foul play, Reynik fumbled in the dark to find some coins. When he had found some, he laid them down on a paving slab at the edge of the lit area and cautiously moved on, taking a wide line around the man standing under the street lamp.

'Bless you,' the man said. Then he suddenly yelled, 'Look out!'

Reynik had been so intent on the old man, he had not noticed another figure closing in on him from further down the street. The warning was timely. Reynik's sword cleared his scabbard in a flash and, by instinct, deflected the new stranger's blade several times. The ring of steel on steel sounded loud in the quiet evening street.

Forced back by the dark figure, Reynik moved into the dim pool of light given off by the street lamp. The stranger followed him, his sword constantly in motion.

'Leave him alone!' the old beggar yelled out, grabbing his

coins and staggering off down the street in a shuffling run. Over his shoulder he shouted again. 'He's doing no harm. Leave him alone.'

'Brother Dragon!' Reynik grunted, as he realised who he faced.

'Brother Wolf Spider,' Shalidar acknowledged in a rasping whisper as he whipped his blade around in a slashing stroke. Reynik barely deflected it. He could just see a sneering smile under the shadow of the assassin's hood.

'What are you doing? What of the bond of the Brotherhood? The creed? Why are you trying to kill me?'

Shalidar paused in his assault for a moment, his sword held poised. 'The Guild does not tolerate traitors to live, Reynik. You should have completed your mission this night. The Guild offered you a place in our family. A man cannot give allegiance to two families without creating a conflict of interests. As you're also working for the Emperor, you're doubly a traitor. I will enjoy telling the Guildmaster he was wrong about you, but I will gain even greater pleasure from collecting the fee that was to be yours. Now I must send you to join your father. The bounty for a traitor's head is sure to be substantial.'

Reynik's heart was sinking as Shalidar named him a traitor to the Guild. Had the assassin told anyone else? If Reynik could kill him, would he be safe to go back to the Guild headquarters? Then he froze as the import of the last few sentences sunk in. Shalidar had killed his father ... Shalidar had *killed* his father! The feeling in his stomach switched from cold, leaden dread to white-hot rage in the blink of an eye.

In those first few seconds it took a supreme effort of will to hold back from launching into a berserk attack. A combination of his military training and his lessons with Serrius saved him. The gladiator's words in particular flashed back into his head.

'Never fight angry; I allowed my opponent in the arena to get me angry and look what happened.' Reynik had seen Serrius' scars before, but the visual impact of the entry and exit scars where the gladiator had been run through had lost none of their value. 'Peace and balance must be at the centre of your being, or you will lose awareness and poise. Be at peace. Focus. Control your breathing. Allow your balance and speed to be your strength.'

Somehow, Reynik clamped down on his anger. He was not in a mental state of peace and balance, but he kept his emotions under control as Shalidar attacked again. The assassin was a master swordsman, but he was expecting an opponent with little more than a basic military training to draw on. It took a moment, but Shalidar soon realised that this was no ordinary young soldier.

Reynik met Shalidar's attack with flowing strokes and fine balance. There was no woodenness about the way he handled a sword. The drills that the Legions favoured in developing fighters who could work together in lines without maiming the person next to them were not in evidence. Reynik held his ground, matching the assassin stroke for stroke, and countering with some elegant blade work of his own.

The ringing tones of the two blades meeting in rapid sequences sang loud, echoing down the street. Sparks flashed from the blades with each impact. Reynik could see that Shalidar was superior in skill and technique, but what he lacked in skill, Reynik made up for with speed and fitness. After an extended exchange of blows with neither protagonist breaking through the other's defence, Reynik began taunting the assassin in an attempt to provoke him.

'What's the matter, Shalidar? Lost your touch? You've got slack, that's what it is. You're so used to stabbing people in the back that you've lost your edge.'

Shalidar ignored him. He knew exactly what Reynik was trying to do. It would not work. He began to circle his opponent, stalking him like a big cat. Reynik, too, began to circle, keeping up a string of taunts.

Leaping in close, Reynik suddenly took the fight to Shalidar. There was another clashing exchange, as Reynik drove forward with a vicious sequence of strokes, but Shalidar met every swing with a solid defence. Reynik sprang back, but his assailant followed, catching him momentarily off balance.

Shalidar's blade flashed at Reynik's neck. Somehow, Reynik blocked it, but the follow up stroke was just too fast for him and it impacted his chest plate. He was lucky that the blow was a sweeping one, rather than a lunge, or his light armour would not have saved him. However, as he was already moving backwards, the strike on his chest armour was enough to overbalance him. He fell, deflecting another stroke even whilst in the air. The impact with the cobbled street was painful, and his helmet came loose, spinning off across the stones with a noisy clatter.

The assassin's blade speared down towards Reynik in a

killer lunge. Somehow, with a twist of his body and an inspired parry, Reynik turned the blade aside and the point struck the cobbles a hair's breadth from his body. Shalidar had been forced to come in close to make the lunge – too close. With another mighty twist, Reynik kicked Shalidar's legs out from under his body, dumping him on the cobbles in a fall that was every bit as hard as Reynik's.

Both men scrambled to their feet. Another sound intruded: the sound of running feet – booted feet. A formation of Legionnaires was running along the street towards them, swords already drawn.

Shalidar did not hesitate. He turned and ran. Reynik went after him. The assassin was fast and silent. When he turned off the main road into a side alley, Reynik skidded to a halt. It was one thing to chase Shalidar up a lit road, but quite another to try to follow him into the shadows. He had no choice. He would have to let the assassin go.

'I'll get you next time, Shalidar!' he called.

There was no response. He was gone. The Legionnaires were closing. He could not afford to waste time explaining himself to every File Leader who thought they should know what was going on. He had to get to the Palace quickly. If Femke were to get into the Guild headquarters, it would have to be done quickly, before the Guildmaster thought to set a watch on his room. Reynik turned and ran on up the main road.

'You there! Legionnaire! Halt!'

Reynik did not waste his breath by responding. He took the next available alleyway on the opposite side of the street and disappeared into the night.

CHAPTER FOURTEEN

Reynik gave the password to the guard at the servants' entrance to the Imperial Palace. He was waved through without question. The guard knew better than to question someone who knew that particular password.

Reynik had called at the safe house where Femke had last been staying. It was empty. If Femke was still using it, then she was not at home this evening. Reynik knew there was a chance she could be here in the Palace, but it was a long shot. It was more likely she would be out in the city on a mission.

There was no time to search for her, or to wait until she returned home. Reynik needed help. He needed to talk to the Emperor. Surabar would know what to do next. He had been a military General for years. It was his plan to begin with. He would not have committed them to it without having thought through some contingencies. Of course it was probable this was not a situation he had ever considered. After all, what were the chances of his infiltrating the Guild, getting found out, but then escaping with his life? It was not a sequence of events he would have anticipated.

Racing through the corridors and up the stairs, Reynik approached the Emperor's study. He was not surprised to see light flickering in the high windows that opened onto the corridor. Good, he thought, at least the Emperor is in.

He approached the guard at the door. 'Legionnaire Reynik to see the Emperor,' he announced. The guard looked suspicious.

'Password?'

Reynik gave his password and the guard nodded. 'Very well,' he said. 'Wait here just a moment.' The man knocked on the study door and disappeared. He reappeared very quickly. 'The Emperor will see you now.'

'Thanks.'

Reynik stepped inside. He had hoped that Femke might be in the office already, but the Emperor was alone. He marched smartly forward and stopped with his posture firmly at 'attention'. He saluted and the Emperor smiled.

'At ease, Reynik. It's good to see you've not forgotten all your military training. Now, why are you here? Femke told me earlier that you'd successfully infiltrated the Guild. Have you discovered the location of their headquarters? If not then you've taken a great risk by coming here.'

'No, your Majesty. I've learned nothing new. I'm here because I have a problem. My cover has been blown. Shalidar tried to kill me not half an hour ago. The Guild-master set me a hit, but it was not one that I could carry out. I'm sorry, your Majesty, but I've failed. They asked me to kill Commander Lutalo. I could never do that. Commander Lutalo is my father.'

'You are Lutalo's son? I didn't realise that, but I can see the likeness now.' The Emperor got out of his chair and paced across the room with his right forefinger poised thoughtfully at his lips. 'Did they realise, do you think? Did the Guildmaster know of the relationship before he set you the task?'

'It's possible, your Majesty, but unlikely. I've tried to keep that fact quiet to prevent any talk of favouritism amongst the other men. I don't know how, your Majesty, but despite taking lots of precautions against being followed, Shalidar stayed on my tail and witnessed a conversation between my father and me. We talked about what I was doing. I know I shouldn't have done it, but I couldn't lie to my father. In talking openly, I inadvertently compromised the position we risked so much to attain.'

The Emperor paused in his pacing for a moment and looked at Reynik with his most piercing gaze. 'Don't judge yourself too harshly, young man. Anyone who would kill his own father in cold blood to complete a mission would not hold a shred of human decency in his body. It's a shame that you went to Lutalo first rather than coming here, but the outcome would probably have been similar. Your going to him is perfectly understandable. The question remains – what can we salvage out of this? Have you any clues yet as to who the Guildmaster is? If we knew who we were fighting, it would make anticipating his next move more feasible.'

'All I can tell you is that he's not a young man, your Majesty. The timbre of his voice and his bearing both suggest an older man. I would place him between fifty-five and seventy years old. His speech is cultured and clearly intonated, like that of the Nobility. He speaks as one who is well educated. He is of medium build and height. It's not much of a description, I know, but aside from these things, there is nothing I can tell you.'

'Hmm! If the Guildmaster is a Nobleman, then he's not one of the old-school Lords. If he were then the Guild would have made a concerted effort to kill me.'

'The creed prevents them from killing you, your Majesty. They are not allowed to do anything that might cause the destruction of the Empire.'

Surabar gave him a twisted smile. 'Ah, but it does, Reynik. It's all in the interpretation. I'm aware of the creed, but you see in the eyes of the old-school Lords, having a commoner for an Emperor is the beginning of the end for the Empire. They view my removal as essential to the Empire's survival. Therefore, by killing me, they would be saving the Empire from destruction. I think we can safely rule out the idea that the Guildmaster is one of the old-school ranks, or I'd be wading knee deep in assassins by now.'

'Well, your Majesty, maybe Femke would be able to find out more. It's very risky, but I could still get her inside the headquarters. If we're going to attempt it, then it's now or never. She must be in place before a watch is set on my rooms. Do you know where she is?'

'Yes, she's here in the Palace. We had a meeting about half an hour ago. She has a room here. Do you know where it is?'

'Yes, your Majesty. I know it. What are your orders? Should I attempt to get Femke inside the Guild, or is the risk too great?'

The Emperor's brow furrowed as he considered his response. It was a difficult choice. Femke was such an effective spy that he was reluctant to send her on so dangerous a mission. The chance of success was very small, but if anyone could find out the identity of the Guildmaster and the location of the Guild, then it would be Femke. His mind ran in circles, which was unusual for one used to making life and death decisions. He was torn. Was it worth the gamble? She was his most reliable source of information. Was the potential reward worth spending the life of his most valuable spy?

'Go,' he said, his face serious. 'Get Femke and get her inside the Guild. But, Reynik . . .' he added, as Reynik instantly saluted and turned for the door. Reynik stopped and looked back.

'Yes, your Majesty?'

'Try to bring her back in one piece, would you? She's a damned good spy. I don't have many like her.'

Reynik grinned. 'Don't worry, your Majesty. Femke is one very capable young lady, but I'll do my best to help her in any way I can.'

It was not far to Femke's room. Reynik knocked at her door and it opened instantly. It was as if she had been standing on the other side waiting for him. His heart skipped as she smiled at him. She was still wearing the nondescript street clothing he had seen her in earlier, but she looked lovely no matter how she dressed. His mind rebelled at the idea of placing her in such dire danger, but he had no choice.

'Femke, the Emperor wants me to get you inside the Guild. We have to go now. The Guild knows I'm an impostor. Shalidar tried to kill me not more than an hour ago. If I'm going to get you inside, then we need to go before Shalidar has a chance to organise the Guild into setting a watch on my rooms. I suggest you wear something dark. Nowhere in the Guild headquarters is brightly lit.'

'Just give me a moment,' Femke replied, catching the urgency in his voice. 'Come in. Take a seat. I'll only be a few seconds.'

Reynik stepped through the door and closed it behind him. Femke's room was quite large, but there was no private dressing area. To Reynik's acute embarrassment, when he turned around again he realised that she was already throwing off her clothing as she walked swiftly over to her large wardrobe cupboard. Colour flushed his cheeks as he made a determined effort to look away. Femke talked as she rummaged through her wardrobe, pulling out a selection of dark clothing.

'How did they find out? Were we seen in the marketplace earlier?'

'No. Well, I don't think so, anyway. I was given a hit this afternoon. By chance, or design – I'm not sure which – the Guildmaster tasked me with killing my father. There was no question of my doing it. Unfortunately, despite all my precautions, Shalidar managed to follow me. He overheard me warning my father that he'd become a target. Shalidar . . .' Reynik choked, unable to continue.

'What is it, Reynik? What's the matter?'

Femke walked across to him and placed a comforting hand on his shoulder. Reynik looked up gratefully, but instantly lowered his eyes again as he realised Femke was not yet wearing much clothing. A tear rolled down his cheek.

'Shalidar killed him after I left,' he stammered.

'Oh, Reynik, I'm so sorry.' Femke gave him a quick hug, but was not blind to his embarrassment. It was clearly not the time to tease him for his prudishness. She stepped away and threw on her change of clothes. True to her word, she was dressed again within a very short time. 'Come on. I'm ready,' she said, catching his hands up from his knees and pulling him to his feet. She hugged him properly this time. 'Let's crack open the Guild and see that Shalidar gets his just reward,' she whispered in his ear. 'You've done a great job, Reynik. Now it's my turn. Lead the way.'

Reynik's heart was pounding in his chest. How could he take her to the Guild headquarters? If she were killed there, he knew he would never forgive himself. But he had no choice. If they were to succeed, someone must get the information they needed. He could not deny that Femke was the person best qualified to get it.

Reluctantly, he eased away from her and met her gaze. Did she realise how he felt about her? Would she have hugged him like that if she did? All the feelings bottled up inside him ebbed, building with a pressure that threatened to explode out like a flash flood. Somehow he contained them. The only leakage from his well of emotion was the visible tear tracks still staining his cheeks. Reynik did not move as Femke gently reached up and wiped them away with the back of her finger.

'Don't give up, Reynik. It'll all work out in the end. Trust me. Come on, let's go.'

Reynik could not find words to answer her. Instead he nodded. A quick visit to the Palace stores resulted in Reynik changing his apparel for dark clothing similar to that Femke had chosen. Like silent shadows, the two figures dressed in black slipped into the corridor, through the Palace and out into the night.

'Wolf Spider's an impostor – a spy sent to scout us out. He's one of the Emperor's men.'

'Really? You have proof of this?' The Guildmaster's voice was full of scepticism.

'I followed him to Lutalo's tent and listened in on his conversation. He admitted a lot of things to Lutalo about what he'd been doing. I heard it all. It appears that Brother Wolf Spider is a serving member of the First Legion. More importantly, though, Lutalo is his father. Did you know of their family ties, Guildmaster? Was the hit designed to test his loyalty?'

Shalidar's unspoken implication was clear. If the Guildmaster had known of the relationship, then the test was a harsh one. Shalidar doubted many of those in the Guild would have fulfilled such a contract. There were a few amongst their number who might have made the hit if the fee were high enough, but they would be the exceptions rather than the rule.

'No, I didn't know of the relationship. However, it

277

appears chance has worked in our favour, Brother Dragon. My unwitting choice of target exposed a most convincing infiltrator. It's strange. Even with your testimony I still find it hard to believe Surabar would order the deaths of Kempten and Lacedian in order to get someone inside the Guild. If such hypocrisy were made common knowledge, then he would be discredited as a ruler. No one would ever trust him again. The bizarre thing is that his reputation is so spotless few would believe it even if we were to release such information. I wouldn't put it past the canny old fox to have relied on this when he sent the lad on the mission in the first place. I knew Surabar was a wily General, but I had no idea he was this ruthless. You know, I think I'm beginning to like him!'

Shalidar looked up sharply at the Guildmaster's admission. The old man was leaning on the front gate of Shalidar's booth. Even in the dim light, the assassin could just make out a hint of a smile under the Guildmaster's hood.

'What would you have me do, Guildmaster?'

'Kill the boy, of course. Brother Wolf Spider must not be allowed to live one second longer than necessary. He has seen the inner sanctuary. His treachery to the Guild must be punished. I will send Brothers out to watch his transfer points on a rota until he is found and killed. I'll also set a watch on his rooms in case he somehow gets past the outer defence. You're to track him down and kill him. I shall send Brothers Viper and Bear out on a similar mission—'

'That won't be necessary, Guildmaster. I can handle Wolf Spider,' Shalidar interrupted.

'I'm sure you can, Brother Dragon. Nevertheless, I'll send them to make sure. Whoever gets to him first will collect the fee. At least with a bit of healthy competition you should remain focused. I know how easy it is for some of you Brothers to get distracted by lucrative side ventures. Don't. The Guild will pay double the normal traitor kill fee to ensure your concentration does not wander.'

'Double! Yes, Guildmaster. I'm on my way.'

'Good. You can be sure that Viper and Bear will be hard on your heels. I'm going to see them right now.'

'OK, Femke, this is it. Once we touch the talisman to that stone over there we will be transferred to my living room in the Guild complex. It looks like we're in time. I can't see any watchers, can you?'

Femke shook her head. They had scouted the alleyway without seeing any sign of danger. If someone was watching, he was well hidden and most likely freezing. The temperature had plummeted during the last hour. Frozen air driven straight from the Vortaff region gave the wind a vicious bite. Femke's face felt as if a thousand needles were pricking it, and her fingertips were numb with cold. Nobody could stay still for long in these conditions, she decided. The alley must be clear.

'Remember, the disorientation will last a while. I'll carry you through to the bedroom and leave you under the bed. Stay put until you feel fully recovered from the effects of the transfer. I'll try to cause a diversion. With any luck, it will give you a chance to look around before I come back for you. You'll have two hours – no more. Find out what you can in that time and then get back to my room. Happy?'

'Ecstatic!' she said with a forced grin, trying not to think about what she would do if Reynik could not get back.

'Right, let's go then,' he said decisively, rising from where they were crouched together in the shadows.

'Wait!'

'What is it?' he asked, ducking down again.

Femke leaned forward and kissed him firmly on the lips. 'For luck,' she whispered. Reynik looked dumbstruck. Shand but you're stupid sometimes, Femke, she cursed silently. You want him to be clear-headed, sharp and focused, so why confuse him with unneeded emotion now? Did you learn nothing in Mantor? Have you lost your mind? Allowing feelings for Danar to develop had been a mistake. This could be worse.

To his credit, Reynik was quick to recover his outer poise. Femke was relieved, but knew she had not helped their cause.

'Thanks,' he muttered, giving her a forced smile. 'Come on, we mustn't delay any longer. The Guildmaster is no fool. Shalidar's information will provoke a rapid response. Let's go.'

Reynik grabbed her hand and they both ran forward to the transfer stone. To Femke it looked little different from the other stones around it, save for eight small indentations in its surface. Reynik drew out the silver talisman with his left hand and put his right arm around her waist.

'Hold the talisman with me,' he instructed. She did as he asked. Together they touched the spider to the stone.

Reynik had described the transfer to her, but though he had tried to convey the sensations she would experience, the reality was mind-blowing. For a moment it felt as if the wind had whipped her inside a tornado, spinning her so fast that she lost all sense of position. Femke felt dizzy and sick. Was Reynik still with her? She could no longer feel his arm.

Tiny stars danced around her as if she had somehow grown whilst the universe had shrunk so much that she dominated the heavens. She felt god-like in proportion. Then came the explosion. Reynik had told her what to expect, but nothing could have prepared her for the feeling of exploding into a million tiny particles, smaller than the swirling motes that surrounded her.

The coalescence was every bit as disorienting as Reynik had predicted. Femke sensed rather than felt him catch her weight as they re-materialised in the underground chamber. Despite her best efforts at maintaining consciousness, Femke's mind could not cope. When she surfaced again, she had vague recollections of being carried. There had been shouting and the sound of running feet. Had it been real, or a dream?

Femke opened her eyes. It was dark. The air felt strange – close. She tried to lift her hand to her face, but it impacted something wooden just a few inches above her body. Of course! The bed, she realised. Reynik had done it. She was under his bed.

The stone floor had sapped much of the heat from her back. Her bottom, her upper back and the back of her shoulders felt numb. How long had she been here, though?

There was no way of telling. Time was of the essence. She had no idea how long she had before Reynik was due to come back. For all she knew he could be due back any moment, or worse, he could be overdue. All she could do was to explore the complex as swiftly as possible. She would learn what she could and then return here in the hope that Reynik would make it back.

Easing herself inch by inch sideways, Femke edged her body silently out from under the bed on elbows and heels. All was silent – silent and dark. Moving slowly, Femke first sat up and then struggled to her feet. She took a moment to massage blood back into her posterior. The restoration of blood flow brought pain, but it was a wholesome pain, tinged with the relief of a return to normal. She flexed her thighs. They felt perfectly normal.

There was no time to dwell on discomforts any further. She had to get moving. A doorway was visible in the darkness. Light was spilling around the edge of the door. She crept soundlessly across the room towards it and listened. She could hear nothing. If someone were in the adjoining room, then he was remaining very still. Femke waited at the door for at least two minutes, straining her ears for any sense of movement or sound on the other side. Still nothing.

Reaching down, she drew a throwing knife from the holster at the top of her boot. Then, in one smooth, silent motion she opened the door and dived through it, tucking into a silent roll. Her acrobatic manoeuvre brought her back to her feet. She scanned the room. Nobody was there. The flickering light from three torches filled the living room.

She took a moment to absorb a few details. The first thing she noticed was the predominance of spider imagery. She shuddered. Spiders had never been among her favourite creatures.

Femke noted the lines of books, the richness of the furniture and the spider motif emblem over the onward doorway. Her eye was caught by the stonework around the door arch.

The chambers had been carved from solid rock, but someone had clearly then tidied up the shape of the rooms by building in standard shaped doorways using cut stone. Whoever had made this doorway was a master craftsman. Femke looked back at the doorway to the bedroom. It had been made to a similarly high standard. There was something familiar about the way in which the stones had been fitted together around the doorframe that niggled at her memory. She had seen masonry work like this somewhere before . . . but where?

Whatever the answer, it was not ready to leap straight to the forefront of her mind. She took a close look at the doorway to memorise the pattern in which the stones had been fitted, then she moved on. The door out from the living chamber was already open. Again there was nobody outside. Whatever Reynik had done appeared to have drawn all attention from his rooms. She pushed forward as fast as she dared, slipping along the corridor, ghostlike in her silence.

At the end of the corridor was the doorway into the central chamber. Femke slipped into the shadow-filled stall that looked out into the meeting place of the Guild. As she entered, she heard someone else entering through another of the stalls. Ducking down as low as she could, she crawled forwards and crouched in the forward right hand corner of the little booth. Footsteps approached. Was it one set, or two? It was difficult to tell.

'I'd rather be out hunting him, Guildmaster, but I'll take the first watch. Sadly, I can't see him being foolish enough to return here again. I'd like to have been the one to nail him. To be honest, I'm surprised he came back at all once he knew his disguise had been compromised. I can't imagine what was so valuable that he felt he had to retrieve it. Fox is taking over from me? Good.'

Femke listened to the man's voice as he approached. It was not Shalidar. She would have known his rasping tones anywhere. It was clear the second set of steps she could hear was the Guildmaster's. She silently prayed that he would speak so she would get a chance to hear the voice of the man whose identity the Emperor wanted so badly. It was not to be.

A hand appeared over the gate at the front of the stall. Femke shrank back as far as she could into the corner. The man opened the latch and swung open the gate. It opened towards her, shielding her further from the man's sight. He stepped into the booth and allowed the gate to swing shut behind him. As the gate swung shut, she could see the tall figure of the assassin in the dim light. For a second she thought he would see her, but he turned and exited through the back of the booth.

Femke released her breath in a silent sigh of relief. The quiet retreating footsteps of the Guildmaster were audible, so she risked a peek over the rail of the booth. A figure in black was near the central podium. Even as she looked at him, he started to turn back towards her. She ducked back down, wondering why he was turning back. Had he forgotten to tell the other assassin something? Had he somehow sensed her presence?

She waited silently for a few moments, but there was no sound of returning footsteps. After about a minute Femke decided to risk another peep over the rail. When she did, she found the central chamber empty. Curious, she thought. Where had the Guildmaster gone? She had not heard him leave the chamber, yet his footsteps had been clearly audible when he walked across the chamber to the centre. Did he have a transfer stone there somewhere? She decided to find out.

With one final look around the chamber to make sure it was clear, she slid over the gate and crept across to the pulpit-like structure in the centre. When she reached it, she noticed the black hole in the floor. Walking closer, she realised that it was not a hole but a steep, descending spiral staircase. That was why the Guildmaster had turned towards her. He had to in order to step down onto the first step. It was good to find that this disappearance was not magical in nature.

Did she dare go down? Reynik had told her the assassins all had chambers that were accessed through their relative booths. By the same token, it seemed likely that this stair-well led to the Guildmaster's private quarters. If this were the case, then he was unlikely to be surrounded by guards. After all, this was a very secret headquarters with a unique entry and exit control system. She decided to risk it.

As soon as Femke put her foot onto the first stair, she realised why she had not heard the Guildmaster descend out of the chamber. The stair had a small triangle of carpet attached over the central part of the step. The next was the same. She grinned. No doubt this was useful to the Guildmaster when he wanted to make a silent entrance. Used in reverse, it would allow her to descend without worrying about him hearing her approach.

With her knife held firmly in her right hand, she stepped down into the darkness. After half a dozen steps, she discovered a handrail to her left, which allowed her to steady herself with her left hand, whilst still keeping her blade out in front.

The staircase was narrow and steep, but the stairs were flat and well cut. After roughly two full spirals in total darkness, a dim light shone up from below. Step by step, she continued to descend, crouching down and leaning forward so that she could see as far ahead around the spiral as possible. The bottom of the stairwell came into view. Femke stopped to listen for signs of movement. To her horror, the sounds she did hear were not coming from below, but above. Someone was coming down the steps behind her, and he was not far above.

There was no time for caution. She fled silently down the last few steps and found herself half-way along a lit corridor. Left or right? It had to be an instant decision. She opted to run right, sprinting forwards silently on her toes, her heart hammering in her chest. A little way along the corridor there was a recessed door on the right. She ducked into the recess and pressed her body back against the door.

Her every muscle was taut. Despite the adrenalin and the after effects of the sudden sprint, she held her breath to listen. At first all she could hear was her heart pumping. Then she could no longer hold her breath against her straining need for air. Slowly – ever so slowly – she exhaled and drew in another lungful. Relief. The quiet sounds of retreating footsteps were as music to her ears, giving her leave to begin breathing more normally again.

Femke decided to risk a quick look along the corridor. The retreating figure was dressed in a set of brown robes. Must be a servant, she thought. Was this the servants' level? That didn't make sense. Why would the entrance to the servants' level be in the middle of the assassins' meeting chamber? No, it was more likely that the servant was on his way to do something for the Guildmaster. With a little luck she might discover where he was. If she could just steal a look at the Guildmaster's face, she would know if Reynik's assertion that he was a member of the Nobility was correct. Femke knew all members of the Nobility, major and minor, by face and name. It was required knowledge for one in her profession.

The servant went all the way to the far end of the corridor and knocked on the door there. He must have received a response, for he entered. Femke wasted no time. She raced out from her hiding place and down the corridor to listen at the door. There were sounds of movement within, but no talking. Come on, come on, she urged silently. Say something!

'Will you be wanting your meal soon, Guildmaster?'

There was a pause. Femke's anticipation reached fever pitch.

'Thank you, Jurre, that would be wonderful. What's on the menu today?'

Femke's jaw dropped and her heart sank into the pit of her stomach. For a moment the urge to scream 'Traitor!' was overwhelming. There was no longer any need to see the Guildmaster's face. She would know that voice anywhere.

CHAPTER FIFTEEN

Reynik took Femke's weight as she slumped. He was ready for it. Had she come through that first transfer without passing out, he would have felt most inadequate. There were so many things that Femke was good at, he was pleased to see that she reacted to this situation in the same way he had. He was ready to drop her if there were anyone present in the room, but all was quiet. It seemed the Guild had not yet set a watch on his quarters. He doubted they had long before someone thought of it.

Dipping to sweep up her legs, he lifted Femke into his arms and carried her through to the bedroom. She was completely out cold. He guessed it would take a good few minutes for her to come around. He could not afford to wait that long. It would be better if he created a diversion to draw attention away from his rooms and out into the streets of the city. Then, when Femke awoke, she should stand a chance of looking around the complex without having to wade through a line of assassins to do it.

Gently, he lowered her to the floor. For a moment his eyes lingered on her peaceful face. Her lips looked soft and inviting. The temptation to lean down and brush his lips against them was huge. Why had she kissed him? Did she feel something for him after all? He had assumed she was only friendly because they were working together. Did it go further than that? Had she begun to feel a romantic bond?

It was not easy to slide her under the bed. In the end he had to be quite forceful. He tried to be careful of her damaged ribs, but it was not easy to find other suitable areas to push on. If she suffered bruising as a result of his rough handling, he would find it hard to forgive himself – especially after that kiss.

'Snap out of it, you idiot!' he chided himself, in a whispered growl. 'Grow up and concentrate. This is no time to be thinking about such things.'

He pulled the blankets down so they hung to the floor on the near side of the bed. No one would see Femke now unless the room was searched with purpose.

A noise drew his attention back to the door. Someone was coming. He had to get out fast. He ran to the door. Voices were approaching the door on the other side of the room. Reynik decided to make a run for the transfer stone. It was not far, but the door on the other side of the room opened at the same time as he broke into a run across the room. It was the Guildmaster and one of the other assassins. He did not know which one. Whoever it was reacted very quickly.

Ripping the spider talisman from its leather cord, Reynik

dived for the transfer stone at the same time as the assassin drew and threw a knife. Out of the corner of his eye, Reynik saw the spinning blade cutting through the air towards him even as his hand stretched out with the talisman. He gritted his teeth as he waited for the blade to bite, but the anticipated pain never came.

The spider talisman made contact with the transfer stone and initiated the magical translocation. Reynik could have sworn afterwards that he felt the blade pass through his body, but it was most likely his imagination.

As he entered the translocation in a dive, so he exited it, complete with all of his initial momentum. This made him doubly fortunate. He emerged in his flat out dive, crashing to the ground in a most ungainly fashion. As he did so, however, a crossbow bolt smashed into the wall where he would have been standing. Whoever had fired the bolt had not waited for the telltale sparkling lights to finish coalescing before loosing the shot.

Reynik scrambled to his feet and started running. The watcher must have arrived only moments after Reynik and Femke had made their transfer into his quarters. In a bizarre flashback he suddenly recalled something his father had told him years before.

'*There are times when it's better to be lucky than good, son.*'

How right he had been!

It would take the archer a few moments to reload his crossbow. Reynik did not intend to be within range by that time. He sprinted out of the alleyway and into the side street. On instinct he turned right. If he were to fight for his life, then he would do it in the heart of Shandrim. There

291

would be regular patrols of Legionnaires and militia there. If his luck held, they might prove useful.

'Go! Wolf Spider transferred to his shared stone. If you're quick, you'll get there hard on his heels.'

'Yes, Guildmaster,' Cougar replied, but he hesitated as he reached the door. 'But what about the watcher? He has orders to shoot any that emerge there.'

'Duck. If you're lucky, Firedrake will have enough sense to realise that it would be impossible for Wolf Spider to materialise twice in quick succession.'

'Yes, Guildmaster,' he responded through gritted teeth. 'And guarding the rooms here?'

'I'll fetch someone else to do that. Young Wolf Spider won't come back in a hurry. He knows we'll be waiting for him if he does. Go!'

Cougar left at a run. 'If Firedrake hasn't been distracted along the way, the spy should be dead already,' the Guildmaster muttered to himself. 'Well, young Reynik, if that really is your name,' he added, addressing the transfer stone as if his words could somehow bridge the magical gap between them, 'you seem to have a knack for getting out of tight spots. Therefore I suppose it shows prudence to make sure. Firedrake's waiting for you at the exit point, Cougar's on his way there, and Dragon, Viper and Bear are all out in the city looking for you. You won't last long. One of them will collect the price on your head. They always do.'

Reynik raced to the nearest tavern and burst in through the door. People all around the crowded bar room looked round at the sound of his explosive entrance. The sound level dropped noticeably for a few seconds as he instinctively paused in the doorway, panting, then rose again to a higher volume as people either returned to their conversations or fell to speculating on the reason for the young man's abrupt arrival. He assessed the room in a second and pushed forward, weaving his way through the people and tables, apologising at every other step but not slowing.

When he reached the back door, he rummaged amongst the weapons in the large rack to the left of the exit. Bows, swords, staves and belt knives were stowed here as a matter of policy. The Landlord was very strict about it. Anyone found in the main bar area carrying a weapon about his person was instantly banned. The no tolerance policy had served him well over the years, for damages and visits by the militia had been kept to a minimum.

'Got you!' Reynik uttered with a triumphant note in his voice. He drew out a staff from the rack that end to end was about a hand span longer than he was tall. There was a sword of his in the rack as well, but he was reluctant to take it, as it was hard to run fast with a sword strapped to your side whilst also carrying a staff. After a few seconds of inner debate, he decided to sacrifice speed for weaponry.

From a cupboard to the right of the door, he drew out a mail shirt and leather jerkin. As he had decided to forfeit fleetness, it would be as well to protect his body as best he could. He was so glad now that he had thought to pre-place so many useful items in public locations. The mail would offer some protection against thrown and thrusting weapons, though it would not save him from a well-aimed crossbow bolt.

He threw off his cloak and slipped on the tunic. There was no time for fancy lacing. He ran the laces through a couple of the holes and tied them off. The mail shirt went over the top, followed by a bright blue cloak from a nearby peg and he was off again – out into the night and away from the vicinity of his transfer stone.

The narrow street with its dim oil lanterns and crooked overhanging houses felt hostile. Menacing shadows loomed everywhere. The hairs on the back of Reynik's neck prickled with nervous fear. The road was pocked with potholes and missing cobbles. A dangerous surface for running in such dim light, Reynik thought grimly. Well, he was not about to run again just yet. Running would only draw attention. Let the assassins get in close to properly identify him before attacking. Armed as he was now, he felt a lot more comfortable about confronting members of the Guild at close quarters.

Heading in towards the city centre, Reynik walked with an air of purpose. He did not rush, but lengthened his stride to cover ground at a good pace. He had not gone far before the first assassin caught up with him.

There was no warning. The first awareness Reynik had of his assailant was a knife striking him square in the middle of the back. With the protection of the chain mail and the leather, it felt as if someone had punched him hard. He stumbled forward as the blade fell harmlessly to the ground and skittered across the cobbles.

Firedrake was already moving forwards, knowing in the

moment he released his blade that the throw was good. His move was premature. Had he remained in the shadows, he would have been able to make another throw before being seen. Reynik picked him out instantly. With his balance quickly restored, he moved to intercept.

'Damn you! You have more lives than a cat!' the assassin grumbled, drawing his sword. 'Come on then, traitor. You've used your last. It's time to die.'

From the way Firedrake approached, Reynik could see he had never fought against someone armed with a staff before – at least no one competent. His confidence rose a little. It was tempting to say something, but he knew it was better to remain silent. This was no time for taunting or gloating. Finish it quickly and get away, he thought.

The assassin swung his sword hard and fast. Reynik deflected it easily and jabbed the end of the staff hard into the man's stomach. The blow deflated him, all the air rushing from his lungs in a single whoosh of expelled air. Reynik followed up by stepping back and whirling the staff around such that the other end struck his foe a mighty rap on the left temple. He fell like a pole-axed cow. Reynik hit him once more on the head for good measure.

He knew it would be in his best interests to draw his sword and finish the man off. For a moment he considered it. Then he dismissed the thought. Killing Lacedian in cold blood had tainted him in a way he did not want to repeat. He did not want another life on his conscience – even that of an assassin.

As he turned to walk away, Reynik caught a slight movement out of the corner of his eye. Someone else was moving stealthily down the street towards him. There was little doubt it was another Guild member, for he was hugging the shadows and moving fast. Another one already, he thought, horrified. How were they finding him so quickly? Were the streets crawling with killers?

Knowing there was another assassin who had latched onto his position, Reynik began to use some of the techniques Femke had taught him for throwing off followers. He started by moving away quickly towards the city centre. It was impossible to ignore the fact that someone was most likely closing up behind him with deadly intentions, but he did his best not to look back more than would be normal for one walking the streets at this time of night.

It occurred to Reynik that it might be better to double back and confront the man head on rather than allow him a chance to strike without warning. He did not want to fight at all, but if he had to fight, then he would prefer to dictate the terms. Then he realised his thinking was based on an unproven premise. How could he be sure that the man he had just incapacitated was the person who had fired the crossbow back in the alley? He could not. If he openly turned back and the man now behind him was the archer, Reynik would become an easy target. An open confrontation was too risky. He would have to use guile if he was going to survive.

He lengthened his stride without changing his pace. The subtle acceleration took him swiftly around a corner and out of his pursuer's direct line of sight. The moment he was sure he was out of the assassin's field of view, Reynik was up on his toes and running as fast and as silently as he could.

There was an alleyway to the right. He took it. It did not lead towards the city centre, but he knew one of the arterial roads was not far away. By going this way, he knew he could intercept the main road quickly and then turn back towards his eventual destination. It was not yet late. There would still be a good amount of traffic on the main route through the city. It should be easy enough to blend in with the general mill of people and leave anyone attempting to get to him with a far more difficult target.

The alley was dark, forcing Reynik to slow down. He did not want to make any noise that might attract unwanted attention. Stepping carefully, he concentrated hard on using the techniques Femke had taught him for moving silently in dark places. The assassin, Viper, had seemed to glide through the dark on the evening Reynik had followed him through the back streets and alleys. Reynik had not mastered the techniques to such a degree, but he made a worthy attempt at duplicating what he could remember of Viper's style of movement.

As he approached the far end of the alley, he could hear hoarse whispers. Looking towards the light at the end of the alleyway, he could clearly see the silhouetted outlines of three men bent over a fourth. It looked as if they were rummaging through his clothing looking for items to rob. Was the man dead, or were they holding him down?

Another dilemma! Should he tuck down in a corner and wait for them to finish their business, or help the unfortunate victim? If the assassin trailing him were to come this way, he might pass Reynik in the dark and be forced to tangle with the thieves in his stead. The assassin might even think Reynik the victim, and that the thieves had done his work for him. On the other hand, he might pause in the same place as Reynik to debate his own course of action. If he did, the killer would most likely find his prey within seconds.

Whatever he decided, Reynik knew he could not afford to dither. The man on the ground began to struggle. One of his assailants dealt him a hard, backhanded blow across the face that stilled him again. The fact that he was alive ignited Reynik's sense of justice. He could not stand by and watch while the three thugs carried out their villainy. He had to do something.

Moving forwards with careful stealth, Reynik closed in on the men until he was almost on top of them. With no warning, he attacked. A vicious jab with the end of his staff struck just behind the ear of the first man, who went down without uttering a sound.

'What the—'

The second man did not get to finish his sentence as Reynik whipped the staff around into a powerful sweeping blow that caught the man across the bridge of his nose so hard that it all but lifted him off the ground. The third man drew a knife, but got no opportunity to use it. A single spin of the staff and it cracked him across the wrist, sending the knife flying from his grasp. A jab to the groin, followed by an overhead smash to the back of the head, and it was all over.

Reynik checked the victim's pulse. It was strong, and he was beginning to regain consciousness again. Reynik did not want to wait around. He could not afford to get further involved. His attack had only lasted a few seconds. As fights went, it had been remarkably quiet and efficient, but there had been some unavoidable noise. He would be surprised if his pursuer had not heard it.

At close quarters, Reynik's weapon of choice would always be a staff. However, it was not a weapon in common use in the city. Fighting with staves was a pastime normally left to the country folk. Assassins were predominantly city dwellers, so they were unlikely to be well trained in the art of fighting with, or against, someone wielding a staff. This gave Reynik a distinct advantage in a hand-to-hand fight.

Unfortunately, it was impossible to hide a staff. Following the trail of bodies in Reynik's wake, any assassin worth his fee would not now tackle Reynik at close quarters unless he had no other choice. The staff had to go, but he did not want to leave it here. It would be better for his tail to be looking for someone with a staff.

Reynik slipped out of the alley and into the street. It was not far from here to the main north road. He had to act quickly. On his toes and running again, Reynik raced down the narrow street. His senses strained to garner any signs of pursuit whilst he sought somewhere to dispose of the staff. He sensed nothing, nor found anywhere obvious.

He reached the main north road and slowed to an inconspicuous walk. It was not busy in the true sense of the word, but there were people moving both into and out of the city. Reynik crossed the street and turned towards the city centre. A wagon drawn by a plodding horse was not far ahead. Reynik quickened his pace and moved alongside. Straps holding the upper canvas to the wagon structure offered him the perfect stowage for his staff. He slipped it horizontally behind four sets of straps. It was tightly enough wedged that it was unlikely to fall out, he thought happily.

'Where are you bound, friend?' he called up to the driver.

'To the Imperial Palace. I've a cargo of foodstuffs for His Majesty's kitchen,' the man answered.

'Any chance of a lift?'

'Well, it's hardly far, but if you really want a lift, I see no reason why not.' He halted the wagon. 'Climb on up.'

'Thanks. I appreciate it.'

Reynik threw back his hood and climbed up onto the driver's bench next to him. The driver immediately flicked the reins to get them moving. The horse sighed heavily, but leaned into the traces and they lurched forwards, rumbling and bumping across the cobbles.

As he looked across at the driver, Reynik saw a dark figure emerge from the side street out of the corner of his eye. The figure paused and looked around, scanning the people on the street for signs of his target. Reynik turned his head back to look straight ahead and laughed aloud.

'What's so funny?'

'I was just thinking your horse is about as enthusiastic about her work as I am about mine,' he replied, keeping his voice normal, but low enough that it would not carry back to the assassin. All the killer would see would be two friendly wagoneers chatting to pass the time.

The driver chuckled too. 'If you think the horse's bad, you should meet the wife!' he said. 'Meera'll tell you that keeping our eight children amused and fed should be considered work. Honestly! I don't know what's wrong with the woman.'

Reynik raised an eyebrow at the wagon driver, who chuckled harder at his quizzical expression.

'Gaetan's the name. And you?'

'Reynik.'

'Good to meet you, Reynik. You chose a good night to ask for a lift, my friend. Normally I'd have told you where you could go, but tonight I'm in a fine and generous mood.'

'I'm not sure whether I should ask why, but I'm going to anyway.'

Gaetan glanced across at Reynik again with a twinkle in his eye. 'I'm going home tonight for the first time in several weeks,' he said happily. 'Meera's always pleased to see me when I've been away for a while, if you take my meaning.'

'Ah, yes!' Reynik mumbled, colour rising to his cheeks. 'Then I'm sure you're in for a fine evening, Gaetan. Tell me, have you made plans for where you'll keep more children?'

The wagoneer laughed again. 'No need, young Reynik, no need. Meera's already expecting our ninth, so I hardly need think beyond that one now, do I?'

They rode on into the centre of Shandrim. Gaetan babbled on about his wife and his brood of children with excitement and pride. Reynik lent a polite ear to his chatter, but all the while monitored the progress of the shadowy figure following on behind. He felt sure he had not been seen, but it looked as if the follower had a sixth sense. Despite his giving no indication that he had spotted

Reynik, he followed along the main road behind them as if dragged by instinct.

They were not far from the Palace when Reynik decided that enough was enough.

'This will be fine for me. Thanks for the lift, Gaetan. I would ask you to pass my regards to your wife, but I suspect that you will be somewhat distracted. I hope I'll be able to return your kind favour some day. Take care.'

'Goodnight, Reynik. Good fortune.'

Reynik leaped down from the driver's bench and, while the body of the wagon hid him from the eyes of the man following behind, he retrieved his staff from where he had wedged it through the strapping. It was only a few paces to the dark shadow of a side street. Reynik stepped smartly across the short distance and slipped into the deepest shade of the corner building. There he turned and waited to see what his tail would do.

To Reynik's relief, the hooded man showed no signs of noticing him. There was little doubt in Reynik's mind that this was another Guild member. From the way he was walking, Reynik suspected it might be Cougar. Cougar had accompanied Reynik on his early sorties out from the Guild complex in order to ensure Reynik was not incapacitated by the disorientation caused during transfer. The man had been cold as ice the entire time they had been together.

Reynik watched as the assassin passed abeam his position and continued up the main street towards the Palace. The further along the street the man dressed in black went, the more relaxed Reynik felt. Content that he was safe to go his own way without fear of further pursuit, he was about to turn when a second figure, also dressed in a black, hooded garb stepped out of a dark shadow and greeted his original tail.

Heart in throat, Reynik watched as the second figure engaged the first in quiet dialogue. It would have been impossible to hear even a normal conversation at his range, but when the second figure pointed towards his current position, he knew his troubles were far from over.

'Shand alive! Where did he come from? Have I got a big sign on my back saying, "Kill me. I'm the infiltrator"?' he muttered angrily.

The two figures dressed in black set out towards Reynik's position, both striding forwards with deadly purpose. He wanted to run, but he knew that fleeing now would do little good. He would have to confront them at some point. He was unlikely to shake them easily. They were too practised at trailing a target to be thrown off the scent by his repertoire of tricks. Taking on two assassins simultaneously seemed tantamount to suicide, but he was out of options. The first assassin he had faced had clearly been unfamiliar with the techniques needed to fight someone armed with a staff. Could this be a weakness he could exploit again? There was only one way to find out.

Reynik stepped away from the wall to ensure he had enough room to manoeuvre freely. He was still standing in dark shadow, but he had no doubt that the two assassins could see him. They were closing fast, so he settled into a defensive stance. When they reached a distance of about ten paces, Reynik whirled the staff in an experimental sequence to see if either of the men would show any signs of caution. They did not. There was no hesitation in their approach.

As Reynik finished his sequence of twirls, he ended it with the staff upright and gave an explosive 'Ha!' sound in an effort to show confidence. By freak chance, as he barked out his defiance a knife that Reynik had not even seen thrown, impacted the staff right in front of his face. The point erupted through the wood just above his handhold. For a split second his eyes crossed as they tried to focus on the point no more than a hand span in front of his nose. It was a miraculous chance of luck, but to the approaching assassins, it appeared deliberate. He would not have been inducted into the Guild if he had not been an efficient killer. For the slightest instant, their confidence waned.

Reynik seized the initiative and leaped forward. One man had drawn his sword while another throwing knife was in the hand of the other. There was too much ground to cover for Reynik to engage the knife thrower before he threw again. He was too fast. The second blade launched towards Reynik, this time directly at the centre of his body. Reynik managed to turn slightly, though he could not avoid the blade altogether. It impacted his chest at an angle and was turned aside by the chain mail armour under his cloak.

The assassin did not get a chance to throw another. Reynik deflected the sword of his partner, and hit the knife thrower hard in the chest with a stabbing jab of the staff. He fell back, clutching the impact point.

The swordsman assassin was fast. Worse, he clearly had

experience in facing men skilled with the staff. Although Reynik had deflected the man's initial swing, defending against his blade during his subsequent sustained attack proved increasingly difficult. The knife stuck through the staff did not help. The extra weight on one end made the staff feel unbalanced and unwieldy. Compensating was difficult, but for the next few seconds, Reynik's mastery of the double-handed weapon enabled him to cope.

The second assassin was recovering. Reynik knew that if he allowed them both to mount a simultaneous attack again, then he would die. In a daring manoeuvre that cost him his staff, he launched himself at the swordsman. The assassin's blade impacted the centre of the staff, breaking it in the middle but not cutting clean through. Even as his momentum carried him forward, Reynik twisted the tangled mess hard, wrenching the swordsman's wrist. The twist completed the break, the staff becoming two sword length pieces of wood with splintered ends outward.

The swordsman had been staggered by the wrenching of his wrist. Before he could move to defend himself, Reynik jammed the splintered end of one piece of staff into his face. He screamed and fell to the ground, his hands clutching at the wound.

Reynik sensed movement behind him. He spun, instinctively clubbing aside the blade of the second assassin with one piece of wood and smashing him across the side of the head with the second. The killer did not go down, but he was stunned. The follow-up spinning kick finished the job. Both assassins were at his mercy.

Breathing hard, Reynik paused. Now he was faced with a

worse choice than before. He had already left one enemy alive. Here were two more. Could he really afford to leave them here in the full knowledge that they would come after him again as soon as they were able? He drew his sword and walked over to where the first assassin was writhing on the ground clutching his face. Killing him would be easy. It was the safe option, but no matter how sensible it was, Reynik could not bring himself to do it.

'Get up!' he ordered harshly, kicking the man hard on the thigh. 'Get up, or by Shand I'll run you through and be done with it!'

Without taking his hands from his face, the man contorted his body until he first got to his knees, then to his feet.

'Who are you? Which icon do you carry?'

'Cougar. I'm Cougar,' he moaned.

'I thought so. And your friend?'

'Viper.'

'Ah, perfect!' Reynik said. But he was not talking about the identity of the second assassin. A patrol of Legionnaires had rounded the corner a little way up the street and was marching towards them. Assuming he could convince the lead soldier to do as he asked, Reynik now had a third, more palatable option.

CHAPTER SIXTEEN

Femke was boiling with fury, the like of which she had never known. Lord Ferdand, her mentor, was Guildmaster of the Guild of Assassins. How could he do it? After all his lectures to her about only killing as a last resort, here he was, the next best thing to death incarnate!

So intense was her anger that for a moment she lost track of the conversation on the far side of the door. Had her concentration held firm, it would have been obvious that once Ferdand had confirmed he was ready for his meal, the servant would be quick to go and get it. It was a shock for both Femke and the servant when the door suddenly opened. For a moment they simply stared face to face.

Femke was quicker to overcome her surprise. A quick, stiff-fingered blow to the throat sent the servant reeling back into the room. For just an instant, she locked eyes with her old mentor who was relaxing in an armchair on the far side of a plush chamber. Like a fat, old spider holed up in his lair, she thought bitterly.

'Liar!' she spat. Then she turned on her heels and ran.

Ferdand recognised her immediately. 'Femke, wait! I can explain everything.'

Femke was not about to stop and listen. He was the enemy. Ferdand had violated her trust in a way she could never forgive, no matter how good the explanation. Her mentor had always been eloquent. His lessons during her education as a spy had always left her in awe of his intelligence and logic. Now, however, she did not want to listen. How could he leave her to think he was dead these past years? If he had cared one iota for her, he would have let her know he was alive, she thought bitterly.

It was easy to see why he did not want her to know what he was doing. For all his fine words and noble gestures, he was nothing more than a hired killer – something he had always protested he disliked about Shalidar. Femke's entire sense of order crumbled as she ran. Her eyes welled with tears that were part sorrow, part pain and part pure, unadulterated rage.

She reached the stairwell and raced up the pitch-black spiral staircase on all fours like a monkey. It was not elegant, but there was no one to see her in the darkness and it was most effective.

Femke reached the central chamber of the Guild very quickly. As she peered out of the hole into the chamber, she felt dizzy from her rapid, spiralling climb. No one appeared to be around, so she scrambled up the last few stairs and sprinted silently across to the booth with the wolf spider logo on the front gate.

Vaulting the gate, Femke landed lightly inside. She

dropped to a crouch. A slight twinge of pain in her ribs caused her to wince. It seemed that every time she thought her ribs fully healed, the pain came back to haunt her. She drew a knife from her boot. Somewhere ahead was the assassin who had been sent to Reynik's chamber to guard against his return. Pain or no pain, he would have to be dealt with if she was to get out of here alive.

There was not much time. Ferdand ... 'The Guild-master,' she told herself firmly. 'I'll not think of him as Ferdand. Lord Ferdand no longer exists. He is dead. There is only the Guildmaster.' The Guildmaster would not waste time. He would have her captured as soon as he could. He knew her capabilities. He knew the danger she represented.

Femke slipped through the door and into the corridor behind it. The torches along the walls guttered in the slight through-flow of air created by the open door. If the man were alert for someone coming from this direction, then the flickering of the torches alone would put him on his guard. Careful not to make any noise, she eased the door closed behind her. It was likely he was concentrating on the potential re-appearance of Reynik. There was no reason for him to expect an attack from this direction, she reasoned.

Like a stalking cat, she crept along the corridor to the door into Reynik's living room. She had thought herself soundless, but as she reached the open door a voice addressed her.

'Come in, Foxy lady. You're early. Does that mean you've come to play? Wait a minute! You're not Fox . . .'

The man had been relaxing in a chair with his back to the

open door. It was only as he stood and turned to look at her that he realised his mistake, but by then it was far too late. Femke's knife hit him square in the chest and he sank to the floor with a groan of pain.

The wound was a mortal one. She had seen enough knife wounds to know the man would not survive long. Even as he fell, she heard the door open at the far end of the corridor. Multiple voices were audible and closing fast. The Guildmaster had gathered his forces even quicker than she had anticipated.

Femke threw the door closed and dragged the armchair across to wedge it shut. She tilted it such that it fitted under the handle. It was heavy, but not heavy enough to prevent a determined assault on the door. The angle it was propped at would help, but not for long.

She looked around for more pieces of furniture with which to barricade the door. The dahl table was easy to move, but did not add much weight. The bookcase to the right of the door looked more promising. She ran around to the far side of it and, putting her shoulder as low down the side of the bookcase as was comfortable, she pushed it with all her might.

There was a juddering scrape, and the heavy-laden wooden frame slid across the floor until it was hard up against the armchair already wedged under the door handle. Pain stabbed Femke's ribs once more, causing her to clutch her side. Only the very end of the bookcase was blocking the door, which would not be of much use. Bending lower, she grabbed the back of the bookcase. It was easier to spin it round than it was to push it across the floor. The handle of the door turned even as she moved it the final few hand spans into position.

'Open the door, Femke. Barricading it will do you no good. There's no way out. We will break it down if we have to.'

Femke did not answer. She had nothing to say to Ferdand. Her focus was on holding out until Reynik came back for her. There was no question of falling back to the bedroom as a second line of defence. This was the room that Reynik would transfer in to. Her stand had to be here.

The chaise longue was next onto the barricade. Again, it was not as heavy as she would have liked, but it might just delay them a few more seconds. What else was there? Not a lot that she could move alone, she realised.

A loud thump rattled the door. They were beginning the process of smashing the door in. It would not be long now.

'Come on, Reynik!' she muttered, standing behind the pile of furniture and looking anxiously at the door. 'Please come soon.' Another loud bang reverberated through the room. Femke's eyes strayed just slightly from the door to the stonework around it. Uncommonly good stonework, she noted again. Familiar stonework – familiar from where, though?

It was there, hovering in her mind just beyond reach like a word that feels to be on the tip of one's tongue, but is refusing to be articulated. Where was it? It did not feel like a recent memory, so she must have been quite young when she had seen it. Like crawling up the side of a muddy pit, Femke felt she was nearly there. She could almost reach up and grab at the goal, but it was still tantalisingly out of reach.

Without warning a vice-like grip clamped around her ankle and her feet were pulled out from under her. She managed to extend her hands in time to break her fall, but her ribs spiked another protest of pain through her body. The assassin she had written off for dead had used her distraction and the noise of the people trying to break the door down to conceal his snail-like progress across the floor towards her. Dying though he was, the killer was not willing to go without a fight.

Femke saw his other hand rise with a blade ready to strike. Panic surged through her, lending her strength she did not know she possessed. Twisting like a snake caught by the tail, she kicked at the assassin's raised knife hand, sending the blade flying from his grasp. Spinning through the air, the knife bounced off the wall, hit the stone floor and skittered under the display cabinets. A strange, writhing struggle ensued with neither combatant able to get into a position to hurt the other to any great degree.

Locked in silent combat, Femke could do nothing about the continuing assault on the barricaded door. There was another crash. This time the wooden door splintered. Another surge of adrenalin rushed through her body but, despite her desperate efforts to break free, the assassin's grip held firm. She was helpless.

'Thank you! You won't regret it, I promise you,' Reynik called over his shoulder. He broke into a run, heading back through the streets towards his transfer point.

The Legionnaires had taken a lot of convincing. It had looked at one point as if he would have to meet with the patrol's File Leader before they would take him seriously. Fortunately it had not come to that. The senior Legionnaire present had over-ruled the others, claiming he would take responsibility for the decision to take in the two injured men as prisoners and let Reynik go. Reynik knew he owed the man more than a few drinks for taking on that responsibility. Questions would be asked. It was inevitable. It was the military way.

There was little chance of his meeting another assassin now. Cougar had been quite informative under threat of instant death. A series of rapid-fire questions before the soldiers reached them had revealed that Shalidar was in the Imperial Palace looking for him, whilst Bear was somewhere outside the Palace in the city centre. As far as Cougar knew, there were only four of them out in the city actively searching for him and a watcher at each of his transfer points.

Reynik knew there was a distinct possibility Cougar was trying to feed him misinformation. However, there was something in the man's voice that rang true. Strange things happened in a man's mind when he faced death. Even the strongest in appearance could break under such circumstances. For now, Reynik decided to take the information at face value.

By a process of elimination, Reynik knew he had dealt with one of the watchers, so it made sense to head back to the same transfer stone he had left by. He would still need to exercise caution when he approached. There could have been a shift change, but it seemed unlikely. The watcher he had confronted could not have been there more than a few minutes when he had emerged.

The streets were quietening. Midnight was drawing ever closer. As Reynik sprinted through the dimly lit streets, he found it hard to believe that so much could happen in a single evening, and it was not over yet. He still had to get back into the Guild, meet Femke and get out again. There were plenty of things that could go wrong with that sequence of events.

When he had left his quarters, the Guildmaster and another assassin had been entering. Did that mean there was to be a guard inside his rooms as well as at the transfer points? It did seem likely. If so, would Femke have been able to leave the bedroom? Reynik nearly chuckled aloud. It would take more than a single assassin to keep Femke from doing anything that she really wanted to do, he realised. However, the possibility of someone hostile poised waiting for him to appear in his room at the Guild was a serious concern.

He had been incredibly fortunate on more than one occasion this evening. Had he not dived for the transfer stone when he left the Guild, he would have emerged at his transfer point only to be pinned to the wall by a crossbow bolt. Would it be worth trying something similar on his return? The danger if he transferred in with a large amount of momentum was in the direction he emerged. There were no guarantees that he would not crash straight into a table or chair and make lots of unwanted noise. Drawing attention to his arrival could get him killed as easily as if someone were waiting to skewer him as he emerged.

Reynik reached the back street from which his transfer stone alley branched. Concealing himself in the shadows, he took a few moments to recover his breath. How long had it been since he left Femke? It felt both ages, yet not long at all. Would she have had enough time to explore the complex? The questions were meaningless. There was no way of telling without going back in to find out.

Taking conscious control of his breathing, Reynik took a deep breath in and held it. After a few seconds, he exhaled slowly. He repeated the process twice more. Then, breathing normally again, he concentrated for a few moments on not hyperventilating, but regulating the speed and depth of his breaths until he felt his body could continue automatically.

The discipline helped clear his mind. This was not a night for questions. For Reynik it was a night of action. He knew he could not delay. If Femke had not yet finished her spy work, then he would have to wait for her in his rooms, or seek her out. Events were boiling to a head. He must move with the flow or risk the tide sweeping him away.

Content that his breathing was quiet enough to proceed, Reynik flitted through the shadows until he reached the entrance to his alley. Standing in silence for a full minute, he scanned the rooftops overlooking his transfer stone, and listened for any sign of movement. There was none. This was no guarantee that all was safe, of course, but it was the best he could do. He dared not wait any longer. He had to go back in.

Somewhere in the heart of the city a single bell began to

toll. Even as he was about to step into the alley, he paused to listen. It was a deep, sorrowful sound, unlike any bell Reynik had ever heard before. He wondered what it heralded, for it was certainly not giving the time. Femke would know, he thought. Femke was a mine of information for such things.

Without further pause, he stepped boldly into the alley. If there were a watcher, Reynik knew he would be seen no matter how stealthily he tried to approach the stone. His reconnoitre had not revealed anyone, so he decided to be positive. He walked over to the wall in which the stone was embedded. Rather than trying to be too clever, he knelt down next to the wall and reached up with his spider icon. At least he would not be the target shape anyone waiting for him would expect, he thought. Here goes nothing.

Lord Tremarle sat bolt upright in his armchair when the solemn bell began to sound out its doleful toll. A grin spread slowly across his face and his tongue instinctively ran across his lips.

'Shand alive!' he breathed. 'He's done it!'

Placing aside the book he had been reading, he pushed himself up out of his chair. The old Lord walked over to his drinks cabinet and poured himself a large glass of brandy. He felt alive – more alive than he had in months, maybe even years, he reflected. Euphoria swept over him as he sipped at his freshly poured drink. The flavour of the fine old brandy set his tongue alight, the alcohol warming his throat as he swallowed and sending a wave of heat all the way down to his stomach.

Unbidden, a chuckle started from deep within that grew until Tremarle was doubled over laughing. With some difficulty, he checked his mirth. He could not afford to be seen reacting like this. People might suspect something. A wrong word by a servant and he could be strung up on the city walls before he could blink.

Composing his features into a controlled mask of sobriety, he crossed to the writing desk and lowered the front to form a writing surface. He reached inside and drew out the roll of parchments from the slot at the far right. With trembling fingers, he leafed through the sheets of parchment until he reached the final sheet. He placed the others aside, drew out his quill and removed the stopper from the ink well.

Taking a deep breath, Tremarle calmed his excitement as he signed against his name. Lifting a candle from a nearby holder he held a red wax block to it and melted a small pool of wax onto the parchment below his signature. Into the wax he pressed his seal – the seal of the House of Tremarle. All that remained to secure the future of his House was the signature of his designated heir, and the lodging of this document with the Clerk of the Imperial Court.

'What a son he'll make,' Tremarle muttered. 'The House of Tremarle will live on after all.'

CRASH! The door splintered again. The damage this time sounded far greater. They would be through within a minute, Femke realised, kicking out at the assassin with every ounce of strength she could muster. It was no use. No matter what she did, he refused to let go.

317

Suddenly there was a hollow sounding 'clunk' and the assassin's grip loosened.

'Quick! Let's go. Now!' Reynik's voice was urgent. Femke did not need telling twice. She had not seen him arrive, but she was more than glad to see him. Before she could move Reynik grabbed her hands, pulling her to her feet so fast that she overbalanced into his arms. In a half-tangled hug they staggered across the room to the transfer stone. There was another wood-splitting crash. The barricade lurched, as the remains of the door broke apart. Reynik grabbed her hand and placed it on the spider icon. As she felt him touch the spider to the transfer stone, Femke looked into his eyes.

She knew what was going to happen this time, but it did not help. The spinning stars, the swirling vortex and the explosion were all as horrible and disorienting as she remembered from the first time. The coalescing in the alley-way left her feeling nauseous and weak as a newborn baby, but she held onto her consciousness with vicious tenacity. Passing out was not an option this time. Reynik could not carry her far. Pursuit would be swift. They had to get well away from the alley before the other assassins got there. Every step they could get clear of this place was crucial.

Stars swam before Femke's eyes and her ears were ringing. 'Put me down,' she slurred, as she felt Reynik lift her into his arms. 'I can walk if you help me.'

Reynik did as he was bid. She felt him loop her right arm around his neck and place his left arm behind her back to lend her support. She tried to walk, but was half carried, half dragged from the alley. At the turn into the side street,

Reynik started to head out of town. To Femke's surprise there were lots of people on the streets, far more than there had been earlier in the evening, with more leaving their houses all the time. Whole families were on the streets and all were heading the same way – in towards the city centre.

Was there something going on this evening that they had overlooked, she wondered, as they struggled along the road against the flow. A festival perhaps? Whatever it was looked as if it was going to draw a big crowd.

'Stop!' Femke said suddenly. 'That's not my head ringing, is it? That's the Imperial bell!'

'Is it? If you say so, I suppose it must be. What does it mean? It started ringing just before I came in to the complex to get you.'

'You don't know? Well, I suppose that's not altogether surprising. It hasn't rung for some time. The Imperial bell only rings at the passing of an Emperor, Reynik. It means that Surabar is dead.'

For the next few seconds Reynik turned the air blue with one of the most amazing collection of swear words Femke had ever heard strung together. 'Shalidar!' he spat, having temporarily exhausted his repertoire of bad language. 'It must have been Shalidar. Before I handed him over to the Legionnaires, Cougar told me that Shalidar was in the Palace looking for me. It seems that Shalidar decided to break one of the cardinal rules of the Assassins' creed.'

'You don't know that for certain,' Femke said, her voice sounding more lucid. 'Any one of a hundred things might have happened. He was not a young man.'

'He was strong as a horse, Femke, and you know it. I'd

319

lay my last copper sennut on Shalidar having killed him, but why? Why now? If he wanted to kill Surabar, I'm sure he could have engineered the Emperor's death before now.'

'Shalidar has always had his own agenda, Reynik. Surely you've noticed that about him. He's a maverick. What amazes me is that the Guildmaster has let him live this long. The two of them have always disliked one another.'

'And just how did you figure that out?' Reynik asked, his tone sceptical. 'Did you drop in on the Guildmaster and ask him?'

'In a manner of speaking – yes. I know the Guildmaster all too well, Reynik, or at least I thought I did. He's my old master, Lord Ferdand.'

Reynik's jaw dropped. 'Really? I've heard about him. My father said he was a most interesting character: very intelligent, loyal to the Empire and particularly to the Emperor. He was quite outspoken on some issues, I believe.'

'Loyal! I'll give him his due, he convinced me and I'm not deceived easily. Damn him! He had me hanging on his every word. It's hard to admit, but he was a traitor all along: a traitor to the Empire, a traitor to his high-falutin ideals and a traitor to me. I'll never forgive him for this. When I think of all his lessons on ethics . . . and all along he was killing for money. Shand, but I'd like to know what made him do it! Why would he compromise his position in such a way? I can't believe it was for money; he had wealth of his own. What would make him join the Guild?'

'Um, Femke, I don't mean to sound rude, but do you think these questions could wait until we've reached some

320

sort of safety? We're out in the dark here, and I'm not talking about this street. Without Surabar we have nowhere to go.'

'Don't be foolish, Reynik. You know that isn't true. We still have our fallback plan.'

'No, Femke. We've lost control. I'm beginning to think that we should just go and find the deepest hole, or the darkest cellar we can, and hide in it for the next five years!'

Femke froze. All her muscles tensed.

'Say that again,' she said slowly.

'Say what again?'

'The part about the hole and the cellar.'

'I said we should go and find the deepest hole, or the darkest cellar we can, and hide in it,' he repeated uncertainly. 'What is it, Femke? What's the matter?'

'That's *it!*' she said excitedly. 'Reynik you're a genius!'

Femke threw her other arm around his neck and kissed him soundly on the lips. If he had been surprised before, then he was astonished now. Femke laughed at the lost expression on his face.

'Well, I'd like to say "Of course!" and bask in the glory, but as I don't have the faintest idea what you're talking about, I'll settle for an explanation.'

'Very well, but not here. You were right. We must keep moving. We would be a lot less obvious if we went with the flow. But Ferdand would expect me to try to disappear by melting into the crowd. It was he who taught me how. Therefore, we shall do the opposite. Come on. Let's get as far away from this place and the Palace as we possibly can. A large crowd is normally a good place to hide, but not today. Ferdand will have all his people sweeping the crowd in front of the Imperial Palace looking for us.'

They started moving again. Femke had regained her focus. He was impressed. It had taken him much longer to recover from his second transfer using the spider icon. He could see she was hurting from the discovery of Ferdand's treachery, but she was not letting it dominate her. He could not think of anyone else who had the ability to hold such a strong sense of purpose under such trying circumstances.

What he could not see was that Femke was hurting on many levels. A flood of questions was assailing her mind. Why had Ferdand joined the Guild? Why had he trained her to be a spy for the Emperor if he was working for the Guild the entire time? How had he concealed his hypocrisy from her for so long? She had thought she had known him well, but she was just beginning to realise that she had never known him at all.

Aside from the treachery of Ferdand, every toll of the bell sent a wave of guilt ringing through her. It was she who had convinced the General to take the Mantle. Now he was dead. As a spy, Femke was not unused to losing people to death, but this was different.

She had felt a particular sense of responsibility for Emperor Surabar. She was sworn to his service: to protect and obey. It was an oath she took very seriously. His death filled her with both a sense of great loss, and a sense of failure. He had been a good man: true to his purpose, generous of himself and filled with an uncommon sense of justice. Thinking of his qualities made her all the more angry at the betrayal of Ferdand.

Reynik too, mourned the death of the Emperor, but for very different reasons. He did not know Surabar well. To him, the Emperor had been like any other senior officer – someone to be obeyed without question. The respect with which he was held by the Legions meant more than his personal feelings for the man. Reynik's real sense of loss was a selfish one. He had lost his top cover. Without the Emperor, he only had Femke to vilify him in the event he was ever questioned over the death of Lord Lacedian. As far as the rest of the world was concerned, he was a murderer. With Surabar wearing the Mantle, he had felt secure in his mission, but questioned how much weight Femke's word would have if it came down to a trial.

Femke led the way, keeping always to the back streets. This avoided the need to battle against the larger flows of people going into the city centre along the major roads. Reynik felt a little disappointed that she no longer needed his support. She had kissed him twice tonight. He smiled at the thought. Once was an occasion, but twice was almost a habit. He hoped it would become a habit that would grow.

A quarter of an hour later she led him into another alley and they sat down on a stone step to rest.

'I would judge we're clear of imminent danger,' she said thoughtfully. 'You wanted an explanation. I have one. Did you notice the stonework around the doorways in the Guild complex?'

Reynik thought for a moment and then shook his head. 'I can't say that I did. There was nothing strange about it that I can remember.'

'You're right. There was nothing strange, but there was

something distinctive. The stonework was of a very high quality, and the door archways were made in a style I've only seen once before. I was combing my memories for where I had seen such masonry work, but it eluded me . . . until you spoke of a deep cellar. Your words sent my mind back to the deepest cellar I've known. Would it surprise you to know that the stonework in that cellar is an exact duplicate of the stonework in the Guild complex?'

'Really? You're sure? Where is this cellar?'

'Oh, I'm sure. What's more, having realised that the same stonemason did the work in both cases answered the most puzzling mystery of all for me. I did not wonder so much how the Guild headquarters was cut from the rock. Such things have been possible for many centuries. The question that troubled me was how those who did the work concealed such an undertaking. After all, the people who mined out those chambers would have needed to dispose of thousands of wagonloads of rock. It would have taken many workers years to complete. The scale of such a project would be huge.'

'Yes, but surely if the site were remote enough, then this would not pose too many problems.'

'If it were, then yes, I would agree with you, Reynik. But this site was not remote. It had to be close to the centre of Shandrim because of the limitations on the magical power provided by the icons and the stones. If I told you that the place I'd seen stonework like that in the Guild was in the lower cellars of the Imperial Palace, would you see my thoughts?'

Reynik's eyes widened with wonder as he absorbed her words.

'The Guild complex is under the Palace?'

'That's what I believe. Yes.'

'Could you prove it?'

'I believe so. I suspect that the ventilation system of the Guild complex opens alongside that of the cellars in the Palace. My bet would be that if you were to count the ventilation shafts leading out of the cellars and then count the grated openings around the Palace grounds, you would find a considerable discrepancy.'

'But why has no one noticed this before? Surely someone must know,' Reynik protested.

'Why? Who would think to check such a thing? I suspect there have been few members of the Guild of Assassins wandering through the deepest levels of the Palace cellars. You would not find many prominent targets down there. I only went there because I posed as a Palace servant for several months as part of a training project set by . . . my tutor. You saw nothing unusual in the masonry. Why should a trained assassin be any different? I noticed because I was taught to notice details everywhere I went. It was drilled into me.'

'Fine! We know the location of the Guild headquarters. We also know the man behind the organisation. But what use is the knowledge? If Surabar's dead, then we've lost. I refer you back to my earlier comment. We might as well go hide in a hole. I can't go back to the Legion – the Guild knows about my history now. They'd find me in no time. You can't go back to the Palace. So what do you plan to do?'

Femke sighed. 'You're being very negative, Reynik. I agree, the situation is not ideal, but Surabar did prepare for this eventuality. He always knew there was a possibility that the Guild of Assassins would finally get annoyed enough to ignore the creed and dispose of him. I, for one, am not willing to give up on his goal. Now that I know Ferdand's behind the Guild, I want to see them destroyed more than ever. Surabar was right. There is no place in our society for a Guild of killers, no matter how they dress up their morals with their blasted creed.'

'I'm not going to argue with your intentions, but how in Shand's name do you think you're going to succeed without the Emperor to back you up?'

'I may not have Surabar, but I'm not totally without resources. There is also Lord Kempten. We mustn't forget him. He believed in what Surabar was doing. The Emperor put him out of harm's way for good reason. You've realised you have nowhere to go. Will you help me finish what we started?'

Reynik looked into Femke's grey-blue eyes. They sparked with determination and purpose. 'Of course I'll help,' he replied, his voice calm and steady. 'Shalidar has taken my uncle and my father from me,' he added silently. 'I'll be damned if I'll let him take you as well.'

**If you enjoyed *Imperial Assassin*,
look out for the third book in the sequence,
Imperial Traitor, coming soon!
Here's a taster of what's in store . . .**

Shalidar drew a deep breath and held it for a moment before slowly releasing it. He drew another. His turbulent thoughts began to calm and his dark eyes glittered with cold, calculating malice. He had come this far, he did not have to make the decision tonight. It would not hurt to scout the security surrounding the Emperor. Knowledge of how seriously Surabar was taking his personal protection now would be useful.

He slid out from the doorway and moved noiselessly forwards into the depths of the Palace. It was late. The passageways were quiet. Getting close to the Emperor's study without being seen would not be difficult.

He had come to the palace to look for Wolf Spider. His reason for being here was legitimate. The Guildmaster had tasked him with killing the young man who had infiltrated the Guild, and Wolf Spider's links to the Emperor were beyond doubt. His commission gave Shalidar further reason to consider making a hit on the Emperor tonight. But how could he make it look accidental? If his target had been anyone other than Surabar, he would not have hesitated to use Wolf Spider as a smokescreen. But the Guildmaster was no fool. It would not take him long to work out what Shalidar was about.

The assassin moved like a phantom through the Palace, gliding smoothly from one dark recess to the next. There were some sounds of movement from rooms on either side of the passages, but no one disturbed him as he threaded his way into the heart of the Emperor's domain.

The smell of cleaning wax hung heavy in the air, as it always did in the palace passageways. Despite the high ceilings and the inevitable smoking odour from the burning torches that lit the inner walkways, every door, every wooden panel, every surface was scented with polish and gleamed with the effort of generations of Palace staff.

As he expected, two guards held post outside the Emperor's study. They were dressed in full ceremonial armour for their vigil and were armed with swords, knives, and what looked like miniature crossbows. Crossbows! That was a development he had not considered. It was most unusual to arm indoor guards with mid-range weapons.

Shalidar held his position. He was hidden in the deep shadow some distance along the corridor from where the two men were standing silent and alert. Torches were lit in the Emperor's study. He could see the light shining through the narrow windows that opened high up in the wall of the corridor. Surabar was there, but the assassin had no way of getting any closer to the Emperor's study without revealing himself to the guards. The passwords for the outer Palace gates were easily obtainable from his many sources, but the more secret inner passwords he knew were long out of date. It was unlikely he could bluff his way any further. He needed a diversion: something to draw the guards away from the door, or distract their attention sufficiently for him to approach without being noticed.

Fire was always a good diversion, but if he were to kill

the Emperor, it was unlikely to help his cause with the Guildmaster if he burnt down the Imperial Palace in the process. No. He needed something spectacular, but not life threatening – an occurrence that would catch everyone's attention. If it drew the Emperor from his study too, then all the better. Once Surabar was out of his lair, he would be far more vulnerable to attack. The gold plating on the pommel would be if Wolf Spider were drawn into the open at the same time.

'Ah, now *that* would be neat!' Shalidar breathed as the thought crossed his mind. 'Or Femke – I'd be more than happy to settle my score with the Emperor's pet spy!'

The question remained. How? The longer he lingered, the more determinedly blank Shalidar's mind became. Nothing. He could think of nothing that would have the effect he desired. It was no good. He would have to go away and think on it. Improvising a hit was one thing, but to do so under these conditions would serve little purpose, other than to end his career in a hurry. Frustrated, but resigned, he turned and slipped silently away from the vicinity of the guarded study. There would be another time, he vowed silently. He would return with a viable plan. The Emperor would not live long.

It was as he reached the ground floor that the seed of an idea germinated within his mind. To his surprise it flourished and grew into a fully-fledged plan within seconds. It was genius, he decided. Everything he needed was here in the Palace.

IMPERIAL SPY BY MARK ROBSON

In a world of magic and murder, Femke is entrusted with a vital foreign mission by the Emperor. The task appears straightforward, but the young spy quickly finds herself ensnared in an elaborate trap.

Isolated in a hostile country, hunted by the authorities and with her arch-enemy closing in for his revenge, Femke needs all her wit and skills to survive. Only Reynik, a soldier barely out of training, appears willing to help. But with no knowledge of her true mission, Reynik soon discovers loyalty is a dangerous business.

ISBN: 1-416-90185-X